ALSO BY VENETIA WELBY

FICTION

Mother of Darkness (2017)

DREAMTIME

VENETIA WELBY

SALT

CROMER

PUBLISHED BY SALT PUBLISHING 2021

2 4 6 8 10 9 7 5 3 1

Copyright © Venetia Welby 2021

Venetia Welby has asserted her right under the Copyright, Designs and
Patents Act 1988 to be identified as the author of this work.

First published in Great Britain in 2021 by
Salt Publishing Ltd
12 Norwich Road, Cromer, Norfolk NR27 0AX United Kingdom

www.saltpublishing.com

Salt Publishing Limited Reg. No. 5293401

A CIP catalogue record for this book is available from the British Library

ISBN 978 1 78463 241 0 (Paperback edition)
ISBN 978 1 78463 242 7 (Electronic edition)

Typeset in Monotype Apollo by Tetragon

Printed and bound in Great Britain by Clays Ltd, Elcograf S.p.A

For Charlie

LIGHTS

ARIZONA, USA. September 2035.

'So, where is he then, your dad?' Carter's hand is creeping towards her bony hip. Very illicit. 'Won't he come to your Family Week?'

Sol does not answer. She thinks about how Carter sold his house to pay for this – if that were true. Would it be worth it? This sober life?

Carter lights another cigarette, squinting. It's still standard to chain-smoke through rehab, just as it is to treat deeply personal questions like they're in any way acceptable. Smoking real tobacco in retro papers is something of a statement these days: we who have lived on the front line of life do not vape.

'Meds!' a voice yells out from the squat white complex that houses both Detox Unit and Pharmacy.

Sol watches the inmates swarm to the call. One by one they swoop in to pick up their fun-size plastic pot of drugs. Once upon a time I was like you, she thinks – but now her sad little pill pot contains only probiotics. Detox is complete and there's no going back to the downers they gave her in the first month. She takes a drag of Carter's cigarette instead.

'What's up next?' he asks her now, his fingers tracing the line of her hip with growing insistence.

Sol looks at his kindly face, wolfish beneath the greying eyebrows. She recalls the languid way he removed her skirt in one of the dangling Meditation Pods by the pool last week.

Not today. Today, the end is actually in sight. Her three months are nearly up and she has to meet Belinda in a few minutes. Carter, though he's been a lifeline, is not worth an extended sentence.

Disentangled, she walks alone past the palm-tree-fringed pool to Belinda's office. Like everyone else on the programme, Sol has a personal psychotherapist assigned to her. Belinda – they're all on first name terms only – is supposed to be some sort of mentor. 'Appropriate Reparenting' is a popular phrase.

Lights would look like a holiday resort, with its pristine villas and manicured tropical gardens, were it not for the heavies who patrol the place like a pack of dogs, muttering intelligence into walkie-talkies. Constant vigilance, their only mission to prevent escape and inappropriate touching. The first one's a waste of manpower. If anyone did fly off through the Sonoran Desert that extends around them for miles in every direction, how far could they get? The snakes, the spiders, the scorpions ... the sun! Even the goddamn sun, her namesake, is lethal. As with all the more affluent places in Tucson now, the outdoor spaces in Lights are in fact indoors, air filtered and conditioned beneath heat-reflecting structures of Perspex and steel. The carbon footprint of this place is off the scale. If they must go outside, people tend to drive from dome to dome, park beneath the ground in vaulted caverns of cooled air.

Arizona is a bad place to be homeless.

This is meant to be the best rehab in the western hemisphere. It's certainly a successful business, with an army of clients so satisfied they want another round. It costs a Tucson bungalow to be here, but for Sol this stint is instead of a jail sentence.

Ultraluxe rehab centres have sprung up all over America for the rich, louche and disaffected; meanwhile prisons bulge with the drugged-up poor, a situation only inflamed by the climate refugees. These inner states may be baked, but land still uncompromised by sea is all too desirable. Sol is a fortunate beneficiary of the latest pro-equality initiative: the state-sponsored rehabilitation of local reoffenders within these plutocratic shrines – an effort by the new government to draw the two cliffs of the abyss closer.

She'd found the first couple of weeks unspeakable, that much is true, toxic waste seeping from her green complexion, intangible horror hopping from muscle to muscle. Worse than that, having to wake up at dawn, at least half a day before her usual call to action. She hadn't much liked the tests they'd done on her either. The hit of relief, though, was spectacular: the all clear after a small lifetime of rolling the dice.

Above all, of course, she'd missed Kit. Sol had been waiting interminably for him to visit, yet here no one comes in and no one goes out, except for Family Week. And that approaches – for now Sol is steeped in a new language of Step-based recovery. She leaks pseudo-Eastern philosophy bound by Western capitalist ideals. There's still an aimlessness within her; she knows it, she fears it: the void that threatens to empty her from the inside out. All these years alive and so little to show for it, just track marks and fallout. And she's about to turn thirty, for god's sake. It's a miracle she's made it so far, frankly.

Belinda is lying in a tie-dye hammock outside the therapy room; the great UV lamp at the top of the glass dome – a gentler substitute sun – glances off her silver toe ring and anklet, the henna swirls on her tanned foot. She skips out, bird-like, and hugs Sol. Hug Therapy is a big thing here – hugging meditation, tree hugging, horse hugging. Sexual hugging is not a thing.

Belinda gestures for Sol to take the hammock and she hops in, feeling the warmth of the lamp rays on her face. Sol swipes her short hair forward into prickles and begins to talk, freely associating word after disassociated word as she has been encouraged to do since she arrived – 'to warm up the unconscious'.

Sol's warm-up always starts the same way: 'Uh … Percocet …'

'Good, Sol. Go on.'

'OxyContin … Percocet … uh … fentanyl …'

Taking therapy in the hammock is a privilege she has attained through persistence with Her Recovery. She must say 'My Recovery' a thousand times a day.

Better than jail.

As she talks, Belinda manoeuvres her body into unnatural shapes on the sand, illustrating Sol's post-hammock routine for today. She teaches a dawn yoga class here too. They are super keen on dawn stuff here – sage-smoke rituals with an eagle quill, prayers to the animal spirits, ancestral dances … You name it, dawn's the time for it and an elder appears from what's left of the Cocopah Reservation to give it. They dine at four in the afternoon and the evening, a time not of spirituality but of wickedness, holds only sleep. This has been tough for a night bird like Sol, but on the other hand boredom is a great soporific, and sleep a great propeller of time.

'Well done, Sol. That's enough now.' Belinda extracts a slender limb from the pretzel she has become. 'Are you in enough of a safe space to assume your vulnerable position?'

Sol gets out of the hammock and Belinda, now fully unravelled, slips back in. Sol breathes and bends over, palms on the ground, into Downward Dog.

Ass venerating sunlamp, it's still hard not to feel a little shaken up. How Phoenix used to love it when she posed like this!

There's a lot about Lights that transports her to Dreamtime, not least the constant rehashing of her years there in 'Trauma Processing'. Phoenix's place, the commune where she and Kit spent their childhood, was also a secluded desert camp ticking to its own time. And Dreamtime, it occurs to her now, also aped the rituals of displaced native peoples. Way less regimented there though. Unlike Lights, that set-up understood the draw of getting high. The whole thing, apart from the occasional worship of Phoenix, was geared for transcendence, he and his women always seeking the Dreamtime, the Everywhen. His wide Rasputin eyes would soften when he talked about the Australian outback, his supernatural experiences there. Even his beard seemed to slacken its grasp on his chin.

'It's an Aboriginal thing,' he used to tell his kids. 'It's like a time out of time. An eternal time. Oh, you'll get it when you grow up. Now buzz off.'

And then the rites would continue.

'OK, Sol,' Belinda says. 'Well done. Sit up.'

Sol finds she is panting.

'Now' – Belinda fixes her with a laser eye – 'why don't you tell me about you and Carter?'

Sol can't detect any threat in her voice, but wariness is second nature. First nature. So much time spent surviving. 'Well, we've become friends here. He's nice, looks out for me, you know?'

'Would you like there to be something more going on?'

The bruisers in charge make that pretty tricky, but upped stakes were ever an aphrodisiac. Sol shakes her head convincingly. 'No way. He's sixty-five. He's old enough to be my father.' Or grandfather, it occurs to her.

'Carter has suggested to us that there may be a problem, Sol. He is concerned that you're, uh, flirting with him and interfering with His Recovery.'

She is speechless. Carter has been chasing her since she arrived, his lust undeterred by the skeletal wreck she had been.

Belinda takes advantage of her silence to press on: 'You compared him to your father ... I feel that's significant. Tell me what you mean by that.'

'No, I just said he's old enough to be my father ...'

'And we know, don't we, *we have established* that that's been part of the draw in the past. You lost your father at such a young age.'

Losing implies a kind of carelessness. Her father left in the night, that's all Sol knows. Like a fox stealing out of a chicken coop. And then what? Phoenix, and the sad parade of pseudo dads that came after. Life in foster care is bleak; the stretches in between are worse.

Her father's vanishing has been absolute – astonishing now that the whole world is instantly accessible, trackable, visible online. Sol has been trying to locate him for as long as she can remember, even at Dreamtime when there was no online to help. She'd drag Kit along on brave forays into the desert – all they knew – to hunt him down. Her mother Janet refused to tell her anything she could use later in life. The details Janet let slip on a comedown – 'Jo Jackson, no, not from here, I don't know, he did some carpet fitting at one point, dark hair' – did not narrow down the list of North American candidates she found when, at eleven, the vast virtual world of the internet was revealed to her.

Still, Sol persisted.

She figured Jo must have skipped Tucson long ago. Hadn't Janet said that he'd left town when he left her? But it was always at the back of her mind, a little thrill of fear and ... something else, harder to define, when she escorted a new client to a dinner or a party. What if this time, this one was her father?

Belinda clears her throat. 'Look, Sol, I'm not gonna lie. You only have another couple of weeks. You're well on track and I feel confident that you have a strong relapse-prevention programme in place.' She raises her head from the hammock and looks Sol in the eye. 'But you deserve better than this ... this pattern that's brought you to rock bottom. If you want that shiny new life, I'd encourage you to keep working on your relationship with your father.'

How the fuck can she do that? 'He's not here.'

'I'm talking about therapy, Sol. Your dad doesn't have to be here with you, bodily, for you to heal.'

He does. Find him, break the spell, save her life, save the world.

First get the big B off her back. 'I'm glad you reached out,' she says. 'I got this.'

'You got this!' agrees Belinda.

Surviving this place has involved a lot of guesswork – knowing what to say, what to hold back, how to make it clear that progress is being made. The phrases that work. Same as surviving Dreamtime, except here she's alone. No Kit to keep her sane. It's funny, all her life she's been running from institutionalised life. And all her decisions have led her back to it. As if whatever it is you think you're looking for, you can only find what you already know. Sucks.

'I think Family Week's gonna help you a lot,' says Belinda.

'Really? Will Kit be there?'

'I think let's keep the whos and whats a surprise. Anticipation will only get in the way of the process, you know?'

Sol coughs. Historically, family surprises have not been all that.

The sound of a cymbal interrupts: Gong Bath time. Sol can see the savage sun sinking behind the glass and is thankful she can't feel its obliterating heat. Carter told her part of Lights had melted before they had the Perspex fitted. They should have rebuilt it underground. *Homo subterraneus* – the Survivalist bunkered future.

Funny name, Lights. It's meant to inspire hope and illumination, but it reminds Sol of the feathery lungs of crabs, the 'lights' Phoenix called them. Lights and 'dead man's fingers' – the grey gills. All of it had to come out.

It was the only trip they'd ever taken from Dreamtime, driving west across the desert to San Diego, now under water of course. The group had set up camp on the beach: Phoenix, his enchanted women, their offspring. That was the first time she'd seen the sea; she knew freedom when she saw it. The red desert feels like death. She dreams sometimes that she is eating fistfuls of its dry sand, choking on dust.

Those barbecued crabs tasted so sweet.

The sunset Gong Bath sometimes takes place outside the glass dome so inmates may commune with the hiss and hum of the desert. But it's a hundred and twenty-five degrees today, so they will be washed clean by a tsunami of bells, Himalayan singing bowls, ancient bronze gongs, wind gongs, sun gongs, Burmese singing gongs, shofar and conch in one of the larger therapy rooms.

'Welcome in, guys. Love and light,' says the Bath Leader swinging a gong mallet like a golf club.

Carter is there, holding open the door for her. She scowls at him and sits on the far side of the room by the gongs.

Even as she is slipping into the alpha brainwaves of relaxation, anticipating the deeper theta of meditation, she can feel his eyes upon her.

The bite of his betrayal, she thinks, will keep her tethered to reality, but as the waves of the wind gongs crest and crash through and through her, she sinks below the surface.

She dreams of her father: like her but bigger. Safer. Then, inevitably, of Tucson and the myriad highs she might lay her hands on there. She dreams of many-hued narcotics raining down upon her, of cruising on a lilo in a sea of vodka, leaning lazily over one side to lap at the intoxicating nectar, a cat beneath a cocaine sun.

Family Week was always going to be a problem for Sol. Runaway dad aside, the only person she wants to see is Kit, and he's not even family. Does that matter? She's talked loudly and often about him in the hope that Belinda will put him on the list. He's the closest thing to a brother she has – the pair grew up together. Kit is a year younger than her, though he sometimes seems older, and their mothers had been friends in the commune. All the children at Dreamtime were encouraged to see Phoenix as their father and in most cases, certainly Kit's, he was. But he was not Sol's. Phoenix loved her anyway and she suffered for it. 'You do invite it,' he told her.

Who counts as family now in any case? Not Chase, that's been her main specification. Given that he's doing time in Arizona State Prison, it's unlikely he would have made it over anyway. He's still her husband legally, sure, but spiritually she has flown. She wonders if he's run into Phoenix there yet. A reunion – Chase had at one point been the commune's dealer, or so he claimed. That should have been warning enough.

Sol is dressed in white to symbolise her newfound virginal purity. It has been a febrile night of sweat and sleeplessness. She is not at all sure what to expect. She only knows what she has observed: that those who undergo family therapy here always seem to be on the point of rehab graduation when they start, yet to have added to their sentence by the end.

Belinda has reiterated it several times: be wholly unprepared, be open-hearted, be undefended against the untold benefits of these sessions. Now she slinks up to her looking furtive yet triumphant. 'OK, Sol. Are you ready for this?' Belinda extends her hand for a fist bump.

'Sure. Ready for what?' Sol feebly meets her gesture.

'Don't filter the feelings ... We've managed to get your mom on board. She's just through here.'

'Which one?' asks Sol, dismayed. Which one of the succession of foster parents that couldn't cope with her?

The answer is a jolting thunderbolt of a shock: Janet ... her actual mother. A mother unseen since the commune was shut down. Sol was eleven and taken into care.

'I – I'm not sure I'm ready for that,' she says, starting to hyperventilate. Of all the things thrown at her at Lights, this is the least tolerable.

'I think it will be very helpful for you to see her,' soothes Belinda. 'It will be in a controlled environment. We will be here; Security will be here too – she can't hurt you.'

'I'm not worried about her hurting me. It's just, it's been years and years, you know? Why dredge up the past?'

'Sol, if we don't address the past, it will be moved to constantly address us. Lights' family therapy is one of the most radical and effective programmes out there. Trust me. And anyway, she's here now.'

Sol had seen an unknown woman earlier, escorted by guards through the back of the complex. Could that have been her mother? She hadn't been able to make her out clearly, but the pose was a familiar one. All the Dreamtime women had been led away by the feds. Then the social workers came for the children.

It is 9 a.m., a time for suits and schoolchildren, but here it's late in the day. It is nearly lunchtime. She has already had an hour's kundalini yoga session, attempting to open her clam-like root chakra, a vedic chanting session and a macrobiotic cookery lesson, fermenting soybeans to make *nattō* and hearing about the dangers for 'people like us' of residual alcohol in kombucha.

Full of dread, she follows Belinda along the pebbled Twelve Steps path, a priapic monument at each juncture. Some way past a locked gate stands a guard by a circular thatched hut. The door requires them both to duck.

Inside, she is blinded by the sudden darkness. The light of the UV lamp outside dances like neon in her eyes, obscuring what is there. A hand takes hers and she hears Belinda's voice: 'Welcome to the Rebirth Hut,' she begins importantly. 'Now, research has shown that birth is the first big trauma we experience. The screaming, the blood – I mean, guys, you know, it's no fun for anyone. At Lights we believe that most of our patients are suffering from a kinda PTSD that stems from this: the initial terror of being expelled from the birth canal. Here we aim to replace this trauma with a more positive experience for baby, and for momma too.'

Someone grunts, presumably Janet.

Sol is used to surrendering to the idiotic – weird shit happens all the time at Lights – but she could never have predicted this.

'I want you to come and lie down over here, Sol. On your left-hand side, that's right. Now curl up. Like a foetus. Got it? Now, Janet, you move in a bit closer and put your arms around Sol.'

'Uh, OK ...?' Her skin tingles unpleasantly as she feels flesh enclose her from behind, breath in her ear. Janet's herbal smell is overwhelming: here is childhood. She can feel her mother smiling.

'Right,' says Belinda. 'Welcome to Womb Therapy. It's a seriously powerful tool, so take it seriously, guys.'

Sol's solar plexus spasms as Janet squeezes her rigid form.

'Sol,' Belinda urges, 'it's very important you don't think too much about this. There's a lot to process here and your rational mind will only get in the way of that. So try just to go with it and let your inner child take over, yeah?'

How is she supposed not to think about this? As far as she understood it, her mother had disappeared off the face of the earth after Phoenix's place was shut down. It wasn't like she hadn't looked for her. Janet's nebulous clues were the only hope she had of finding her father. But people can change their name, can hide in virtual reality or whatever. Sol grew used to the idea of being unwanted. When she was on the streets, she sometimes thought she'd seen Janet – but it always turned out to be someone else.

'My little Sola,' whispers her mother.

'OK, guys. Talking is thinking in action so we're not going to do much of that. We're going to let your bodies heal the severed maternal dynamic here.'

Sol's ear is full of her mother's sighs. Contentment or frustration? Janet is fussing with her dress. Sol longs to turn round and look at her captor. It's still pitch black.

Rhythmic whooshing and thumping starts to emanate from unseen speakers.

'These are the sounds you'd have heard in your mother's uterus, Sol. Close your eyes and just let yourself drift back there.' Her voice slows to a mesmeric drone. 'That's good … That's great … We're going to perform a mother-child meditation here together like this.'

Oh, this is right up her mother's street. Just typical of her to reappear in some hippy bullshit ritual after nearly twenty years. She's probably been sucking on Sonoran Desert toads this whole time, worshipping the scorpions and mainlining peyote. She can hear Janet breathing deeply and peacefully behind her. Sol has never breathed deeply and peacefully. It's Janet's fault, she thinks, tense as a taxidermied mouse up against her mother's scalpel hands.

'At the end of the meditation, Sol, you'll be ready to ask your mother a key question. Don't think about it! The little child inside you will be the one asking. Be quiet and you'll let her speak. Listen to her; give her your silence, your time and understanding.'

One question! There's only ever been one: where is he?

But now she finds this displaced. There are others. Why couldn't you protect me? Why didn't you come and find me? Why did you ruin my life? Do you know that you did? Do you care? Where have you been? What happened to you?

But she must not give Janet the satisfaction of knowing she cares.

She forces herself through the next god knows how long, toxic with murderous thoughts. An eternity. Finally, Belinda's voice intones, 'Let the child speak. What does little Sol want to ask her mom?'

But Janet interrupts: 'Actually, there's something I need to tell you, Sola.'

Sol exhales blackly.

'Janet,' Belinda chides in the same hypnotic chant.

'Just shut the fuck up, will you? I came here to tell my only daughter something important before I die.'

There is silence in the darkness.

'Sola, look. I'm sorry I kept this from you. I thought I was doing you a favour at the time, but that doesn't excuse it, not really. Your father's name is not Jo ... Jackson, or whatever I told you. It's Jonny – Jonathan – Quiss ... Will you let me speak! Listen, he didn't work in carpets. He was a GI. He was in the marines when I met him, in Tucson on leave, and he got me pregnant – with you, obviously. He said he'd stay and do right by us, and he did ... for a while. He kept coming back anyway, every few months or so. But one day – you'd just turned three – he returned to Japan and he ... just never came back. No, I don't know where he is now, or really where he was then – Tokyo? He was always moving about and all those Asian places sound the same to me. But it shouldn't be too hard to look him up now you have the right information, if you want to. I just thought, with everything changing as it is, time is running out ...'

'You're dying?'

'No, girl. It's just a figure of speech. I mean with the world changing ... What, you don't get the news in here?'

'Why are you telling me this?'

'I'm righting my wrongs all over the place these days.' She laughs. 'It's part of My Recovery.'

THE GROUNDING

The hotel where Kit works is not all that far from Lights. The Tucson Grand Resort, part of a worldwide chain though it pretends to be boutique, is proud to offer no-expense-spared, predictable luxury among the saguaro-strewn foothills of the Sonoran Desert. Kit must casually strike up a chat with diners – the kind of breezy syco-phancy that the robots in cheaper establishments still can't quite pull off. The guests expect it, and it ensures his tip hovers between the twenty-five and fifty-per-cent mark. Essential, as he's not paid much besides. To be honest, he's lucky to be employed there at all. He's had to tame his shaggy, sun-streaked hair – some strands made their way into a bonanza breakfast – and clothe himself in a jaunty, upbeat persona. His black-and-white bow-tied uniform couldn't be further from his usual T-shirts, jeans and baseball caps. Makes him feel like a cat in a jacket.

'God, it's so beautiful out there today,' Kit sighs, bearing down upon a Chinese businessman who flinches as he approaches. He places the man's wedge salad on the table before him and assumes the position: hands on too-thin hips, he stares – yearns – through the floor-to-ceiling glass windows out to the rocky desert, a heat haze hovering above it. 'Wow, I could look at those mountains all day.'

Fakeness clogs in his pores: blue-cheese dressing oozing into the cracks and crevices of the iceberg lettuce. He feels the old sensation tightening around him, of being trapped in his own skin, two tiny fallible eyes his only access to the world. Kit dreams sometimes of waking up blind, fumbling his way across a hostile, burning earth by smell and touch alone.

A creature flashes by the long window, a cat perhaps, then slinks back and stops to stare at them through the glass. Kit sees to his surprise that it is some kind of desert fox, its fur bright orange beneath a grey-sprinkled spine, ears large and alert. It must be a kit fox. He thought they'd all died out in recent years; they'd been on the verge of it for decades, like most of the non-terrifying wildlife. The giant crab spider's doing fine, naturally. Thriving, even.

'Look at that!' Kit instructs his diner. 'They're super rare, and in any case nocturnal ... This one's acting like a house cat.'

The man, despite being alone and therefore a prime candidate for Kit's advances, does not appear to be biting. He grunts and returns to his Virrea, erected in a silver holder beyond the salad and adjacent to the bottomless Starbucks flask that sits on all the dining-room tables.

The man stabs a fork into the architecture of the wedge, and Kit lingers, watching the tiny fox scurry off. As its amber eyes meet his, he realises it's a coyote. Of course it is. Those great American tricksters have somehow thrived where so many Sonoran animals have not. It must be a pup, that size. Cunning dogs. He shudders, ten years old again, remembering Chrissie ...

He reshuffles his attention and tries again. 'May I recommend the barbecue restaurant tonight, sir, if you're staying with us? The king crab legs are out of this world. Guaranteed clean! From Alaska, not imported.' Has he no pride? There are better ways of getting money, that's for sure, but not so legal … He needs this job. He sure as hell needs its tips.

'I could bring you a jar of our barbecue sauce, sir, as a special present – if you like, I mean.' He bares his teeth in a smile.

Kit's shoulder is starting to hurt. He's back with his parents again; like he'll never be able to break out on his own. They're still fostering, so he's sleeping in a blue polyester bag in the living room. Temporarily! He falls asleep on his back but inevitably curls up into a foetal position in the night, jamming his shoulder against the laminate. But how fortunate he'd been with these people. Kit was the only foster kid they'd ever adopted, suckers for his angelic looks: wide blue eyes and a golden mop. He's more like a scarecrow now. How generous they are still, though; how different from all those forever families that took in and, as quickly, kicked out Sol, returning her to the group home.

He can't wait to see her later.

The man at last looks up from his device and says through a mouthful of smashed-up lettuce, 'That's really quite alright. And thank you, but I'm meeting friends in Tucson for dinner, then catching a late-night flight back to Tokyo.'

For a Chinese citizen to be here in the States is one thing, but to be back and forth with their allies too, to be based in Tokyo … Well – Kit feels a little thrill in the base of his spine – perhaps the man is a spy.

'Do you live in Tokyo, then?' he asks airily.

The man exhales heavily and makes an exaggerated turn away from his salad to face Kit. 'I'm just tying up some loose business ends before the ban.'

'What ban?'

'Do you not get the news here in America?'

Debatable whether they do, actually. Seeing as the same rich prick owns both the world's largest virtual reality company and the most popular news channel.

'I haven't seen the news today, sir.' Few bother any more. It's too depressing. 'Has something happened?'

'Your president has finally agreed to end commercial aviation. It won't be possible to fly anywhere by the end of the year.'

That ban. The Senate's been talking about it for years, but no one ever thought it would go through. And so soon … Kit is silenced; he can hardly believe it. People have largely stopped acknowledging the quiet death sentence upon them. They have come to accept inertia and stasis in the face of climatic catastrophe and the invading seas.

'Do you mind if I have a look?' Kit gestures to the Virrea. The customer pretends not to hear for a second too long, then nods at it.

There's an expert in a suit allaying fears about the economy. 'Yes, there are various more environmentally friendly ways of flying,' he's insisting. 'And when these electric planes are fully viable, and proven to be safe, limited flights will be permitted once more. This cessation will be an incentive for the big airlines to divert their resources into speeding up this process.'

He supposes they'll invest in VR too – it's already so much a part of people's lives, sometimes indistinguishable from reality. The Virrea guide even dared to suggest it might offer a more authentic experience of a country. Stare at the Taj Mahal at your leisure, free from the squalor and the tourist tat. Do it with an American beer in your hand. Do it in the comfort of your own home. In bed. The whole experience made Kit feel not just trapped in his own body but wallpapered over – with posters of places he would never see.

'I guess there'll still be boats, if people really need to travel,' Kit says hesitantly.

'I don't know about that; all travel spreads pollution and disease. Climate migrants as well,' the guy adds with sudden vigour. 'Keep them where they are.'

Kit knows too many in Tucson who think that way. America for Americans. America first. In a way, it's surprising the government didn't stamp down on travel sooner. They sort of have. None may come in, but the world is theirs. The Silicon Valley billionaires have fled to their New Zealand estates.

The Chinese leaves without tipping a single cent.

Kit is enchanted to see Sol transformed. She is as luminous now as the white temperature-controlled empire of wellness around her. Brown eyes glitter in her elfin face as she takes his hands in hers over the yoga mat, a fragment of a second before they are dashed apart by their Lycra-sprayed coach, an implausibly glowing woman named Belinda. Touching, it turns out, is only permitted in the more advanced poses of partner yoga, and they come later, Kit.

He is inflexible to the point of breaking, too rangy for Sol's slight and springy form. He will swallow the pain: her beauty, her pixie wildness is before him. She is free even in incarceration, freer certainly than when she was brought here, her childlike frame emaciated, long hair matted and sprays of livid acne across her now clear and lovely face. That dark hair has been cut and it stands up over her darker eyes in protest at its owner's imprisonment. More boyish now, there's definitely something of Phoenix about her – it's the colouring. Brings back all the old doubts. Kit reminds himself that he looks wholly different from Phoenix, who is certainly *his* father. Colour means fuck all.

Under Belinda's gelid eye, they stretch, independently, and chat as if they have never been apart. Sol is fixated on her father again. She seems crazed with the idea of tracking him down.

Sol has had various obsessions over the years, most of them substances or inappropriate older men – con artists and pimps, drug dealers and sugar daddies, and in her sham marriage to Chase, all of these combined.

Kit, it seems, has had only one: Sol.

'Yes, my mother! You know. Janet. She was here!' Sol is trying to convey the magnitude of their reunion, but it's the magnitude – the strange drama of it all – that's at the root of Kit's confusion. He understands that Lights has unorthodox methods, claiming as they do to 'itemize and utilize' healing wisdom from all over the world – but Sol's foetal intercourse with her mother sounds bananas. Not unlike Janet though. Yes, of course he remembers her from Dreamtime; can picture her raising the slack arms of her rainbow kaftan, her eyes elsewhere. She had not been seen since he and Sol were placed in care. His own birth mom he saw around all the time, on the street clutching a can.

'So, she's in another commune now,' says Sol in more measured tones. 'Some prepper set-up in Maine.'

'Figures. Less imposing weather, harsher laws on climate immigration. She was always thinking of others, good old Janet. She been there all this time?'

'I didn't get to find out. She left in, uh ...' – she flicks her eyes at Belinda – 'kind of a hurry.'

'I see.'

'She said she wished she'd known her own father. That she was "righting wrongs". And she told me who my dad really is! And where he is! Japan!'

'Oh, only six thousand miles away then. Why there?'

'He's a marine apparently. Or at least he was, when he left.'

Could this be true? He'd love it to be true: to know that Sol is not also Phoenix's child.

A change in gear takes Kit closer to understanding the bizarre ritual she'd undergone with Janet. The two are guided through the deeper poses by Belinda, who repeatedly exhorts them to liberate the emotions from their hips ('The hips are like a great big sack of dirty emotions – Get rid of them!') and wash out their pelvic girdles with purity and light.

'Can't we just sit and talk like normal people?' Sol asks a little desperately.

'You've been sitting and talking like normal people all your life. How's that working out for ya?'

Sol sighs and straddles him apologetically. As she speaks Kit feels an unbearable longing to hold her and bury himself deep inside her, but the pain of her pushing his bent knees to the ground on either side, as instructed, is sufficiently agonising to distract. Sol, unaffected by the pseudosexual extravaganza, says that all she wants now is to find this man. Jonny, his name is. Jonny or Jonathan Quiss.

'I just keep getting it all so fucking wrong, Kit. I mean look at me – back to square one again. But this is the last time. I have another shot at life and … I want my father in it. I'm going to be thirty soon. Thirty. I know who my dad is now. I know *where* he is. I have to find him!'

'I'm sorry to ask this, Sol, but what if the guy's just not interested? I mean, he walked out, never got in contact …'

'But he did! That's the thing. Another thing Janet hid from me, said she thought she was protecting me. Yeah right! He sent a cheque for me every birthday, every Christmas until just a few years ago. There's a stash of money there. My mother spent some of it, "naturally", but she's handing the rest over, now I'm clean. She said it would have been irresponsible to give it to me while I was using. Like, she's had her spies here – said Phoenix had written to tell her I was here. Phoenix!'

The invocation of his name makes Kit shiver.

'But the point really is,' she goes on and he feels a crunch as his right knee, conquered, flops, 'that he was thinking of me, looking out for me. Loving me! Maybe he would have come back for me if I'd written to him, acknowledged his cheques.'

'Was there a return address?'

'No. But they came from a bank in Tokyo, so that's where I think I should go.'

'It's quite big, I hear.' Way fewer people in it since the earth-quake, though. The damage was monumental. But the images of new Tokyoites scurrying around a reconstructed skywards city are impressive and inspiring. Life goes on.

Kit is aware that he's resisting Sol's enthusiasm; he came here wanting to fuel it, to excite her about a future beyond addiction and Chase: a future, perhaps, with him in it. And now he can feel all that slipping away; Sol is going to flee across the world chasing phantoms instead. The world is closing! She can't have heard in this bubble – no Virreas allowed. The flight ban will change everything. If she goes now, there's no guarantee she'll be able to get back.

But she has heard. It's what's driving her urgency. Janet, for once, has been the conveyor of factual information from the outside world. 'She thought she was going to persuade me to come and live with her, that I'd just say, "Sure, Mom, thanks for the abandonment, the lies and this paternal bombshell – yeah, I'd love to come and live with you in your new cult."'

Kit flinches at the word. They had, he thought, made a promise not to use it. They rarely talk about those days anyway and never about Chrissie. He dreams of Chrissie though, sees her all over the place. Maybe Sol does too. But Chrissie's death was his fault, wasn't it? Well, it certainly felt like it. Obviously he would be the one she'd haunt.

'Janet wanted to get me up there while the flights were still running. But I have a better idea. I've just found out all this stuff about my father, and at the same time, it's my last chance, possibly ever, to fly – and find him!' She grins at Belinda. 'It's a message from the universe.'

Belinda's head is cocked. Shouldn't she be encouraging her to use this money wisely? Isn't it an opportunity to set up some kind of life here?

He looks more deeply into Sol, searching for their childhood code, her real feelings. He can sense the old intractability there; once she's had an impulse she must act on it. Then, and only then, can limiting thoughts be admitted.

They shift positions. 'It really helps to see things from different perspectives,' says Belinda.

Sol pulls his arms back, stretching his chest, opening his heart and sending all the blood there rushing downwards. 'I want you to come with me. Let's go together. What d'you say?'

'That's great, Sol!' shouts Belinda. 'Be your passion; speak your truth! Also, time's up here.'

Kit, bewildered, finds himself hustled abruptly back through the winding streets of Lights, unable even to say goodbye to Sol or answer her question. He mounts his electric bike with regret and an extravagant erection.

Later, erectionless, he stands outside the pharmacy in the swelter of the night air, warming up from the blasting air con inside. Kit's back doing the overnight shift for his parents as part payment for his floor space. A job and accommodation. It's a step up from last year. The pharmacy has no choice but to stay open twenty-four seven if it is to limp on another year – the robot-staffed chemical dispensers never shut, after all.

He is about to cross the road when he sees something moving at speed, low to the ground. A cat? No, it's the same small russet coyote he saw earlier and it stands stock-still, opposite him. Has it followed him here, all these miles from the hotel? He feels a sudden chill, even in the inferno. The Navajo say that if a coyote crosses your path you should turn back and not continue your journey. It might be a witch, they say, a skin-walker in coyote form. You can never tell.

He jumps as he hears a wail from next door; one of the two foster kids has nightmares. The boy wets the bed practically every night.

Apart from a commune trip to San Diego, Kit has never left the state of Arizona. He has long clung to the prospect of escape but by that he means north and inland, away from the prowling seas eating away the coastal states, away from the deathly desert and its warlord, the sun. Escape, yes, but to safety. The prospect of travelling to the other side of the world – to the ever more volatile East – is almost more than he can comprehend. Japan might as well be the ends of the earth, hard by the great enemy, China.

But Sol! She wants him with her. Could it be that she has finally realised? Is this his chance? And OK, another Janet-conjured name of a dude with a random story is hardly definitive proof of his and Sol's separate paternity, but it sure as hell is something. And then there's the money. That's real. Proof enough.

It's hardly surprising Sol wants to find her father, but Kit's not convinced an addressless cash dump twice a year is a sign of great paternal affection. It's guilt money, if anything. But if she loses this chance to seek him out now, maybe she'll never know. There's been talk, too, of clamping down on devices: the aviation industry, in its defence, has been citing the massive carbon footprint of the world's Virreas, suggesting the government terminate them instead. How could a person find anyone without search engines, without flights? She'll always feel the grief of letting some sort of hero dad slip through her fingers. She'll spend the rest of her life fucking the aged, seeking a substitute.

Maybe better the delusion of a hero dad than the stark truth of his own genes. To have Phoenix running through his blood, to wonder if he's capable of the same things ... He hopes Sol has been spared that poison.

Phoenix was a failed magician. He had always been full of tricks. Kit learnt that online, where he also discovered Phoenix's real name. The news (though who can trust it?) did not shy away from calling Dreamtime a cult, though Kit prefers not to think of it that way. It makes him feel like he was brainwashed, somehow altered and manipulated there in a way beyond his own power and understanding. As if he does not know himself – and therefore cannot trust himself.

Phoenix and his female followers believed that when the world ended, the Dreamtime would open. Sol was pretty excited about this prospect; wasn't the Dreamtime what the grown-ups were constantly trying to access, ever kicked back out to the loneliness and despair of their solo egos? They tried to fight their individual flesh casings through communality, through sex with Phoenix, and through the acid and peyote they ate to access the shared unconscious.

Kit remembers the crags of his father's bearded face as he sermonised. Phoenix appeared lit from within, like a jack-o'-lantern. 'The Dreamtime will engulf you in its loving wisdom, permanently!' he said, raising his arms and his voice. 'All the products of our human imagination and experience are real entities. We created them! All our creations will die with us as humans go extinct, but first they will all become visible: as the world around us breaks down, so the barriers to this other world – our collective unconscious – shall be lifted!'

Much whooping.

'In the Golden Age, gods and monsters lived alongside men. Then we all moved into cities. We banished the mythical creatures and ghosts with our bright lights and *civilisation.*' He spat the word. 'We lost our humanness! Our connection to the wild. But we're taking it back, humble and dying as we are. You can already see signs of the eternal present around us. Can't you? Our forays into shared consciousness are ever longer and some elements of that dimension now remain in this. Soon, when we die, we can live in that dimension forever!'

Kit didn't understand everything, but he felt the same prickling of hair on his forearms and up his neck, the same ineffable dread he always felt when Phoenix was aroused. A date for the great ending was set; the Dreamtime they called it, which was a bit confusing as they'd already named so many things that, not least their camp. The day arrived, and the whole commune prepared to leave the earth and live in a perpetuity of enlightened consciousness. It was a surprise when they all woke up the following afternoon.

The women redoubled their efforts to open the portal, ascend and transcend. By the time of the accident, the parties were every night, the children left to their own devices in the desert. That was when Chrissie –

But Kit does not want to think about that.

FLIGHT

⚡ *Yay Sol V, your Holograb has sent!* ⚡

Hey again Jonny, or would Dad be too weird, ha ha?

Look, I've called a lot of people Dad over the years and they've all been total assholes.

But you're not – I can tell – you seem lovely, by the way.

I can't wait to meet you!

I feel like I might finally start to know myself, y'know?

Well anyway, I'm not much like Janet – ha ha – that much is clear.

She's still a bit batshit, in case you were wondering.

So I must be like you, no?

Do you think we look alike?

Same nose, I guess. Now I know who to thank for that!

Joking.

So, I guess I'll see you next week …

Thanks for saying I can stay! Your place looks awesome.

Such perfect timing, can't believe I'll be there for my birthday.

Can't think of anywhere I'd rather turn thirty, or anyone I'd rather be with.

Tokyo here I come!

Goddamnit, I'm less excitable in real life, I promise you.

OK, gotta go now.

Bye!

Bye, Dad!

I lost my father in the war.
  We all did.

TOKYO DREAMING

TOKYO, JAPAN. Friday, 14th December.

Jonny Quiss's apartment seems too small for his ample frame, the furniture too low, the walls too close. Kit must shrink against those walls for Jonny to pass. Jonny appears underwhelmed – in fact pretty furious – about his chaperoning presence here with Sol. Why hadn't she mentioned it? Kit wonders.

In the former shock of neon that is Shibuya, central Tokyo, the towers that remain since the shattering earthquake look weary and worn around the edges, an ageing that these modern buildings do not wear well. It's quiet to the point of eerie in here and the rooms are forbiddingly bare, as if Jonny is the sole occupant of all these two-bedroomed apartments. They have not yet seen or heard a single other inhabitant, the elevator doesn't work and even the concierge in the lobby is no longer in evidence, though the desk remains.

This ghost block is not so tall as some of its neighbours, a mere five storeys, but squat and wide. The cracks are showing though, and Kit has seen piles of rubble on their walk from the subway.

Shibuya Station itself and the once hectic Scramble Crossing looked fully regenerated – all ad screens looming, leering, screaming. This is what you see on the news: TOKYO RESTORED. But the shiny footage conceals as much; the place is half-wrecked still.

Sol is to sleep on tatami mats in the tiny second bedroom; Kit is to sleep on the floor – this is clearly to be his role in life – in the kitchen that is also the sitting room. 'Sorry, buddy, no more mats,' Jonny states with evident enjoyment, before directing Kit to a convenience store to feed himself; Jonny had been expecting only one guest, he explains for the seventh time, and therefore only bought sufficient pot noodles for two.

It is a wakeful night. Jet lag has him in its claws. It was the first time he'd flown anywhere, and one of the last planes the sky would see.

The flight west from LA to Tokyo had taken them back across time through a thousand-coloured dawn to darkness, a glowing red sun just beginning to rise. For eight hours they hovered in this uncanny light, ever one step ahead of a day on the verge of emerging, a world between worlds. Kit felt as if aviation itself were reversing its path, humanity folding its creations back into itself, like a mother gathering up her children as she prepares for the end. At one point between wake and sleep, he worried that the sun might not rise at all this time. He found his hand was touching Sol's arm, the comfort of her sleeping skin, and she angled herself towards him in flower-like response.

Kit listens to the unnerving creak of the tower block – as if it's swaying in the hot wind. He filters Jonny's answers to his many and varied questions and deduces that this is most definitely the wrong Jonny Quiss, if that is indeed his name.

'He doesn't even know which part of the States you're from! Or your mother's name ...' he adds definitively to the list of charges laid at Sol's tiny and perfect feet on Saturday morning. Oh god, please don't let her be his sister after all.

'People forget things.' She sniffs. 'He's been in Japan for a long time. And children don't always look like their parents, do they? In any case, there's something about his eyebrows that's very me.'

When Quiss surfaces, Kit inspects these eyebrows and agrees that they are indeed curiously slender and manicured for a dude.

Sol starts smiling at him again.

In the evening, Jonny Quiss takes them (Kit has to insist on coming too) to a nearby *izakaya*, a Japanese pub. It is a den dug into the ground, air thick with fumes of smoke and sake. Sol is wearing a whiskey-coloured silk slip dress that Kit hasn't seen before, and heels that she hands over reluctantly as they descend into the nook of dark wood. She appears to have magicked an entire wardrobe into her bag and he, feeling red-eyed and underdressed, has conceded a white shirt, the only one that made it out here. In their shadowy booth, carved off from the rest of the bar by ornate latticework, a teak tabletop divides him from Sol and Jonny. Beneath it the floor is lowered, a pit for hairy legs in shorts. Sol's are curled up on the flat cushion next to Daddy. At some point Jonny's arm creeps around Sol's waist. Every so often Kit sees his fingers twitch up, or down, and he feels a little electric shock of outrage. Sol is completely unperturbed. If anything, she nestles into Jonny a bit more.

At the heavy wooden bar, three suited salarymen loll forward, fast asleep and statue-still, as if time has stopped – imprisoned and immortalised them.

Jonny resumes his campaign to get Sol pissed. 'You were named after my favourite Mexican beer, darlin' – it'd be a crime not to.' Kit tries to catch her eye but she won't meet his. She seems enchanted by the city, high on it after the bloodless hush of the residential block.

Eyeing Jonny's expansive flesh, Kit reflects yet again on the obscene flattery of his hologram. Back at her post-Lights halfway house, reunited with her Virrea, Sol had shown him an animated shot of Jonny's Holograb. The man was reclining suavely against some brightly coloured cushions, softly lit by something resembling a chandelier. It's not how Kit would have pictured a marine abroad. He'd agreed that the two had a slight nasal resemblance, the same strong jaw and cheekbones and slanting brown eyes, features which sometimes seem too large in Sol's slight frame. His avatar's hair was greying where hers is dark brown, and swept back with a slight wave to it where hers is set in spiny disarray, like a sea urchin. But any likeness at all is hard to see now, other than perhaps a slight upward tilt of defiant jaw.

He could have doctored his hologram to match hers, Kit supposes. He'd certainly enhanced his living quarters.

Jonny orders sake and three cups. Sol, who had protested half-heartedly about the beer, murmurs approvingly. 'What?' she says, finally allowing her eye to be caught. 'I went to Lights for opiates, not booze.'

'Yeah, give the girl a break,' says Jonny, lighting a cigarette and pushing the blue Mevius pack over to Sol. He looks like he's spent a lot of time in places such as this over the years.

The men at the bar suddenly reanimate and order more drinks. One stands up, starts to sing something with enthusiasm and falls over. The robot barman zooms to help him out, extracting his wallet and, therein, the yen he has spent here. Japan is one of the last cash societies left on earth – strange, given their almost total reliance on the virtual. As the man stumbles into the street, no longer in the care of the establishment, Kit has a memory – or is it a premonition – of Sol at that stage of inebriation, a danger to herself and others. The time she found an unlocked car on Fourth Avenue: teenage Sol careering, unlicensed, through the centre of Tucson until a flower-shop window stopped her rampage. She should have been in Lights for booze.

Jonny extends a fleshy forearm to fill Sol's cup with sake and then smacks the table buzzer with force. There's a quietness here, a respectfulness in the way people behave with one another. Jonny highlights this by contrast with his own noise as he places an order with the scurrying robot waiter. He is loud in a way that takes up more space than even the trio of drunk Tokyoites.

Not once are they interrupted by the staff, nor is Kit able to detect the tip-seeking behaviour so essential to his own survival in Tucson. Suits him. And why would robots require tips? Kit had sold his beloved bike to contribute to costs, but it is Sol who bought their flights, using her father's guilt money. They were lucky to fly at all. She had only just scraped these tickets – all too close to the New Year cut-off – and she thought they were fake until the plane actually took off.

Kit watches Jonny talking to Sol, leaning across her, blocking him out. He's holding forth about his upbringing in Miami before the sea levels rose. Sol's elated face looks ever more intrigued.

'So, Jonny, when did the marines bring you to Tucson?' Kit tries a new line of questioning.

'I was just passin' through, Ket. Met Sol's ma and decided to stop passin'.' Some octopus tempura lands on the dark wood between them and Jonny dives at it with chopsticks. 'Octopus,' he declares through a mouthful of it, 'is one of the few things left in the sea that can cope with all the shit in it.' He laughs uproariously.

Kit persists: 'So then the Marine Corps sent you to the Pacific?'

'This guy's hilarious.' Jonny nuzzles into Sol's echinate hair as more survivor specimens are delivered to their table: pickled jellyfish, noodle-wrapped squid, beetles seduced by something sweet and sticky.

'The Japanese have always been imaginative and brilliant chefs,' Kit had read in the airline's valedictory magazine, 'and nowhere can this be seen more plainly than in their culinary response to the toxicity of fish.'

Seeing the abundance of tentacled sea creatures in this *izakaya*, Kit wonders how these can be safe to eat. Just because some species have grown strong on detritus – the fighting crabs of the deep sea, say – that surely doesn't mean it's a good idea for humans to eat them.

He stabs a lacquered beetle with a toothpick and gingerly bites down, cracking the carapace and letting the juicy innards fill his mouth.

'What's it like, Kit?' Sol smiles at him and he finds himself grinning back, that involuntary mirror response he always has with her.

'Kind of like a sugared shrimp.' It's really not that bad. Growing up it would have been weird and repulsive to eat the kissing bugs and robber flies of the desert. The fear of the tick in an earhole, the scorpion in a shoe. Us and them. Phoenix had called it: the future will mean eating things like this, he'd said, dangling a giant crab spider horribly as Kit squirmed.

From his side of the table he can see two chefs working with studied patience behind the bar, one attending wholly to the turning of two single skewers of asparagus and shitake mushroom. Robots are not up to this job, then.

He wonders, suddenly, what they feed Phoenix in prison these days. Those big old huntsman spiders would be poetic justice, but it's more likely nutrient pills. As a teenager Kit thought he'd also end up in jail, like father like son, a chain gang of dodgy DNA. Sol said once – in a rare moment of self-awareness – that people who feel guilty believe, on some level, that they should be incarcerated.

They're unable to stop themselves trying to bring about that result again and again. How narrowly she'd avoided prison this time.

Anyway, he is guilty. Had he and Sol not wandered off on another desert quest to find Sol's father, Chrissie would still be alive and the commune would still be ticking along. Imperfect, oh yes, but what is not?

He dreams of the place often. He dreams of his half siblings, now dispersed like fallout on the wind, and he dreams of being back in that small private world with Sol, protected from the outside. Japan is alien; it throws open the vastness of the universe and exposes him, a small bleating creature trapped in its own skin.

He took Sol to see the old camp once. Not for long, though: there were bright-beaded Gila monsters swarming all over it. Terrible lizards.

Kit swings his legs out, using his halting Japanese to ask the robot waiter for the restroom. He's learnt a little on his Virrea, immersed in a virtual Tokyo that looked quite different from this real one. Unnecessary really, now that translation pieces are so much more sophisticated (they've each bought the full set – eye, ear and tongue) but he wanted to try. The waiter replies in perfect American, before whizzing in the direction of the bathroom and beeping an order at the door. Within, Kit finds several pairs of red slippers and more robot creatures vying for his attention. I just want to have a piss in peace, he thinks.

When he comes out, squirted in unreasonable places by jets of water and hot air, he sees Sol snuggling up to Jonny Quiss in a way that is distinctly unfilial. He hears her saying something about the memories you form before you are three; what she remembers of him, her father. Feeling safe.

Kit feels the need for fresh air.

Standing in the street, wearing the pub's outdoor rubber slippers, fervid water batters him from the skies; as if his bathroom experience has been a mere appetizer for the weather beyond. The world is used to tropical storms now; it's hard to remember a time when they made front-page news. Still, a change from the drought he left in Tucson.

They'll be back there soon enough, mission accomplished. Sol has found a father contending to be hers – and maybe that's as good as the real thing, someone prepared to stand up and claim her as their own. He inhales the rain, wishes he had some weed.

An urban fox slinks past, carrying its brush like a flame in the wet street. It seems unnaturally large. Its tail in particular is enormous and bushy, as if concealing many within that one's marvellous flourish. Kit moves to follow it, to get a closer look, in spite of the downpour bouncing large drops off the shining street. But as he steps out of the doorframe, the fox, startled, runs off, a blaze of red fur turning sharply left down the next alley.

He jumps; a hand on his shoulder. Sol, out of nowhere, is behind him.

'Let's go,' she says, sliding her hand into his as she did when they were children. Even then it gave him an inexplicable thrill.

What has happened in there with that fat fuck? 'Are you alright?'

She doesn't answer. The rain eases without warning, as it began. Sol leads him away from the *izakaya*, along the road and then left down the alleyway where the fox had disappeared. The effects of the earthquake can still be seen here. Buildings lie in disarray, unloved and abandoned.

'Where are we going?' Kit asks her, aware of his heartbeat in strange places.

Again Sol ignores him. She looks flushed and somehow electric, taller.

His feet feel flat and unfleet, and he realises he is still wearing the jelly shoes.

Kit sees various signs outside the houses, lurid in pink and green, lying on their sides. They say:

REST [2h]   ¥3,500~
STAY   ¥8,000~

These must be love hotels that no one has yet thought to restore. He had heard that even before the earthquake buildings lay abandoned throughout Japan. People liked to photograph these dilapidated ruins – old hospitals, theme parks, schools that had fallen into disrepair with the economic crash. A Japanese guest at the Tucson Grand had once shown Kit some of her own pictures. 'Japan,' she told him, 'has always been on the front line in the war with nature.' The earthquake must have brought more economic struggles, more modern ruins. But you wouldn't know it if you weren't right here.

The neon signs are all out. The street is barely lit but for the sudden moon, huge and full, ripping through grey-sodden layers of sky.

Sol stops.

The moonlight catches the silver of a cage, a picture of a cat pinned to the wall above. But the door is open and the cat of this love hotel has run free. Behind it, a building: the door is hanging from its hinges and nature has started to reclaim it, a crop of moss spreading upwards through the dead neon.

Sol looks back at Kit and he follows her. He will always follow her.

She leads him through what must have been the hotel reception, the jade slab chipped, giant Chinese vases smashed on either side and a telephone squatting like some arcane toad deity on top. No one has phones any more. A ripped screen depicting Chinese women in various stages of undress shows an unlit vending machine through its gaps. Beyond, a doorway to a corridor of further dark doors.

As he steps forward, his senses hotwired, he is aware of a patch of collapsed ceiling, the corner of a bed coming through. This place is not stable. The floor is dusty with debris; the lights hang down above him, broken. Sol is behind him now, her fingers dancing on his back. Kit wonders if he is dreaming. He has longed for her to touch him like this for so many years ... It very nearly had happened once – and then it never, never happened again. For good reason. He still doesn't know who her father is. Stop.

'Here,' he says, running his hands over an open door on the left. He turns to face her, but she has already darted inside.

He can barely see a thing in the small glow from Sol's cigarette lighter, just feel shapes rise up before him and impede his progress. He jumps as his foot makes contact with clanging metal. Sol's lighter meets a candle and the little light throws its shadows across the room.

The metal, he sees now, is a helmet. A suit of armour stands to attention in the corner, even as its head lolls on the red-carpeted floor. Medieval knights gallop across peeling wallpaper brandishing lances as blushing maidens cheer them on from the galleries. In the centre is the bed. It's still wearing the attire in which it met the earthquake, but the sheets and pillowcases have slipped, revealing a stained mattress beneath. The smell of damp and green growth hangs heavy in the wet air. A vine has crept through the wall and interwoven itself in the iron bars of the bedframe, which itself resembles a chariot. A deep round bathtub is on the far side of the room; within it an inch of stagnant water and a dead bird. Kit thinks he can hear live birds thrashing about upstairs.

Red velvet curtains curl around alcoves of armchairs and Sol rips one from its moorings and throws it across the bed. What is happening? The unpleasant thought that she is treating him like one of her clients creeps into orbit. He never wanted to know how far she went with those men. 'Escort' is a term of loose boundaries; he knows that. She's taking off her silk dress now and dropping it on the mouldering floor and he feels angry; she can drop the silent femme fatale act. He wants her, body and soul – he'll risk breaking the laws of nature and man for it, he knows that now – but she seems to be playing some sort of trick on him. It's not her; this is not how she behaves, with him.

'Sol,' he begins, searching her eyes for truth, the only part of her unconcealed by skin, that great and lying barrier.

'What's the matter, Kitten? Isn't this what you want? What you've always wanted?' Her eyes are glittering with … desire?

'Yes,' he says simply. Why deny it? 'But not like this.' He wonders if she has taken something. Or what, drunk from two cups of sake? 'You're not yourself.'

'I've never felt more myself,' she purrs, straddling him, snaring him like the serpentine vine watching them. There is a sort of orange glow around her. Her dark hair gleams red in this half-light. 'And I feel the same way about you. You know I do, don't you? I think I always have. It's just taken coming here to realise it.' Her eyes hold his, hard. She looks at him as if she wants to eat him. He is her stunned prey.

Sol kisses him and his mouth – a second's resistance – seems to dissolve beneath hers as with a rush of heat her body is up against his.

Her touch beneath his shirt shocks him; makes the feeling of his own imprisoning skin, the only thing that separates them, vanish.

And then, like the storm, she is upon him. His mouth is on her breasts, her hands ripping at his fly, all the hands and mouths in the world everywhere, electrifying every inch of him, on and on.

When the moon, which has been hiding in cloud again, at last casts light on the scene, Kit can barely see, he certainly can't think. His very lifeblood has flooded to one point: the pinnacle of his being and all he is now as Sol becomes the shaking earth beneath, around, above — a confusion of tortures, the stuff of dreams.

You know, we had never seen anything like it when war came to us.

My father lived simply, working in the sugar-cane fields; I didn't even have shoes.

We knew about the Japanese wars of course – their victories all over Asia.

We thought our colonisers would probably take over the world.

Japan was an unforgiving new parent: we were second-class citizens, banned from our own culture and language.

Every morning we had to bow down low in the direction of the Imperial Palace.

THE SOLDIER

Sunday.

Sol lies there, unwilling to open her eyes but aware even so of the strangeness of her surroundings. Her brain is battling the confines of her skull for space and she is shiveringly hot. She can feel material – damp dress, or sheet … is she naked? – clinging to her back, the residue of something chemical in her blood – but no memory to hang it on.

Eyelids unstuck, sunlight bears down on her through opulent open curtains. She sees that she is somewhere she has not been before, somewhere fraught with exotic decor. She is inside a red and black lacquer box. She is not in her father's – that man is not your father! – in Jonny Quiss's falling-down apartment block …

So where the hell is she? And where has Kit gone? Her Virrea is on the intricately carved table by the bed, and Sol reaches for it, pushing off the unfamiliar object on top: a leather wallet. Not hers. She swipes through her device for signs of Kit but there is nothing. Starting to record a message, she is startled by the scratchy bass of her voice, when here he comes; the bedroom door is opening.

'Hey, sugar. Brought you some breakfast. How's the head?'

Not Kit.

She shrinks back against the pillow, tries to place this stranger. How afraid should she be? The man is so very tall and muscular that the grand red room seems obscenely small with him in it. A few well-placed lines suggest he's quite a bit older than her, but they suit him. They animate his tanned face, youthful only because it is, she has to admit, terrifically handsome. She guesses he's in his fifties. He has one arm bound up in a sling – his right – and she can just glimpse the hard white cast reaching up from his great hand.

She does not reply. God, her head.

The giant hands her a plastic cup of coffee. 'From the vending machine downstairs. Drink it – it'll help.' He has a strong Southern accent. 'Y'know, a guy down there told me there's actually a robot butler you can call to your room.'

Sol notes an all-American smile of implausibly white teeth, many and strong, the troops perfectly drawn up for battle.

He approaches the bed and stands by a red velvet chaise longue at the end of it – is this ... a brothel? Even the muscles in his face look powerful, his jaw broad and sharply defined, cheekbones underlining light green eyes and a low-fade haircut, dirty blonde with a sprinkling of steel. He's mature: there's something knowing about that grin, despite its openness.

'Uh, you don't remember anything, do ya?' The man puts his good ursine paw in front of his mouth, but Sol can tell he is still smiling by the lines that fan out from his eyes. Is he mocking her? 'Hey, hey, don't worry – there's nothing to be worried about. You're completely safe. Nothing happened, you can relax about that.'

Sol coughs. She brings herself upright and quickly and silently inventories herself. Her hair feels congealed, her body desiccated as the desert it came from. She still has her dress on – relief – though it's up round her waist.

Some guy Sol shot up with once in Tucson had the gall to imply that fucking should be an easy extension of her friendship, almost a perk of her presence, given the nature of her job. No, she explained, that couldn't be further from the truth. Why is the word 'escort' so confusing to people? And in any case, sex is a valuable commodity, not to be given away freely. If it were given away freely, that – *that*, she emphasised – would be a seriously big thing. It would mean something.

'Like a "children of cobblers go unshod" kind of thing,' the man replied before planting the needle in her shy green vein. He was British, she remembers. Dead now.

She stares at the new man in front of her, careful to stay very still; a rabbit playing possum in a fox's jaws.

'Can we start again?' The man looks dismayed at her distress. 'My name's Hunter.'

That sounds vaguely familiar. 'I'm Sol.' She takes a sip of sweet cold coffee.

'Ha, yeah, I know that. And you're here in Tokyo, trying to find your father. Right?'

'Uh, yes.'

'Remember saying you thought he was in the military, here in Japan …?'

'I know that he used to be, that's all.'

'Well, so am I.' He beams proudly.

Sol likes the thickness of the vowel. So am ah. 'You're a soldier?'

The twinkle fades. 'USMC. Marines ain't soldiers – you wanna watch that with your pop when you find him.'

'Sorry, didn't mean to offend you.'

'We got to talking last night in the karaoke bar …?' He raises an eyebrow.

Blank.

'No? Well, that's where we met. You're a great singer.' Hunter walks around to the other side of the bed and sits, asking as he does so: 'This OK? Mind if I sit down? My arm's killing me.' He rests the sling on the pillow.

The whole bed sinks away from Sol with his weight. A creeping sense of shame, then of vulnerability. Why can't she remember anything? Could it be that Jonny had slipped something in her sake? Or this mountain she's somehow spent the night with? It's not like she drank that much, from what she can remember. But after such a long stint of abstinence, no tolerance, she supposes.

Hunter sees her darting eyes. 'Look, the point is, I can help you find your dad.'

The magic words. It is reassuring to discover that even though her conscious self has been off duty, someone in there has continued the good work of her quest. Time is running out, sure, but she has already located and befriended a military colleague. For whoever Tokyo Jonny might be, he is certainly not her father. And with that, something of the night's memory returns, marching in strong-armed and rich with disappointment.

Kit had gone somewhere: to the bathroom or outside; he was gone for ages. Jonny's hand on the back of her neck. He had guided her head down, gently at first – a paternal hug, she thought, as her head reached shoulder level – then down and down, his hand then rigid, utterly unyielding as she pressed up against it. Unable to speak, her face stuffed into his groin, she used the only weapons available to her, biting through the fabric of his trousers.

'You're my fucking father,' she cried, watching tears of pain leak as he doubled up away from her. 'What's wrong with you?' Where the hell was Kit when she needed him?

'Yeah, I'm not, babes,' he hissed. ''Course I'm fuckin' not. Thought that was a game we were playin' ...'

It's all pretty hazy after that to be honest. But she got away, she knows that; she ran out of the *izakaya* after Kit, and – oh – she must have got the asshole's wallet as she left. Slipped it out of a jacket pocket; that's the usual way. She is well-practised at awarding herself tips. Sometimes doesn't even know she's doing it. She wants to see what's in it, but not in front of Hunter.

He sees her looking. 'It's all there, don't worry.'

'It's not mine. It's, uh—'

'Yeah, you told me last night and I'm really sorry this happened to you. I'll sort him out for you, baby. If you like.'

Did she? She flicks through the wallet: some yen, some dollars, several credit cards all belonging to one Mr J. B. Quiss and a business card:

JONATHAN QUISS
Luxury Carpet Installer

MIAMI

What is it with carpet laying? Everyone's obsessed with it. No mention of the marines or Japan, but he could have left and – stop making excuses for the absolute fucker!

Fuck it. He was one Jonny Quiss but he was not *the* one. She needs to get on with finding him. 'Where are we?' she asks.

'It's a hotel. A love hotel – but don't be alarmed! You just wanted to see one, you said. So we took it for a short stay, you immediately passed out and I extended it for the night.'

'Thank you,' she tells Hunter weakly. She can't stop looking at his huge shoulder, the slinged arm. If it's broken, perhaps he's on something for the pain. Something strong. She knows what Belinda would say about that: 'That's the naughty li'l voice of your addiction, Sol.' Sol had, under duress, named this voice Chad. 'Chad'll try to trick you,' Belinda warned, face bursting with conviction. 'Fight back!' Sol breathes an *ujjayi* breath, a rehab parting gift bestowed with love and light. Tries to pull herself together.

Hunter scratches the colossal bicep of his bad arm with his good one and peers at her with some concern, his pale green eyes earnest. 'What do you need?' he asks. 'How can I help you?'

She doesn't trust herself to speak as the wave of last night's devastation shatters over her again.

How had she got it so wrong? That someone would pretend to be her dad, lure her across the world playing out some weird sexual fantasy, is … well, it's what she's come to expect from men, isn't it? All men except Kit, and this is hardly his finest moment either.

But the cheques were real. Money is truth and her biological father loved his daughter enough to send it. He is out there somewhere. Out here. She is finally in the right place to find him. And don't fathers need their little girls to complete them too? The strength of her own need makes it inconceivable that it could only go one way. No, it is an elastic band that binds them, can stretch across continents and oceans. Rubber is made for stretching. It won't break.

Finding her father is the key to everything. How can she ever be happy if she doesn't know who she is? Half of her is him. She thought she could see something of herself in Jonny – a certain volatility perhaps. But he was an imposter … a trickster, Janet would have called him, in that fey way she had. Such a man was the subject of Janet's only story, her sole contribution to the tales of fairy and folk they would tell in the desert at Dreamtime: The Animal Groom. It became something of a running joke in the commune. Janet would valiantly try to vary the details, but the gist was always the same: a poor naïve young girl agrees to marry a strange man who has come to seduce her. At some point before the wedding she gets lost walking in the woods, climbs a tree to be safe from predators as night falls and sees – oh horror – her beloved, carrying a spade. And then something – a claw, a tail – gives him away. With dread she realises he is not human, not who he says he is. She watches and hides all night as he digs her grave and sings the song of her imminent death. In the morning, she runs to her father and brothers – they're always male, the avenging relations, and in Janet's versions every one of them was strikingly like Phoenix – who come to kill the Animal Groom. Phoenix really loved that story.

'Love is a trap!' Janet would say privately to Sol. 'And with men, you never know who it is you're really getting. They're shapeshifters. They'll say anything to get you into bed, like your scumbag father.'

Janet had, she said, sworn off all men in the wake of Sol's father's flight, but somehow Phoenix had insinuated himself in her heart with his ecstatic promises of the everywhen, the neverwhere. He seduced her with the eternal present, the Dreamtime, the world between worlds – 'It's real and it's not real,' he used to say. 'It's not just in your mind but a place created by all minds over all time' – and Janet took her place in his harem apparently without question. If Sol had gleaned anything from their bizarre reunion at Lights, it was that Janet now considered Phoenix's imprisonment to be the defining tragedy of her life. Sol's dad's desertion had faded from view and her near twenty-year estrangement from her daughter barely featured at all.

Janet did not appear to have concerned herself with the disaster that precipitated the commune's end, nor the reasons why Phoenix has been doing time ever since. But then turning a blind eye is her speciality.

'You know,' she says to Hunter, 'I could do with some painkillers actually – you got any?'

He smiles on one side of his face.

'I just wondered, with your arm …' Don't sound too keen. Animal need leaps beneath her ribs and she worries that he can sense it. 'I've got a terrible headache.'

'That's what you said last night. You got a problem, girl?'

'Just this headache,' she replies stiffly.

'Aww, don't look so serious. I'm only joking. You're adorable.'

Had she already tapped him for drugs that she can't even remember taking? That would explain the amnesia at least. Hunter fishes out a white packet and slings it across the bed to her. It's only codeine but she knows that's illegal here, like some other odd choices – consequences of the so-called opioid epidemic no doubt. She used to persuade Kit to lift the good Tylenol from his parents' pharmacy; she'd extract the codeine from its acetaminophen base to sell at school.

She bets Hunter has access to better than this though. You don't just get codeine for a broken arm, surely.

'Missed my flight back to Naha for you, by the way.' Hunter winks, but he looks – what – shy?

The offhand way people mention flying … When there are no flights will people stop talking about travel? Or will it be all they can talk about? The worst kind of spring-break shithole will glow rosy with nostalgia. Her friends – if any remain – will be forever off on shiny virtual vacations, living half out of the real world. Same as heroin. A rush of gratitude hits her: she is one of the last to travel, to experience things for real. She *should* be taking risks, should be meeting new people and living this week to the full. It's never going to happen again. No great disaster here. If anything, her night on the town has taken her closer to the truth.

'So you don't live here in Tokyo?' she asks, testing the waters as she swallows the pills dry – she likes to feel them go down – and senses the inner hand rush up at once and ask for more.

'Yeah, I'm just here on leave. I'm usually in Okinawa – it's where most of the American bases are.'

'Far away? I mean, I guess it must be if you were going to fly there.'

''S not a long flight, two and a half hours or so. But yeah, crazy difficult to catch a civilian plane at this late stage – it'll take longer by train and ferry. Okinawa's one of the islands south-west of here, towards Taiwan.'

'Wait, and all the US bases are there, on one island?'

'How d'ya not know this, kid?' It's nice to be treated like a child sometimes, particularly when you're about to turn thirty. 'It's like most of America has no clue what we do for it. Yeah, a lot of us are there; we're back up to at least forty military installations on Oki now. We need more. Chinese aggression ain't gonna contain itself.'

'So it's likely, then, that if my father was in the marines, he'd have been stationed in Okinawa at some point?'

'I'd say highly probable, yeah. Nearly all of the Marine Corps bases are there. Certainly likely that someone would have heard of him, anyway. The whole island's not that big, y'know?'

'Well, I have to go there then. Right now. My flight back to Arizona leaves a week today.'

'Next Sunday? Ain't no big thing – people go to Oki just for the weekend. You got nearly a week. 'S a beautiful place too, a tropical coral island.'

'I have to find Kit.' Sol's already scrambling out of the bed, pulling down her dress, looking for her heels. Hunter reaches behind him and solemnly presents her with a pair of patent red boots.

'What are these?'

'You don't remember? In the night market? No?' He's acting kind of wounded – boyish, despite his great size. 'Yeah, you were wearing these weird jelly slippers – hot as … yeah, no.' He stifles another smile. 'So I got you these. Bit of an unusual choice, but you said you liked 'em.'

Sol's memories are shadows and none of them feature red hooker boots. And with an amber dress! The noise of drinkers, an arm in a sling … yes, the place was tiny, like a cupboard, and there were only a few seats at the bar. The American music that drew her in there – 'Country Roads', was it? West Virginia, mountain mama … Is that where his accent's from? Hunter giving her his chair – insisting she take his stool at the bar. Hand on her back, some light but persistent stroking. Did she sit on his knee at some point? It seems likely. It's conceivable that she might drunkenly have taken a shine to inappropriate footwear. If the shoe fits …

She just does not understand where Kit, *why* Kit— This is all Kit's fault. It's probably just as well he's not here to see the state of her this morning, actually – he would not approve. She will scrub herself clean and then she will call up his location properly, soberly. But the bath is right in the middle of the bedroom, a grand vermilion tub on gold legs shaped like lions' paws.

'Would you mind giving me a minute?' she asks.

'Aw, sure. If you're sure …'

He leaves, banging the door loudly. Next to the bath, Sol sees Hunter's rucksack, the painkillers poking out of a side pocket. Nothing but a temporary measure to ease the shock of finding out your long-lost daddy is no such thing, just another snake. She swipes as many as she feels might go unmissed and stashes them in – ah, she realises. All her stuff, including most of the cash, remains in Jonny Quiss's apartment.

When the Americans hit back after Pearl Harbor, we were first on the front line: an expendable colony, rolled out to protect the Japanese mainland.

My father and brothers, just children, were forced to fight.

The rest of us ran.

We fled, dodging the bombs and the large, loud white men.

We lived in caves, wandering from one to the next by night, starving, kept alive by potato starch mixed with water.

We died in our thousands.

The Japanese told us the Americans would torture and rape us if they caught us.

Death would be far preferable.

Imperial soldiers gave us hand grenades to kill ourselves if we were captured.

We must use them, they said.

They were gifts of love from the Emperor.

TRAVELLERS NOT TOURISTS

Kit looks askance at Hunter, and at Sol looking at Hunter. The guy's built like a tank, perched ridiculously on a pink stool in the cafe window. He is implausibly good-looking, like some ageing action movie hero where the ageing just confirms his virility. Kit hates him on sight. What has happened here? And when and how, he frets, did these two people meet?

He could ask Sol directly, but he'd rather not in this pink *kawaii* cafe with an armoured car – a marine no less – between them. Behind this military brute, the fashion experiments of Tokyo youth confuse him in the streets of Harajuku. Candy-coloured wigs are piled high with zips, clips and padlocks; faces are cluttered with glittery stickers and the alien glow of green, pink and blue paint. Many have wings. Diaphanous nightgowns float down the street above bumblebee-striped tights and towering platform biker boots. Androgynous teens dangle soft toys from multiple piercings and pile up hats three at a time or pin them to other items of clothing. He sees that one has fashioned a trilby and a baseball cap into shoes.

Kit is a small brown lizard among dazzling chameleons. Even

Sol, still in the whisky silk she shed last night, is now wearing garish new boots and red sunglasses, sucking on a multicoloured lollipop like fucking Lolita. Trying not to stare at her, he feels the dull buzz of alarm one might at a hornet's stripes, or a Gila monster's painted beads.

Kit woke up in the ruins of Love Hotel Hill this morning, rays of sun like lasers burning into him through the wall holes. Still half in a dream, he rolled towards Sol, sleepily seeking her perfect form. But she was not there. His first thought was that he'd gone too far and scared her off. Everything was ruined. He rushed out of the room, stumbling dizzy over debris in the ridiculous slippers he's still having to wear now. His shirt was ripped, too. No sign of her, or anyone, in the street. When he turned his Virrea on, he discovered a furious message from Sol sent this morning, demanding he meet her here. She sounded rough.

Had she crept out of the love hotel when he'd fallen asleep? And then what? Gone to a bar, he assumes, or a few, judging by her red-rimmed eyes. In one of them she met this colossus and now they're best buddies, or worse. Of course.

He feels intense anxiety shudder his so recently thrilling bones. His body is a prison again, a concrete dome dropped over him to keep in the toxic waste. But it's not guilt he feels. Not shame. Not that he is an animal, unable to control himself, unable to resist a person he knows might be his own sister. The guilt, it turns out, was all pre-emptive. Now that the deed is done, now that physical distance between them has reasserted itself like a sea, what he feels is aching loss. All he wants is to do it again. His own biology would surely have warned him if it were wrong. Yes, society can't be trusted but biology can. There's no way he and Sol can be related, he can feel it. He's had it all upside down … Instead of waiting for proof of her separate paternity, why not assume they're not related until it's proven otherwise?

But she can hardly bear to look at him. There is an agitation to her that Kit fears is born of deep regret. Did she make a mistake with him? Is she going to pretend it never happened?

It doesn't add up.

Sol told him last night she'd always wanted him. She's like a different person this morning: her Virrea message made no sense. Damp with sarcasm, her avatar had told him that she could see he was over in Love Hotel Hill (uh, yes – why are you not?), asked him if he was having a nice time and politely requested that, if he could tear himself away, he come to Harajuku. Was that just so she could introduce him to this Hunter, her geriatric new boyfriend? Sol is baffling at the best of times and now she's acting as if it were Kit who had run off into the night and met someone else, and not the other way round.

He needs to talk to her, alone. He keeps trying to make meaningful eye contact but she's resisting with an almost tangible pull.

'Where'd you go?' He asks her straight anyway, aware that it does not fit with the conversation she's having with the third wheel, who is some sort of Japan maven.

She ignores him.

Kit glares past them both to the spectacle of Takeshita Street, sees a giant rainbow sphere of cotton candy on a stick, so big it conceals the whole head behind it. Hunter is talking about taking Sol to some distant Japanese island to 'narrow down the search'. It doesn't seem to have occurred to her that they're flying back from this very place, Tokyo, only next week, on the last flight they could get; Tokyo, where Jonny Quiss is, the whole point of this trip even though it turns out he's a creep and almost certainly not who he says he is. Hunter's age lends him an authority he does not deserve. As, Kit figures, does his rank and his needlessly fluent Japanese. Hunter must be as old as Kit's own father. His foster dad, not Phoenix, who was relatively young considering all the children he'd sired.

Maybe Sol is embarrassed and this is just the cold light of day after any fiery one-night stand. But he's more than that, surely. Is it the drinking? Relapses happen – with Sol more times than he can count. No surprises. He's always been there for her. Sol's sense of shame, such as it is, never manifests directly – it comes out as anger. He wishes she would tease him, something mean. Anything but this cold withdrawal.

What can he do? He will give her space and time.

She points at him with the lollipop. 'Look, Kit, we need to get our stuff back before we can go.'

'Our stuff? Why, what's happened to it?'

He can see that Sol is battling not to say something. She even opens her mouth, pauses, then closes it firmly before nodding obliquely at the other man's unslinged, tattoo-sleeved forearm. 'Hunter's going to help us.'

Hunter's handsome smile lights up the neon cafe. 'Sure thing, ma'am. My pleasure,' he says, practically bowing to Sol, the obsequious shit.

'What's going on? Aren't our bags just over at Jonny's place?' Kit is aware there's something he's not being told. He is being excluded.

'Mr J. B. Quiss is not going to be overjoyed about this.' Sol has the guy's wallet. Seeing Kit's mystification, she adds darkly, 'I promise you he deserved worse.'

'Sol, what happened? Are you OK?'

She does not answer.

'She'll be OK,' says Hunter. 'Can you show me where the guy's house is on your Virrea? I'll go get your stuff and y'all can come meet me at the station.'

'What's going on?' Kit asks.

'If you wanna get to Okinawa, you ain't got a whole loada time. We need to get the bullet train down to Kagoshima, so we can take the dawn ferry tomorrow.'

'You don't have to come, Kit,' Sol says in a small, brittle voice. 'Hunter's going that way anyway.' Her tone to Hunter is quite different. 'I'm really sorry I've made you so late.' She is doing her little girl lost act, fluttering her prodigious eyelashes and placing a hand on Hunter's shoulder where the sling is tied. Kit notices him flinch – an almost imperceptible movement. 'It's my birthday tomorrow,' she goes on.

'Hey!' Hunter's extraordinary grin breaks loose again. 'Ain't no party like a bullet-train party.'

'I'll go back to Jonny's house,' Kit declares, trying to reclaim the situation. 'I'll grab our things and meet you at the train station, Sol.' If they must go …

A feathered fashionista slinks past the window like a peacock and turns to look Kit dead in the eye. There's something mechanical about the square turn of the head and then Kit realises: that's not human. It's a robot model, for some avant-garde clothes designer presumably. Is there no solid ground to land on in this place?

Sudden thunder shakes the clear sky iron grey and jets of rain drench the people in the street.

Hunter gets to his feet, a man of action. 'All set? Can you show me the way, Sol? Jerk needs to learn he can't get off treating women like that. And for sure not a woman like you.'

Sol hadn't mentioned a thing about Jonny's behaviour last night in the ruins. Whatever, now she's gazing at Hunter like she was looking at Kit then. Maybe he exaggerated her grand seduction, some psychosomatic effect of long-term fantasy repression. The shock of the forbidden becoming an option. Yes, son, you may sleep with your sister after all. Your own sister – *not sister* – permits it. Your own mind permits it. Maybe Kit is no better than Phoenix.

He is not going to help matters by being the asshat that stops the big adventure.

'It's in Shibuya,' Sol says, swaying slightly in her red boots and waving a hand at her Virrea. 'Let me call up the map.'

'Everything you can imagine is real.' Some artist said that, Kit remembers. But what if nothing real is true?

The three of them walk to Harajuku station, Sol and Hunter ahead and Kit behind, like their kid. He gazes at the slightly convex curve of her nose, turned towards Hunter, the upward tilt of her profile. She is too hot, too much.

The subway's almost empty again: an anticlimax. Kit had expected giant robots like the demonic gate guardians of Buddhist temples, with fearsome brushes for arms sweeping the stragglers in like so many ants. But it's not as it appears on television or online. Much is not – he realises that now.

When the flight ban drops people where they are, pins in a map, the controlled images of the virtual sphere will be the only story told.

No doubt they'll all fly home before the ban descends: they are tourists not travellers, as Sol would say. Kit fears she thinks that of him too; and it's probably true. The thought of missing their flight back, of never being able to catch another one, displaced like climate refugees ... It is a terrifying vision of chaos. Yet off they go, blindly following the first person to suggest it, to a random place over thirty hours away by train and boat. One hour for each year of Sol's life.

Back in Shibuya, Kit lags by a noodle shop, lost in hungry rumination. Last night's bugs squirm in his stomach.

'Kit, we were just in a cafe.' Sol is standing by a scattering of trees that glow bright yellow, their leaves surreal relics of an autumn that won't end, though it is winter. 'You coming or not?'

Maybe she does, deep down in some dark chasm of her psyche, think Kit is her half-brother. Maybe she has horrified herself.

'What was the code?' Sol asks as they reach the apartment block. '97 something …?'

'974 65—'

'Jeez, the guy's living in here?' Hunter interrupts.

'Yes, this is definitely the right block.'

'Did you not read the sign?'

'Uh, no,' Sol is sheepish. 'Can't read Japanese without a translation lens and we had Jonny to do the translating here.'

'Well, yeah, it's like a demolition notice. Building's not safe – a floor could collapse at any moment. This dude must really be crazy desperate to hang out in a place like this.'

The apartment was certainly sparse, though Kit, jet-lagged and in an unfamiliar culture, had assumed that was the Japanese aesthetic. 'Not his apartment' did now seem a more plausible explanation.

Sol finds it hilarious. She's still laughing as they head up the stairs, crying, 'Of course the elevator doesn't fucking work!'

Alerted by the noise, Jonny is at the door, charm itself at the prospect of this reprieve. 'Hey, you came back!' He opens his arms expansively as she approaches ahead of Hunter and Kit.

'Can I come in?' Kit hears Sol asking smoothly. 'I have something for you.'

'My wallet! Oh you li'l— Oh, there's more of you! Hullo, Ket. Hullo, uh, who are you?'

Hunter is on Jonny in an instant, grabbing the guy's abundant neck with his free and unfractured arm. He slams his head back against the wall once, hard, before drawing back the same massive arm to punch him on the nose. Jonny slides to a confused seated position, nasal drizzle of blood beneath an eye already purpling.

'You go get your stuff, ma'am.' Hunter ushers her through the door, ever the gentleman.

The Americans got us of course.

Our cave was full of injured, dying men who gave us away.

They had staggered in the night before, searching frantically for shelter in the rubble. The horrors of those men were indescribable, unimaginable. I won't tell you.

We heard the Western devils yelling outside.

We were all weak with starvation: me, my mother and two sisters – little Tsuru just a baby. I myself was only eight but I felt old.

It was time to end it.

My mother had the grenade in her hand. It's the only way, she said, and the men who were still breathing agreed. I kissed her, said goodbye, that I would see my sisters in Nirai Kanai.

But then, out of nowhere, I heard my dear father's voice. Would you do this to me, he asked. Let a good man lose all his girls? The Americans may not be as bad as all that, you know.

I ran for my life.

THIRTY

Sol feels pleasingly loose and sunny on the bullet train to Kagoshima. Hunter doesn't appear to have noticed the missing pills and keeps stealthily sending new ones her way. 'It's your birthday yo! We be living that shit up,' he says when Kit visits the john, putting an arm around her. She basks in his vastness. Hunter seems to be displaying a more ghetto sort of quality since the incident with Jonny Quiss. His accent, when he's not conversing in seamless Japanese, is less Southern gentleman, more backstreet Baltimore. The way he speaks can change according to the topic of conversation, and Sol finds him mercurial and fascinating. He's not your typical GI, she thinks, though she's not entirely sure what that is. She's never met one before – unless Squatting Jonny, the Miami carpet-fitter was a marine on the side.

She barely notices the midnight transition to Monday, a one-way street to the thirties she never thought she'd see. At some point on the eight-hour journey they disembark, gather more Kirin lager and self-heating bento boxes, then board another speeding Shinkansen. They all, or perhaps just Sol, pass out briefly. She can't have slept much last night.

There's something familiar about Hunter but an element of the unknowable too. When Kit — repeatedly, the Inquisition again — asks him where he's from, Hunter won't pin a single place of origin down, just lists the many he's been to. A great many, but Japan is his greatest love. He talks about the country like a woman. His worldliness is exciting, and she likes his cavalier attitude to excess too. He reminds her a little of Chase — before the darkness got him. But Chase, however suave, was slender and physically weak. She never saw him beat anyone up for her, though both his arms were unbroken. Sol worries occasionally that he can't be faring well in jail. He is a genius at manipulating people, at least. That should help.

Sol sits in the early hours of the predawn, thirty, looking across the still sea of Kagoshima Bay and beyond at angry red flashes flying out of Sakurajima volcano. The mountain reaches up imperiously, exhaling a drag of dark grey smoke. She feels like one of the last three people on earth. They are sitting at the outdoor table of a cafe — a shut one, obviously — at the ferry port.

She reaches for tobacco in the pocket of her frayed white hot-pants — her favourite pair; she's grateful that Hunter rescued them. Rolling a cigarette, she glances up as Hunter exclaims, ''S never still, that ole volcano, hasn't been for years. Erupts about ten times a day now — part of the world heating up, I guess.'

Nothing in this land is still. Sol likes its unsteadiness.

Hunter eases off his sling and releases his cast-bound right arm. His neck looks even more muscular above the extra expanse of revealed shoulder. 'People live there, y'know? Children have to go to school wearing hard hats, like they're off to work on a building site, in case they get hit by flying debris or lava. If we had more time I'd take you there, Sol. Yes, ma'am. Ever been sand bathing before? You get buried alive in boiling black sand by these, like, eighty-year-old women with shovels and you come out feeling super awesome. Just don't jump into the sea because it'll boil ya alive.' He grimaces spookily.

The hot marine knows his stuff. Sol is impressed.

'Y'know, they call this place the Naples of the East,' Hunter continues.

'Have you ever been to Europe?' Kit asks him. He's worked his way through all the other continents. Never knows when to stop.

''Course,' Hunter replies, grinning. 'Been all over, man.'

Kit is barely concealing his irritation and keeps staring at her with something like questioning concern. Well fuck him. Where was he when she needed him? She brought him here, paid for a trip for the two of them – which she didn't mind doing in the slightest. No, she wanted to. Wanted to have some time with her best friend after all the shit that had gone down over the last two decades. She needed him there at the most important time of her life: fully rehabilitated, turning thirty (for god's sake), reconnecting with her father. And it wasn't just about her. No, she thinks gravely, this is a turning point for all humanity. No more travelling. She wanted to give Kit a chance to see something of the world while they still could. To offer a temporary release from the infernal desert city. But he doesn't get it. He just wants to go home. And all of that would be fine if he'd been there for her when Jonny Quiss started acting out. But he wasn't.

'Are you left-handed?' she asks Hunter, watching his right arm hang down, immobile.

'No, right dominant. I shoot with my right, anyhow. But I'm OK with both.'

'What happened?' She nods at it, removing a stray strand of tobacco from her mouth.

'You did it in Tokyo, baby. Don't you remember?'

Sol laughs drily. 'How hilarious you are. Seriously, what happened?'

'Oh, wasn't no big thing. Bit embarrassing really. I'd been drinking in Naha bars, where we're going. I'd had a few … Guess I'm so big, when I fall into something I hit heavy, do some damage. Still, you should see the other guy! Ha, no. It was a tree. 'S just a minor fracture, be better in no time.' He reaches for her roll-up and she lets him take it, suddenly turned on by the intimate gesture, watching his lips close on the place where hers have just been.

Kit gets to his feet and announces that he's stiff after the long train journey, just going for a walk.

'Really?' she says, sighing, but he just blinks his blue eyes at her and moves off. She's quite pleased to have a little time alone with Hunter actually, but really this is further evidence, if any were needed, that Kit is literally always leaving her. When they were taken into care after Chrissie's accident, Kit and Sol had made a pact: they would stick together, always. Then they were sent to separate foster families. She's never been able to shake the idea that it was because Kit didn't convince in his separate interview. For all his worrying he can appear pretty relaxed about the things that really matter.

Belinda's upbeat perk assaults her unwelcoming head: 'People leave you, don't they, Sol? Loving people's not safe for you, so you get the hell out before they have the chance.' Sol does not think that's true. If anything she loves too freely and gets burnt.

A great, salty heat sweeps over her as the indigo sky starts to splinter into streaks of sunrise. Sol's head is full of the sea. She watches the waves on the surface whirl away from the deeper eddies, and then those give way, like the parting of the Red Sea, to strange new waters where odd creatures spin and suck. Her dreams on the train had already shown her this place, she remembers. She thought she was drowning. It must have been the heat, the thirst.

She has been yearning for the sea her whole life, the opposite of the still desert expanse of Dreamtime, the dust of Tucson. A life of land punctuated only by sky. At Dreamtime, thirty seemed unfathomably ancient. And it is. So few of her friends have made it to that grand old age. Dust to dust. There's a deadliness, yes, to the sea's drift and thrust, its siren's beauty, but at the same time it is the origin of all life. It can destroy because it creates. She doesn't know how the desert gets away with it.

Poor Chrissie.

She'd be twenty-three now. A frequent child visitor in Sol's dreams … and sometimes Sol thinks she's caught sight of Chrissie in real life, fully grown. The little girl appears as different women, but Sol always knows it is her by those long auburn flames of hair. The haunting of the guilty. If Sol had done as she'd said she would and looked out for her instead of dragging Kit off into the desert, Chrissie would still be alive.

'Now you know everythin' about me and I know nothin' about you,' declares Hunter, untruthfully. 'Where ya from, darlin'?'

She doesn't like to talk about her childhood at Dreamtime; it's too easy for what she says to be misconstrued. She knows that from the press, who painted Phoenix as some sort of death-cult villain, an abuser of women, an insane drug fiend and pusher. A great romancer of children. Sol felt free in the commune, though she realises now that she would not have appeared so to most. It was a childhood of strange desert beasts, playing and friendship. Freedom from adult authority, for the most part. She and Kit had the run of the place.

As she grew older, she began to be aware that the very great admiration Phoenix had held for her as a younger girl was waning. She noticed that she was chosen less often for his personal cleansing rituals – definitely the worst part of Dreamtime. He became as remote as it was possible for a father figure to be, with the exception of her own actual invisible father. Yes, she would still sit on his knee occasionally or revel in his declaration of her blossoming woman's beauty, but she was basically untethered. He never tried to control her or curb her. She was desert sister to the band of younger children that were still chosen. She would have remained so, she guesses, until old enough to join his adult women or leave. Phoenix wasn't interested in the female inbetweeners, though he didn't mind the older boys. Kit was still popular at ten.

Nor does she want to tell Hunter about her teenage life in and out of foster homes and care. The fathers that came after were far worse than Phoenix. Hypocritical. Unspiritual.

She doesn't want to talk about her life on the streets either, or her life with Chase, or Lights, or anything really. Consign it all to the garbage and begin again.

'I've been around too,' Sol answers and hopes Hunter will leave it at that.

'Y'know,' he says pensively, 'it's possible for a beautiful lettuce to grow out of a bed of cat shit.'

'Lovely.'

'Yeah, listen: the lettuce takes only what it needs and leaves the rest. Maybe a little heavy metal for character. My own upbringing was pure cat shit, but Japan saved me – or the military, I guess, which was the only way I could ever've got out of America in the first place. Okinawa – being somewhere I can make a difference – it saved me. Maybe it'll do the same for you.' He looks earnest, and avid.

'So you see me as a salad vegetable, is that it?' But Sol is touched by his admission of truth, some suggestion of vulnerability in place of the swagger Kit's questioning induced. Though she liked that too.

Hunter looks deeply into her, and his face starts to move irrevocably towards hers. He is so close she can see tiny blades of stubble about to break the skin, the faint scratch marks on his neck. Then his hand reaches to the back of her own neck and he kisses her across the wobbly table. Sol feels the sea thud, a kind of longing, as if a song is being sung that she is straining, straining to hear; the call of the sea through a shell pressed to the ear.

She feels – strange to say – like she has been here before. She is sure she knows this man. Then again, her whole life seems to be one big déjà-fuckin'-vu. The old multiverse horror show at work, no doubt.

Sol can hear a soft growling at the base of his throat. 'C'mon over here and sit on my lap, ya gorgeous girl.' He is irresistible. She hops lightly on to him, her small figure further diminished by the backdrop of his granite chest. She feels as if she is disappearing into him, melting her own boundaries of self to seep into his, her ear to his heart, thumping and rushing through her veins. Like heroin. Don't think about that. Just like heroin. Stop. Breathe. How easy will it be to get hold of in Okinawa? Don't think about it.

As if reading her mind, Hunter washes a couple of codeine tablets down with the beer. 'How's the head?' he asks her mildly, putting the packet in her lap as he rests his good hand on her bare tanned thigh. 'Take the edge off, don't they.'

Sometimes – often – she wishes she'd never met Chase. It was he who'd pointed out to her that heroin was way more effective than the pills she'd become dependent upon. Easier to get hold of too: he had lots.

Sol had been an enthusiastic consumer after Dreamtime, signed up to Ritalin and then Adderall for her ADHD, and Ativan for her PTSD. Her final foster mother, a devout believer in god and guns, tried to ween her off these. Sol should trust in the cult-like Church of Tucson's power to take away the trauma of the past. But when she had two wisdom teeth plucked out, she found the tramadol prescription really raised her spirits. When she broke her ankle, she knew what to ask for, but a nice doctor instead offered her oxycodone, a stronger surprise. Even Sol is not sure if the back problems that followed were ever genuine. Turned out the pills killed the pain in her mind too and that was worth a little deception, even of herself.

But she, Sol, is a grown-up now, she thinks, nestling into Hunter's chest hair. She has somehow managed to turn the ship around. These are not her problems any more; instead she should be thinking about how far she has come: avoiding jail, getting clean and travelling to the other side of the world to find her father. One slip does not a slide make and she will not go back to the way she was before.

There are many tools at her disposal now; the language of Recovery is in her and she is less ignorant about the way it – and she – works. But she'd question any club that had its own language, had assumed principles at its core – it's slavish, cultish. She'd objected at the time to the 'contagion of addiction' line. 'I'd advise you to look more closely at the way you use food, sex, technology,' Belinda had urged, and she'd said it again when Sol argued that her problem was with heroin not beer, so could she have some. It's never been Sol's way to accept philosophies wholesale; there's nothing like spending your childhood in a cult – sorry, commune, but isn't everything Stateside a cult these days? – to make you question these things. And she didn't feel, doesn't feel, that she's addicted to all addicting things, certainly not to food and technology. Jesus, was it even possible?

'The most important conversation you can have is with yourself' – Belinda again, along with 'rebuilding trust in yourself', 'getting to know the real you' and 'worshipping at your own temple'. The thrust of the important conversation she is having with herself seems to be this: is it not a core tenet of the civilised world that we do not need to tolerate pain unaided now? Shouldn't she, then, be able to take pills as and when required as functioning humans do? She should, and she does now.

Hunter's unslinged hand brushes her left breast sending volts and sparks scattering. She tilts her head up to kiss his shadowed jaw.

The dawn is richly red and somehow viscous; Japanese officials begin to man the ferry terminal, their language unfiltered by her earpiece, unnecessary with Hunter. Drowsily she asks him why he went to the trouble of learning the language. Translation technology is so advanced now that few bother.

He sounds surprised that she would ask. 'Oh yeah, was one of the first things I did when I was sent to Oki. Such a beautiful language. And to be honest I never trusted those earpieces. Never know who's listening in.'

'Oh, you hear crazy things like that about all technology. Maybe there'll be less need for the pieces when flying stops and the borders come down, do you think? Like, people will just speak the language that ties them to their bit of land?'

'Sure, why not? There'll still be Americans in Japan though.' He pauses to listen to an announcement. 'OK, the ferry's leaving in half an hour. Where's your friend?'

It occurs to Sol that maybe Kit has at last reached the compelling conclusion that she is bad news and decided not to hang around. Maybe he's on a train back to Tokyo right now, determined to get back to Tucson before air travel grinds to a halt and strands him here. She would be very sorry.

But at that moment she sees Kit coming round a concrete corner. She swiftly disentangles herself from Hunter before Kit can see and goes to meet him.

Kit smiles at her. 'Here you are, all sorted,' he says. He has bought three tickets and checked everyone in. He sounds in fact much more upbeat than he had in Tokyo or on the train.

Sol finds herself smiling too as he puts a paper bag on the table, producing an unlikely breakfast of three tubs of Blue Seal ice cream. There's always something contagious about Kit's grin, too rarely seen but a real radiant face-splitter when it comes. With a face like his, Kit should be a lot more popular with the girls. Anyone would be lucky to have him, but aside from one girlfriend in his twenties – Lucy she was called, Sol wasn't a fan – she's never known anyone to stick around for longer than a couple of dates. Maybe it's his shyness. Stops people seeing the real him.

'I got the most obscure flavours I could see.'

'Cheers, dude,' says Hunter taking the purple sweet potato. 'This is the best of all the US–Oki hybrids. We live on the stuff. You should have this one, Sol.'

Kit firmly extracts the tub from Hunter's grip and places it in a line with the other two in front of Sol. 'They're all for her,' he says unreasonably.

But vying chivalry is arrested by the soft rain they've been ignoring as it mutates rapidly into hard pellets of hail. Sudden gales start to drive the shards at a sharp angle across the pier, and where they hit, they hurt. The typhoon season is meant to be over, but seasons have ceased to have much meaning in the shifted climate. They seek cover in the terminal.

I ran straight into the enemy of course, but I escaped the blast.

I was delirious with thirst and thin as a pin from eating just potato starch and the odd repulsive adan fruit or cycad nut — famine foods.

But my father had been right.

The GIs were kind.

Kinder than the Japanese had ever been to us.

The revelation was terrible.

They offered me some chocolate and of course I wouldn't touch it — I thought it would kill me!

I remember the soldier grinning at me — he looked like some alien god, tall and blond.

And he put a piece of candy in his mouth to show it was safe.

It was the most delicious thing I had ever tasted.

MONSTERS OF THE DEEP

Monday.

Twenty-five hours on a boat! From Tucson, Tokyo seemed like the end of the world, yet now they are accumulating still more planet, over a whole day and night on a ferry, longer than it takes Earth to spin on its axis.

Kit feels himself being swept further out of his depth, into the territory of the sea, its expanse ever growing in dominion over the land. Habitable land has been shrinking year by year, you hear it on the news – oceans advance, nations recede. But here he can feel it; the growing strength of the water and what creatures now claim it.

He is algae, or some small sea snail, tossed about and around in the waves, soon to be flung up on some incomprehensibly distant shore. He had, it is true, considered turning round at the ferry port and going home while there was still time. It seemed as though this was exactly what Sol wanted him to do, that she was daring him. But his heart, the ache that grew in tandem with the escape plan, would not allow it.

Instead, he seizes an opportunity, securing the last two adjacent spots in the communal sleeping room and relegating Hunter to the other side. Sol does not protest: maybe the weird ice cream has brought her around. The sleeping mats are thin and hard but the victory is sweet.

Whatever portal it was that had opened between them may have temporarily swung shut, but the fact that it had unlocked at all was greater cause for hope than any before. It has allowed Kit to transcend his own fears. He decides that confronting Sol directly is a bad idea. She has her reasons. Denial is a self-protective mechanism and Sol has become skilled in its ways.

Just be more attractive is Kit's new and flawless policy.

Sitting on the upstairs deck trying to ignore the queasy feeling of the swaying boat (seasickness is not attractive), the three of them – for Hunter proves hard to lose and Sol sleep-resistant – see curved black mounds rising out of the choppy waters, splashes of tail smashing on wave. The word '*kujira*' starts to echo around the boat. And then there it is, right before their eyes. The thing emerges in its massive entirety, a vast whale leaping out of the water, forty-ton sea god, a prehistoric giant bedecked in barnacles. The creature twists round revealing its white underbelly and crashes back into the waves, slapping its fins as if initiating a round of applause.

'I thought they'd gone extinct!' Sol is enchanted.

'Ah, you still get the odd one,' Hunter answers. 'You're right though; they've mostly died out. This fella's come over a little early.' There is a disarming tenderness to him, Kit realises disapprovingly, that doesn't fit with his extravagant muscles. False advertising.

Kit has petted plenty of extinct creatures on his Virrea, including whales, but nothing could have prepared him for this one's enormity. He doesn't see what's coming either.

The boat starts to shudder and list. The whale is bashing it, throwing its whole weight against it.

A warning, Kit thinks, terrified. Nature is not dead but livid. Here she is thriving; alive with seething, uncontrollable rage. A devouring Mother Earth despairing of her children, washing them away with floods and burning them with electricity from the sky. And here are her minions, her monsters of the sea.

The whale slams into them again: salt spray soars up and over. How many strikes of its magnificent tail before the boat is history? Who would care if the whole human race was swatted by that whale fluke? Wouldn't matter to the whale, the sea, the earth. They'd all be better off.

He crouches low to the boat's floor, ashamed of his fright, unable to see past it. Were those shadows other whales? Are they coming? Sol is fearless, of course. She puts her arm around him and helps him breathe, as she used to at Dreamtime.

The beast retreats, thank holy fuck, and its comrades are nowhere to be seen. The terrible blueness of the sky and sea around him makes Kit feel even more nauseous, like he is drowning in it, trapped in himself, blue trickling in through all his senses, his own skin waterboarding him. The sea is coming for them all. The human race will be as obsolete as the dinosaurs, their only remnants bony homunculid fossils, like the skeletal feathery birds that fly – a reminder of overlords past. Scenery for some lizard revival, or whatever brave new creatures can survive the heat and the waste. Go to the fallout zones for a clue to what's coming.

Kit has to lie down. He returns to the double-mat arrangement alone.

Still land, but still by the sea. The sea rhythm is outside him, not within, where it had made even his daydreams bob up and down uncomfortably.

As soon as the ferry docks at Naha, Sol insists they go to the beach, as if the sea is oxygen, as if she hasn't been surrounded by it for the past day and night. Hunter brings them directly to Naminoue, the only beach of Okinawa's capital, apparently.

'But we're on a tropical island!' Sol protests.

They come through a park strewn with stray cats and stray people sleeping off the contents of the bottles at their feet. Seeking what's left of nature. Cats and the homeless have multiplied everywhere then.

Tuesday's sun is newly risen, sending spears of light glancing off the sea's ripples. It is searingly hot already. Framing the bright, pale sand, Kit sees not one but three highways zigzagging across each other, built on thick stilts, suspended above the sea, already at full throttle. At the top of a rockface are the red lacquered angles of a building.

Hunter sees Kit looking up. 'It's a shrine, buddy. Kept sailors safe in the old Ryukyu Kingdom.'

'What's that?' asks Sol.

''S what this place was called when all the independent islands were united. There's loads of 'em. The kingdom was a big deal for a few centuries. Yeah, big seafarers, big on trade. Then the Japanese got in on the act, colonised the whole archipelago and renamed it Okinawa prefecture.'

Hunter is the kind of know-it-all no one needs now they have access to all of human knowledge ever online. Kit wonders when – and, more grimly, if – he will fuck off. 'Ryukyu' comes up as 'glazed horn-dragon' on his Virrea. That's what Sol makes him.

'How do you know all this stuff?' It is evidently having the desired effect on Sol.

'Ah, y'know. Been out with a few local girls. Only right to learn a bit about their island.'

The sea looks calm and glassy, jade and turquoise strips of colour showing the seabed. But further out, the bay is blocked from the darker blue by a barrier – long piles of boulders for giant waves to batter. Ingress of the beyond threatens, currents against which the land must defend itself. Kit tells himself he is just paranoid after the shock of the whale ploughing into their boat.

When Kit had finally emerged greenly from the ferry's mattress room, Hunter had gone on and on about riptides, sea snakes, jellyfish – the deadly box, Portuguese men o' war and all the rest of them, each more obscene than the last. 'Whatever you're told about the sea being a dead zone, the extinction of marine life, none of it applies to the place we're going, OK? The coral's all dead but the squid are freaks. They like the plastic – camouflage for the fuckers.'

A sea full of krakens. Great. Whenever an ancient virus is discovered in the not-so-perma-frost, Kit's sense of another age – long buried, rising up again – increases. A pre-man era leaking out into the present like nuclear waste. Not human gods, human lore, the creatures of human imagination and morality, but the psychopath reptiles that ruled before them, slaves of fatal Earth and all her elemental terrors. So much for Phoenix's paradise: the Dreamtime, the return of the so-called Golden Age. Who would want to hurry this version in?

At the ferry port Kit had seen posters warning of all the deadly creatures one might encounter here and assorted emergency procedures. Some of them were just pretty shells, conical and patterned: the sort you might unwittingly pick up, beachcombing. And here on this beach they are all around. His toe just nudged one. But an indignant blue hermit crab poked itself out of the cone and then scuttled away, house and all, from the intruder.

Kit's attention is caught skywards by a great throbbing and stuttering: a grey steel menace wheeling a circle, rotor blades spinning on each wing and each side dipping in turn as it rights itself. The sound – hives of angry hornets in a blender – dwarfs that of the three highways.

'That's one of our boys,' says Hunter as a second judders into view, makes the same sharp turn in its unwieldy way and follows its mate inland.

Yes, Kit knows the metal hornets are military aircraft. They are V-22s, Ospreys, he would have been able to tell Sol, had not Hunter – of course, as usual – got there first. Kit knows things too; he used to collect cards of these. They can take off like helicopters but fly twice as fast, like planes. Tucson had the world's largest airplane boneyard – he'd marvelled at its vast ranks of defunct military aircraft all lined up, barely decaying in the desert.

As a teenager he had bought the military line – it had seemed like the antidote to his unregimented Dreamtime childhood. A way into a decent career, a way out of Tucson. Kit saw and absorbed the reverence the American people had for their defenders: they were heroes just for signing up. He thought it likely that when he finished school he'd join the Marine Corps. He would make something of himself and escape the pain of his forbidden love for Sol. Instead, he took up smoking weed, his muttering anxiety took on a new volume, and he realised he was not the right sort of person for such a career. Sol became the reason he should stay, just to be near her, to be her friend through revolving calamity, though it hurt. The ever-present suspicion that what he wanted most might never happen was a tinnitus of the soul.

Besides, he was too weak, mentally and physically, to be a marine. Hunter must have a hundred pounds on him. Kit would have been a light snack for his corps brothers.

Just then the beach shakes as a fighter jet roars overhead, terrifyingly loud. Kit finds he is clutching himself, trembling a little. Relief and then another deafening metal scream. Their dirt, their ferocity – these must surely be more damaging to the natural world than the commercial airliners.

'What's going to happen to all these planes when the flight ban kicks in?' Kit asks Hunter, the Oracle. And what will happen to you, he doesn't say, and all your kind out here? Will you have to stay put, knowing how difficult it will be to see home again? He considers, too, what Sol's father will do, if he's here. Maybe he has a family on the island. 'Will you just go home now?' he settles on.

'Oh I don't think the ban'll apply to us.' Hunter pauses, thinking. 'I mean, ya can't send troops to the other side of the world and then not allow them to do their job – or to get home again. And you know the situation with China, man. That's not gonna change just because people stop going on exotic holidays. The Japanese need us here to keep them safe. We can keep a very close eye on Shanghai from here – Korea and Russia too ... Yeah, Okinawa needs us, I think – and needs to keep us in the air.'

'They must be very grateful for your protection,' Kit replies shortly. Even on his brief trip through Naha city he'd seen the posters shouting, 'Go home, marines.' A Starred and Striped coffee shop and a clothes store called 'Uncle Sam's' had caught his eye just beyond the ancient Naminoue shrine. Squatting beacons of an alien culture. Then just around the corner, a sign: NO BASE, NO RAPE.

'Yeah, most of them are,' says Hunter, but he looks a little deflated and Kit senses he has touched a nerve. Hunter sighs. 'We do our best by them, y'know – provide jobs, big up the economy, put ourselves on the front line of clear-ups and evacuations when there are natural disasters, which is like every month here in the Pacific

Ring of Fire. But the old folks have long memories, I guess. And a few can't help but give the rest of us military men a bad name.' He brightens. 'But yeah, it's a weird situation, no doubt. I think most have gotten used to it. Those Ospreys are from Futenma – the airbase. Probably doing an off-shore refuelling exercise.'

Sol is sitting by Kit, running broken shells and coral through her fingers, looking longingly at the sea. 'Shall we swim?' she asks. 'It's so hot.'

Hunter leans back against the ivory sand. 'You don't wanna swim in there, trust me. See the sign?' He turns to Kit: 'They used to put jellyfish nets out in the summer; now it's hot enough for swimming all year but the sea has – uh – other problems, so no one does. So, no nets, no lifeguards. Not sure the nets could stop these jellies anyway.'

Kit blanches. 'Wait – you have to swim in a net?'

But Sol is already kicking off her white shorts and vest, running into the water as Kit – and, he is sure, Hunter – can only gaze upon the perfect peach of her black-pantie-clad bottom in breath-holding awe. Her tiny figure seems androgynous when clothed but impossibly curvy stripped down to her underwear, her bra the same black as her panties, the same bra she was wearing in the Tokyo love hotel. Kit is assailed by an image of Sol mounting him, crawling on all fours up his body like some feral cat.

She is waving at him, or both of them, saying how lovely it is in there. She looks like a fucking water nymph. Kit is on the verge of approaching but is suddenly afraid his body will give his thoughts away.

He had imagined they'd be alone together this whole trip, that finally all the hangers-on in Sol's life, and all the leeches she refused to pick off, would be out of the picture. It was bad luck that she'd picked up another father substitute, even on the quest for the real thing. On the same night that Kit's most desperate and sinful fantasy had come true and shown him what this life could be. He'd been under the impression that Hunter was in an extraordinary hurry to get back to base, no doubt to perform some violent operation of great import, but now here he is lolling about on the beach like he's on vacation.

Kit is pleased to see that Hunter looks pale and unslept. He seems to be conflicted. But then he gets to his feet announcing, 'Just once can't hurt,' and starts ripping off his chinos to display hulking thigh muscles bulging below military-issue underpants.

Hunter hesitates again at the sea's edge but runs in when Sol shouts to him. Kit, impotent, stares at his beloved shrieking and bucking, dodging Hunter's broken-armed splashes. His muscled torso, his inflated shoulders, his rock of neck like a comic-book villain's … Kit just does not like the guy.

Sol has always been brave, or defined by the death wish that afflicts the human race. The sea might pretend its clarity and innocence, but they all know it is a filthy writhing thing now, vengeful and unsafe. He half expects the pair to crawl out sleek and sticky with gobs of black oil, like the grebes you used to see before they all died out. He expects them to be coated with plastic waste, dyed by chemicals, sent mad by mercury and rendered infertile by fake oestrogens. Or eaten by mutant radioactive fish, their exploding numbers restoring the lost population of the sea.

They appear to be just fine though.

As they emerge, Kit sees a troop of schoolchildren wearing luminous yellow vests file neatly on to the sand. A teacher eyes Sol and Hunter with alarm and hustles the children away from the water. They disperse to pick up the morning's plastic waste: catch of the day.

'Aren't you needed somewhere today?' Kit asks Hunter when he returns from a trip to the vending machines, seemingly reluctant to get dressed again or leave the beach. Naked, the definition of his many muscles gives him the look of a younger man.

'Yeah,' says Hunter, passing a pack of local Uruma cigarettes to Sol, who inspects the orange, gold and black seahorse on the front. 'I am actually. But not till this evening. I've got time to show you a good, cheap place to stay – would have you to mine but it's not a big place and, well, y'know.'

The three of them walk up from the shore as the growing wet heat hangs heavy in the fibres of their clothes, sticky in the pores of their skin. A series of love hotels set back from the coast advertise their potential on pink-unicorn-embossed boards. 'Where 2 become 1,' invites Hotel Ponytail in English letters. Further into Naha, as soon as they are through the first concrete blocks, they seem miles from the sea – there's no sign of it anywhere – and Kit feels a little safer, less like he has been exiled to a tiny island far, far away even from the main islands of Japan. And Japan seemed pretty far when he was trapped in Tucson, bound by so much dusty land. Everywhere he looks are pylons vomiting electrical wires, buzzing highways, unexotic typhoon-tight buildings. All over the place – the roofs, the front gates – are colourful statues of fierce, goofy creatures that resemble little lion-dogs.

'They're called *shisa*,' Hunter says, stopping in front of a large blue pair. 'See the one with the open mouth? That's the male, keeps the bad spirits away. And the other one is female – keeps her mouth shut and the good spirits in. They're very superstitious here in Oki.'

Kit guesses they need to be with brutes like Hunter patrolling the place.

They turn into a wide street of closed clubs, bars and massage parlours.

'This is the red-light district, isn't it?' Sol asks, peering at the neon signs.

The only place open here in the daytime is, dubiously, a pharmacy. Kit can see a closed door behind the counter, to the left of the bottles and pills; on it posters of lithe and unfeasibly bendy girls advertise what lurks within: SOAPLAND.

'Yeah, it's one of a few, Sol, but it's perfectly safe. Girl like you knows how to handle herself I reckon.' Hunter winks. 'This area's called Matsuyama – fairly central here, not too far to the main drag of town, Kokusai Dori.' He pronounces it 'Cock's Eye'. 'Right, this is the one. It's got all you need and it ain't a rip-off.'

'Hotel Matsu' is written to one side of the revolving door. Inside, the place is small, clean and clinical, with a pervasive air-freshener smell. The lobby, like madness, is a white box. A robot receptionist bows low and visibly switches his settings to American, his face lightening and becoming more Western in appearance. He says in slow English, 'Good morning. May I help you?'

Kit watches a Chinese man, slight of frame and clad of neon, come out of an elevator. Within it a high-pitched electronic sing-song is piping something poetic, the poetry only a box that escorts people to different floors knows.

'Go on then,' says Hunter to Sol.

'Uh, yeah, the only thing is ...' Kit hesitates, reluctant to become too closely entwined with Hunter and his life here, then continues, for Sol's sake, and for the sake of getting home while they still can: 'Shouldn't we be staying near your base if that's where all the Americans are?'

'We Americans are everywhere.' Hunter is quick to cut Kit's line of thinking off and that's fine by him. 'I mean seriously, there are bases like all over Okinawa. Your dad, Sol, could be in any of them, or he could have left the military completely. There's no point taking off all over the island before I've made some basic enquiries.

No, it'll be best for you to stay here in the city while I do some digging and I'll call ya when I've got something, 'K?'

Sol's nodding and Kit is glad this means he'll have her to himself for a while. She's looking sallow and exhausted in the bright overhead light of the foyer. He can look after her, encourage her to start looking after herself again.

He is pleased and surprised when she insists on a double room, albeit with twin beds. There are only Western-style options here, no futons or tatami mats. Just as well, really, as the latter have done his shoulder no favours. Wouldn't she have asked for separate rooms if she was still angry with him?

'We need to save our money,' she says, and he is grateful to her for calling it 'our'. 'Who knows how much further we'll need to go?'

Not very, is his pleading internal response. He is already calculating the diminishing options for getting back to Tokyo in time. No flights, obviously. He checks his Virrea compulsively for cancellations.

'I'm fixin' to get y'all a proper Oki lunch,' threatens Hunter. They leave him smoking in the lobby and take the elevator to their room on the fifth floor. Kit carries Sol's bag and watches her shifting expression reflected by the mirrored walls.

It feels good to be staying at a hotel. Kit's only ever served in them before – and none with robot staff. The room is tiny, all of it variously textured cream except for the dark wood furnishings. The two beds, themselves smaller than Kit's length, are separated by a noodle's breadth, white pyjamas positioned carefully on each, slippers by the door. By far the most notable feature of the room, however, is what appears to be a many-handed person crouching in the corner.

Sol rushes to it immediately, squeaking with excitement. As she approaches, it unfolds itself into a chair shape and speaks English in a casual sort of way: 'Hey, you look like you need a massage! Why not come sit on me?'

'Oh my god,' she cries. 'I love this place!'

Encouraged, the robot continues: 'I can do shiatsu, Thai, Chinese and Swedish. Please make your selection. I can be man, woman or an animal of your choosing. Please make your selection.'

Is this a sexual thing? Better this dude than the one waiting in the lobby.

But Sol is busy exploring. She grows even more animated by a lavatory that speaks to her in Japanese as she enters the bathroom, raising its lid to welcome her to its pre-warmed seat. Kit, having gauged the heartening lack of distance between the two singles, pulls off his old T-shirt, stiff with sweat and dirt, ready for a shower. He feels the electronic eyes of the masseur upon him.

Sol emerges, her hotpants soaking wet. 'I think I pressed the wrong button,' she says, showing Kit a jet of water still arcing from the happily chattering machine. Some expensive-looking bath salts are in her hand: 'Yuzu, to make you merry.'

The lavatory abruptly stops gabbling. Kit is suddenly uncomfortable in the smallness and proximity, conscious of the nakedness of his torso. The fucking robot. Sol is very still, watching him. But he feels awkward and unwashed and weirdly aware again of the un-vanished feeling of siblinghood, such a pervasive fear over the years. He bustles about mopping up the flood, then shuts the door and tries to navigate the equally loquacious shower.

'Have a massage,' he shouts. 'I won't be long.'

When he comes out, Sol has already left, the lure of the masseur all too dispensable.

The Americans took me to a camp.

My people were dying of starvation and malaria all around me.

I couldn't tell what was real and what a dream.

Who were soldiers and who evil spirits.

I left my own family to die – can you imagine what that's like?

To carry on, to survive, that's not something that can be done with a full sense of reality, you see.

By the time they dropped the atom bombs, I'd lost everyone I loved.

No one left was spared grief: nearly a third of our population had been wiped out for Japan.

My brothers were killed in the fighting.

And my father?

The Japanese shot him.

They thought he was a spy, I learned, since he wasn't speaking Japanese.

He was speaking what he always spoke: Uchinaaguchi.

It is, after all, our language.

INTERNATIONAL STREET

Kit is behaving strangely. Even more strangely than usual, Sol thinks, as the two of them walk again, mostly in silence – what is he fretting about now? – back towards the centre of Naha. Kit had insisted they return to the ferry port and buy return tickets for Kagoshima leaving Friday evening, 'The absolute latest we can leave it.' His entire focus in Japan has so far been directed at getting out of it. Sometimes Sol fears he is incapable of living for the moment.

She can feel the brine in her hair, even spikier now after her dip this morning. A necessary ritual, due reverence to the sea god. Kit had just sat rigid on the beach despite her best efforts to entice him in, to shake off some of his travel malaise. The boat, the whale – she recognises these had not been much fun for him. That taken out of his comfort zone he will only try to scramble back in.

Of course she has seen reports of the sea's pollution; but for every one of these there is a conflicting story. If you can't trust what you see in the news, isn't your only choice to live? Seize every experience by the balls. If you thought about the long-term consequence of every action you'd never do anything at all, would you? Terrified into inertia.

She'd thought this short trip would open Kit up, take him beyond his fears. But he's so resistant to change. Not only to the daily adaptation of their journey, but also to her own efforts to reinvent herself. Personality is a trap. She wants to wear her characteristics as lightly as her belongings. Ditch half of them, chuck the rest in a suitcase, start again. But Kit knows her past, her core; he can scent deviation and make her feel shallow and inauthentic.

Here, so far away from the familiar, Sol feels closer to herself. She is freer and more childlike in her reactions to what she sees, in how she thinks and feels. She remembers being a little girl in the desert: as she encountered each new thing for the first time, each response was immediate and unfiltered, forming, she supposes, the prototype of a personality. After that, everything was seen second- or third-hand, through the lens of other people's beliefs or her own cursory judgements. And now, at thirty, when everyone has earned a new self, Sol is finally beginning again — here in Japan, in this daily confrontation with the new and the different. But Kit has gathered up the broken bits of her discarded self in Tucson and brought them with him. He is caressing and blowing warm air upon them, trying to reignite the embers. He can't see that she has soared phoenix-like out of them. That self wanted her dead. An old Dreamtime campfire song keeps playing in her head:

> *Rise, rise, burning child,*
> *Red-flamed, golden*
> *Wingèd bride.*

We can all escape our past, it reminds her. She could have escaped it a lot sooner if her mother had stuck around long enough to pass on Jonny's cheques. How different her life could have been! So much time wasted. She can't throw off the idea that her father is looking for her too, willing her to find him.

Hunter went home to Camp Foster earlier this evening and Sol misses his boulder-like presence, his confidence and charm. He is an invitation to a good time. She and Kit cross two highways via long pedestrian bridges and now Sol sees that they are in a much busier area, though no doubt their red-light part of town picks up later on. There are winding streets in all directions full of cafes, bars and *izakaya*s lit up by red lanterns, and Sol realises it's been a few hours since her last beer. She could certainly justify a drink now without appearing unreasonable, to herself at least, if not to Kit.

The codeine's all gone though.

Maybe it's the dwindling magic of the pills, or the slightly surreal Okinawan aesthetic, a clash of cultures, but she still feels half out of it. At some point on the boat, or possibly the train, in the fug of the painkillers and the beers and the travelling, she dreamed of her father, and the vision has stayed with her. He was wearing Marine Corps kit, green woodland camouflage, huge like Hunter but resembling her, standing out in the sea. She swam to him and, in anger at his distance, began to unpeel him from his layers of uniform, trying to reach his core. But she drew back in awe as she saw exquisite jewels, encrusted shells and horns and whorls growing out of his chest. The hair on it was seaweed and in his hand he held a trident. She rubbed her fragile face against his callouses and cried, 'Daddy, is that you?' marvelling at the blinding beauty of this sea deity. He took her with him down into the deepest caves of the sea, a kingdom of dragons, their fire warming the island that had cradled her father all this time – Okinawa. He made her his queen and she felt majestic and loved, powerful and primal.

The buzz of the codeine was not enough anyway. Like a scale played to just short of an octave – Sol yearns for those top notes.

No matter how she tries, she cannot forget the soft warmth of heroin, the state of divine apathy it lends her. Why wasn't Hunter on something stronger for his arm? Where's the opioid epidemic when you need it, huh? Sol bets he has bros who know.

Kokusai Dori — International Street — is alive with light and sound and the sultry assault of Okinawan, Chinese, Japanese and American cooking. Rich in traffic, the mile-long road is gaudy with tourist tat, vintage military shops, bars, cafes, restaurants and massage parlours. The twangy sound of the snake-covered *sanshin* drifts out of doorways as groups of Chinese tourists drift in. Reports of war must surely be exaggerated when so many Chinese are still coming here for kicks — while the tourist industry is permitted to fly them here at least. They can't all be spies. Women in traditional-looking robes of brilliant colour try to pull them in too, but Sol is not ready to commit, drawn this way and that. 'Christ, look at those!' she exclaims as they walk through a cascade of frog-shaped leather purses, their legs dangling down, tickling the heads of passers-by.

'I think they're real frogs.' Kit stops to examine one, but Sol's attention has already been caught by a bar with a neon bottle in its window. A sign: WELCOME MILITARY PERSONNEL. She peers in, almost expecting to see the man from her dream at the bar, but she can see no one American inside. It's quite early, only half past eight on a Tuesday night. Unlikely the streets of Naha will be filled with jarheads looking for a good time. Yet.

'Yeah, it implies, don't you think,' asks Kit, 'that military personnel are not too welcome everywhere else?'

Sol's not sure about that. Hunter had been pretty open and, she felt, balanced about the situation here. Obviously it's not ideal for a tiny tropical island to host forty US military bases, but China is the real threat. She's never seen a conflicting news story about that.

'The Chinese,' Hunter had declared as they sat down to lunch, 'would've built bases on every single island on this archipelago by now if we weren't here. Not just the Senkakus. Labs too – you know what they're like.' He'd brought them to 'a little place he knew' near the highways. Sol had wanted to see the main street then but Hunter wasn't keen. 'You gotta trust me, they do the best taco rice on the island here.'

'But look,' he returned to China. 'Japan'd be toast. Radioactive toast. The Japanese pay us to be here.' He kept his voice low as every other table consisted of Chinese tourists. 'Try it!' he urged, as plates of mince and rice arrived, topped with orange cheese and salad.

Taco rice had been a classic since the occupation, Hunter said. The GIs had a ton of taco seasoning and salsa but no tacos. Plenty of rice though. Sol liked it; Kit wasn't too sure. Sol noticed that Kit tugged against whatever Hunter was enthusiastic about, balancing it out with negativity. The more Hunter insisted on the dish's popularity, the more nervous Kit seemed to be. Like it might induce instant diarrhoea or something.

Much as Sol wants to go into the military-welcoming bar, she senses Kit's concern. What do you want to *eat*, he keeps asking. Seeing a pharmacy across the street, she finds herself drawn there. She scours the baffling shelves of medicines – the pharmacy is five storeys high, with bottles and pill packets piled into giant towers – but even without the translation lens she can see there's nothing for her here. It's all Korean beauty products made from snail mucus and bird spit, and turmeric hangover-cure drinks. Nothing she's interested in will be lying around on a shop floor like this. Although … there's a screen high up in the corner announcing, 'This medical advance is brought to you by Virrea.'

Sol tries her luck with the tiny woman behind the counter. '*Hai*,' she says, '*Chuu wuganabira*.' Hello, good day. Translation pieces only do Japanese, Hunter had said – 'You'll be surprised how far an Okinawan phrase or two'll get ya.' It doesn't seem to work here. 'OxyContin?' she adds hopefully.

'Ibuprofen,' the woman replies, glowering.

Sol buys them anyway, up for the comfort of swallowing any pill. She hopes Hunter gives them a call soon; he has promised he will. If the American Village is anything like America, she'll be able to get hold of something easily enough. And that, she thinks, is one reason not to regret their imminent return to the States.

'Did you find what you were after?' asks Kit when she re-emerges into the street. 'Aren't you feeling well? Maybe we should go back to the hotel.' The street performers across from them shout '*ah-ye-ah, ah-ye-ah, ah-ye-ah-ye-ah-ye-ah*' in high-pitched percussive chorus, clapping their hands and dancing. Sol feels suddenly inconsolable. Her freedom curtailed again, after all those months in the desert rehab prison. She feels, illogically, that it is Kit who is jailing her. She must talk to Americans – there are plenty around now, with cropped hair and youthful faces, though she has yet to see a uniform. And she must have a drink.

At lunch Hunter had revealed in his languorous Southern way that the military were meant to be observing an alcohol ban. 'This happens every so often, y'know, we're kept on a very tight leash here to avoid upsetting the locals. But really, I mean c'mon, it's not too fair is it, sending young people across the world, asking them to leave their families and risk their lives but not letting them have a beer to unwind?' Sol agreed and, not being in the military herself, ordered two. There's always been something so familiar and comforting about the smell of beer. The scent of a mother's breath, she supposes; a mother who has become calmer and cuddlier, who can face the day. Phoenix rarely drank but he certainly encouraged it in others – the kids too, claiming it was European and civilised.

'Let's go in there, shall we?' She starts across the road for an inviting doorway and Kit has to grab her out of the path of an oncoming moped as the hooting screams into her ears. Feeling too shaky to roll a cigarette, she stops at a vending machine to buy the same Uruma ones as Hunter. They walk into the restaurant, past a tank of prehistoric-looking sea creatures, just for show, for conservation, a museum of Japan's culinary past, not for eating here and now.

'How I love that you can smoke inside in this country,' she says as a waitress gestures, smilelessly, to the seats at the bar. 'How can they be so relaxed about tobacco and alcohol, yet so uptight about drugs? Wouldn't a joint be just perfect right now?' Her laugh, even to her own ears, sounds thin and tight. Kit says nothing. Sol clears her throat and inspects the picture menu.

The robot service industry does not seem to have caught on with quite the same tenacity as in Tokyo. Here, as with the taco rice place, there are real people dashing about, but Sol has to fight to get their attention. She has a strong sense of being *unwelcome*. They are the only Americans here. The closest waitress to studiously avoid them is slight and small. There's a fineness to her sculpted face and a wideness to her eyes that Sol is starting to recognise as distinctly Okinawan.

''S all in the earwax,' Hunter had announced at lunch, leaning in confidentially. 'Yeah, they're not really Japanese at all, y'know? The Okinawans are the ingid– indigenous people but not officially recognised by the Japanese as such. Got completely different earwax.' Unfortunately, his lowered drawl was still loud enough to be overheard by the waitress, but even she displayed none of the animosity they were now receiving. In fact she came up and leaned on Hunter's good shoulder, said dryly, 'Hey man, our earwax is second to none.'

Sol recalled her uncharitable thought about Hunter at the time, how his arm resting in its sling had looked like a great Spanish ham. She had felt a bit put out by his easiness with the waitress, and realised that she'd had his undivided attention since they met. When it was her turn to order, Hunter turned the beam back upon her and she felt reanimated.

'To be honest,' he said, giving up on volume control, 'the Japanese from the mainland look down on them a bit. Treat 'em like hicks. But I like them.' He grinned. 'I like an underdog.'

'How long've you got left in that sling?' Kit had asked, clearly unable to prevent himself from studying it with interest, perhaps also mesmerised by its ham-like qualities.

'Few weeks yet.'

It was obvious to Sol that Hunter didn't want to elaborate, but Kit kept pressing.

'Hunter's a bit …' Kit begins now, as little saucers of something black, hairy and unsolicited are slapped in front of them with a scowl. 'Don't you think?'

'A bit what?'

'I dunno, maybe that's what all marines are like.'

'Kit, you're not making any sense.'

'It doesn't matter.'

'Just say!'

'Forget it.'

'I think he's amazing,' she replies. 'And we need him.'

Kit nods.

Sol extracts a few strands of the black substance with chopsticks: vinegar, then the scent of the sea.

'I think it's seaweed,' she said. 'Try some.'

'Mmmm, you try it for both of us.' Kit is still scrutinising the laminated menu. He looks much younger than he is in the caustic light from above, and totally out of place.

'What shall we have to drink then?' she asks lightly.

'Think I'm going to stick to water tonight.' Is there some hopeful hint of suggestion in his tone? He is trying, she guesses, to make it easier for her to bounce back on to the wagon she was forced upon all summer. Screw that. She's only here for a week; this is no time to shun the local culture. She orders a large *tokuri* of sake with two cups and pushes one Kit's way. He could really do with lightening up.

After some time the waitress returns looking bored.

'What is this please?' asks Sol, gesturing at the black stuff.

'*Mozuku.*'

'I see. Thank you. We'd like this, this, *kore, kore* and *kore,*' she says, gesturing. The waitress moves away and immediately assumes a friendlier demeanour, laughing at nothing with the locals at the table behind them. It is perplexing.

'It's interesting, isn't it,' she says, inspecting the *mozuku*, 'that we can't eat fish any more because the sea is so fucked but this seaweed is fair game.'

'Well, I think we should be a bit cautious ...' Kit sounds strained and his eyes look a little red. 'But maybe it's been grown in freshwater or something.'

'Right. Maybe ...' She eats it regardless, finding it slithery and acetic.

'You know, I sometimes wonder if the whole world is being sent steadily crazy by eating what's come from the water. Like the sea is slowly poisoning everyone to save itself. Vengeance.'

'Ha, like we're all in some sort of mass hallucination before we die, horribly. Cheery, Kit. Thanks for that.'

If he's serious, he is at least smiling. 'Yes, exactly like that. We're stunned, like frozen lobsters as the water starts to boil around them. Whatever crap it's releasing is what stops us being able to do anything about it. It makes us stupider, genetically I mean, and derails our intentions. Like air pollution.'

'Kit, this is no way to live, you know? You simply have got to start focusing on the positive. God, it should have been you on the receiving end of Belinda's Law of Attraction campaign this summer.'

'The pharmacy though … have you been feeling alright since you went in the sea?'

'Ah, that's what this apocalyptic vision's about. We're probably just a bit jet-lagged still, you know. I feel fine now.'

'Maybe we were a little hungover too …'

Sol ignores him, admiring the colourful plates of food banged down on the bar.

'*Goya champuru,*' says the waitress, resuming the mandatory amount of surliness with Americans, and Sol beholds a stir-fry of Spam and snozzcumbers with eager eyes. The frilly green semi-circles are bitter but lifted by salty stir-fried egg, tofu and Spam. It is, somehow, delicious.

'I guess the Spam's another present from our friends in the military,' says Kit in an unfriendly sort of way.

'Try it – it's much nicer than it looks.' So too is a different kind of seaweed, *umibudo*, like clusters of tiny grapes along a vine that pop in her mouth.

You really can get high on the newness of a thing, Sol thinks. Even sobriety was doable when it was new. Is her father built the same way as her? She wonders if he's been here all along, on this strange island of homesick Americans, eating Spam and seeking novelty.

The camp was awful, yes, but one good thing came out of it.

It was there that I met Seko, my light in the darkness.

He was ten and reminded me so much of the father I'd lost.

I think it was our love for each other that kept us alive: as long as we had each other, we could keep the horror at bay.

When we left the camp, my family's land had been stolen, the house flattened.

The Americans had built Futenma airbase on it.

I had no relations left to fight for compensation, which the Americans refused to give anyway.

So I became part of Seko's family, what remained of it.

The Battle of Okinawa had destroyed almost everything, even great Shuri Castle, but not this house.

Look there, you can see gunshot marks on the walls — but it survived the war.

It allowed us to survive.

SIBLINGS

Walking through the backstreets of Naha, Kit reflects again on the giddy freedom of the waiters here. No 'have a nice day' compulsion. No forced fake chats. No tipping! The waiters don't even come near you unless you summon them with a *'sumimasen'*. This is how it should be.

He realises Sol has veered off to the side and follows her attention: a black kitten cowering on a scrubby bit of land. She's always been sentimental about waifs and strays. Knows what it's like, he supposes.

'Do you have any food on you?' she asks him, her voice lowered. 'Anything in your pockets left over from the boat?'

The small creature draws back as Sol approaches and emits a squeaky miaow in warning. This one is so little it is surely too young to have been parted from its mother. Crouching tiger-like and fierce now, it's reacting to something behind them – a woman. When Kit moves out of the way, the kitten comes trotting over and bats its tiny face against her outstretched hand. She turns to Sol and says something in Japanese, or perhaps it's Okinawan. He turns his earpiece on but the woman has already switched to English.

'I'm trying to persuade her to come and live in my bar,' she says, stroking the kitten's ears. Her long black hair is tied up in a ponytail and there is a prominent mole on her cheek. She's older than them but not by much. 'I've come here every night since the last typhoon, when I found her brother all washed up and close to death. He lives in my bar now. He runs it! You wanna come see?'

Sol is almost hypnotised by the street cat and Kit recalls how there were always a couple milling around her in the places she lived with Chase, or where she squatted before he materialised. Feral cats saw something of themselves in her, evidently, and they would follow her to each new building to become remnants of her own past lives, fragments of lost self.

He remembers smuggling Sol in like a stray cat, gamine and mischievous, when she came looking for him at the pharmacy. She'd run away from one or other of her foster homes and he found her in the street, shivering despite the Tucson sun. He was so pleased to see her. He thought maybe he could keep her there indefinitely, hiding her in his room, sneaking food from his plate to bring her in a napkin, letting her out to have a shower when his parents went off to sell their pills. She could share his bed. But of course his father found her. Kit pleaded for them to foster her too, but they distrusted Sol, thought she was a bad influence (they were probably right). His dad told him later that they'd taken advice from a CPS psychiatrist: Kit would do well to put past associations from Dreamtime and traumatic links to Chrissie's death – which would be processed in therapy – behind him. He doesn't remember having any therapy. Too expensive probably.

Sol, the woman and the cat, now scooped up and unprotesting, a small smudge of black against the woman's acid-green denim dress, start to walk back towards International Street, away from the hotel. Sol has barely slept since they arrived in Japan and Kit is aware that this, as ever, is making her act more impulsively. The idea of finding her father – or perhaps it's travelling itself: the freedom, the novelty, something in the air – seems to be bringing about a complete relapse. But he doesn't know why; or how he can protect her, except by making himself the boring one, chaperoning her, being the voice of early nights and sobriety. Meanwhile, all he wants to do is rip off that white shirt dress she's wearing and replay their night in the love hotel. Sol has never been interested in nice guys though, still less dull ones. His position is untenable.

Why does she constantly steer herself away from stability? Why, if she harbours this terror of being out on the street again, alone, afraid and in danger, forced to depend on the kindness of unkind men? It never goes away, he's heard someone else say of homelessness, the fear that it will happen again. And then he thinks that this itchiness of hers, this desire for nomadism is what she knows, that there is safety in its familiarity. This is hers by choice, not imposed upon her by all the things she does not have. Travelling is a state of voluntary homelessness, one she can control. It must affect her nervous system differently from his own. His own must be more nervous.

The woman and her new cat weave through the alleys where earlier in the day, accompanied by Hunter, Kit and Sol had seen what used to be the fish market. Now it's an exhibit: bright blue parrotfish, giant conch, clam and crab. It's rumoured, or so Hunter had said, that the Japanese, unable to embrace this new fishless identity, sometimes buy sea creatures legally as pets – for it's illegal to buy or sell them as food – and then host elaborate banquets with their pets as the star attraction, sashimied, stewed, steamed or soused and served with all manner of nostalgic accompaniments.

Though it is late, the covered street, Heiwa Dori, is still abuzz with sellers of *goya* juice, the green pressing of the bitter gourd, tall stacks of purple-sweet-potato pastries, pink dragon fruits, stone *shisa* dogs, Okinawan donuts and bottles of fiery *awamori*, the Ryukyuan spirit which Kit had seen at the restaurant and in which Sol had perhaps unsurprisingly expressed an interest.

At dinner he'd thought he would talk to her about what happened in Tokyo after all. But when he tried, the memory seemed to stream like mercury through his fingers. Even now it has a dreamlike quality. Parts don't make sense when he tries to pin the butterfly to the board. Sol seemed to have no idea what he was dancing around, and eventually he gave up. Maybe she'd already dismissed it – an embarrassing mistake best ignored. Is it possible she'd been more smashed than he realised and genuinely doesn't remember? She didn't seem it.

Beyond the glitz of this shinily lit shopping street, Peace Street, the light is darker, but at the end of an alley glows the red lantern of hospitality. The woman ushers them in, placing the kitten carefully on the ground, where she is met and gingerly sniffed by an altogether more robust-looking copy of herself.

There is a single customer sitting at one of the dark wooden tables, her back to them. All Kit can see of her is bobbed blonde hair with black roots. She turns briefly to glance at the kittens and Kit sees that she's young, in her early twenties probably. Her pale fringe is very long, falling into her eyes. There's a guy in a tiny cupboard on the left that, judging by the clangs and steam gusts, serves as a kitchen.

'My husband, Ryo,' says the woman who led them here, as the man comes out to greet the new kitten. His hair is sleek and shoulder length, a bandanna drawing it off his angular face, his cheekbones and jawline razor diagonals. 'And I'm Tomi.'

'I'm Sol, and this is Kit.'

'You are brother and sister? Like the kittens?'

'As good as,' says Sol, and Kit realises with a diving sensation that she really cannot see him as an object of lust, despite what happened between them. A tiny hammer in his jaw starts to flutter and he realises he is clenching it into spasm.

The kittens begin to pounce on each other in boisterous recognition and chase each other round the bar, knocking over a bottle of *awamori*, sending an ashtray spinning to the floor and then rolling around on the floor mewing tiny war cries. They make Kit think of that story his mother used to tell at Dreamtime, about the fearsome desert predator, the Cactus Cat. He hasn't thought of it in ages. With a coat of needles instead of fur, the Cactus Cat would slash the bases of cacti with blade-like paws, allow the leaking juice to ferment. The cat would then get wasted and maraud, causing chaos wherever it rampaged. When Sol at twelve cut her hair into spikes and discovered tequila, Kit took to calling her Cactus, a move which did not pay off. These creeping black kittens, hopping crabwise with arched back and hissing maw, make him eleven again: unspiky and uncool.

'What would you like to drink?' asks Ryo through a translator. 'Try our *awamori* perhaps?' He gestures behind the bar to a colourful array of clay pots.

'Yes, great,' says Sol, when Ryo points to one glazed in blue: 'My family make it here in Naha.' She is distracted, laughing as the larger kitten backflips off the smaller.

Kit and Sol sit on a yellow sofa near the back of the room, facing the bar, the *awamori* amphorae and a Virrea screen showing soccer. Tomi places a bucket of ice on their table, a jug of water, the *awamori* in a blue and white ceramic flask, glasses and a cocktail swizzler.

'Can you hear something?' Kit asks Sol. Shouting, chanting, something getting louder as it approaches.

Before she can answer, the bar door is swung back hard against the wall. Three young women stride in noisily, debating something inaccessible to Kit amongst themselves. One is weighed down by a large pile of pamphlets which she dumps on the bar despite a palpable lack of encouragement from the proprietors. The kittens flee for cover and the girl with peroxide bangs takes out a book and stares fixedly at the turning pages.

All three newcomers are stylishly dressed student types. One of them, the long-haired pamphlet carrier with a leader's authority, looks around the bar questioningly and Kit can see that her eyes, behind glasses, are reddened. Those eyes land on his and this seems to be the trigger she's been waiting for as she lets fly an instant and violent flurry of invective upon the bar owners. It's an angry-sounding attack and too fast to travel clearly through his translators. He is glad he can't understand any of it – even her two accomplices seem wary of joining in.

Ryo is holding the door open now, ushering them out. The two quieter girls do not need a second invitation and the vocal one has turned to follow them, collecting half of the leaflets. Kit can see the picture on the front from this angle: a V-22 Osprey in disaster, crashed through the roof of what looks like a school.

Without warning, she turns and yells at Kit in English, 'Military, are you?'

He's reluctant to get involved but she's just hanging there expectantly. 'Absolutely not. We're tourists.' He feels Sol flinch a little. 'We're the last tourists, I guess. From America, but not military.'

'Isn't that a thought, Masayo-san,' says Tomi, eyes warning her off. 'The last tourists.'

'American tourists don't come here so let's just assume you're not, huh?'

'I'm looking for my father here actually,' says Sol, fiddling with the *awamori* array. The blonde woman sits up and looks their way.

'Tell me, do you think it's right that Ryukyuan girls can't walk about by themselves?' Masayo continues, still staring with repulsion at Kit.

Kit copies Sol, pouring some *awamori* over ice, then adding water. More water than Sol. It is cool and clean-tasting, fumy and incisive, but he feels uncomfortable here. Should they go? He takes a large draught of its fire and replies, 'Of course not. Everyone should be free to walk however they want. Can they – can *you* – not here?'

'Not if we don't want to end up raped and dead. No we can't.' Her tears are now fully visible. 'Yui was a student of mine. She had her whole life ahead of her when a man snatched her on the way home from school. They found her bleeding and unconscious miles north in Yanbaru forest – near the US jungle training camp.'

Tomi is looking more and more alarmed by this outburst. 'This is not the way ...' she says in English, for their benefit presumably. She is searching Masayo's face for something. 'You're upset. It's not safe for you to behave like this, you know that, don't you? This is not the way to bring about peace. That's what we all want, isn't it?'

'You don't want anything! You are complicit! Why are you still letting Americans and Japanese in your bar? Why do you have Virrea up there spreading their lies? Our islands are flooding, our fishing is done – this is the end of days for us and you do nothing! You pretend it isn't even happening!'

'Masayo-san, I think you should go now,' Ryo says gently.

But she's looking at Kit. 'Aren't you sorry? Is this *normal* for you?'

Kit looks down at his lap where an emergent kitten is starting to prickle his thigh with whetted claws. 'I'm so very sorry. That's awful. Really awful. Is your friend recovering now? Did they get the guy?'

'No, Yui died of her injuries last week, and no, they haven't caught the American lowlife.'

Kit is very sorry. He keeps saying it. But he dares to ask, too, how they know the criminal's American.

'It's always an American! There's a new thing every week: an accident, a robbery, a rape – a murder.'

'Were there any witnesses? Surely they'll find him.'

'You people always look after your own. What'll you do? Pay a pittance to the family and impose a token few days' alcohol ban? If you had to stand trial in our courts, things would be very different.'

Kit's eyes are drawn to a small woodblock print on the wall, a chain-mail-clad skeleton gleefully lancing a knight from behind. Next to it, three more prints as Death comes variously for a child, a ploughman, an old woman. He shudders.

Sol is unusually quiet and downcast, making her way swiftly through the pure spirit. He removes the kneading kitten from his leg and places it on her. Kit wonders if this conversation is doing anything to put Sol off Hunter.

Masayo's addressing Tomi and Ryo now but in English. Maybe it had been Okinawan initially, not Japanese, and that's why the translators couldn't pick it up. How many people still speak Okinawan here? 'Look,' she's crying, 'there won't ever be any peace here until the Americans withdraw their bases. No one listens to the Ryukyuan people, but we are the ones who suffer. American crimes don't even make it on to Virrea. It's only by telling people what's really going on that anything will be done. I promise you, the world now sees what America constructs as reality. They don't see reality itself. *You* don't.'

The girls outside speak to Masayo, telling her to leave Kit guesses. He hasn't seen anyone this angry since Phoenix. Even as she leaves, she's shouting back towards the bar, 'You Americans helped the Japanese do to us what you did to your own native peoples. You won't stop till we're all gone.'

Silence. Everyone is paralysed.

Finally, Tomi speaks: 'I'm so sorry about that. I'm afraid Masayo's had some bad experiences. Let me get you another drink – no charge.'

Kit tries to demur but even as he does so more *awamori* is arriving. Sol is still unmoving. He sits back down, trying to swallow his distress: anger makes all his nerves go live. 'I'm sorry. Americans do want to know what's done in their name. We do. We know it's hard to find the truth through all the fake news and VR and AR and all that bullshit.'

'We have some problems here but we're fine. We'll be fine,' Tomi says firmly. 'Whatever happens with the ban, we'll cope. Just enjoy your drink, yes?'

The blonde woman drops her book to smile at them with something approaching warmth. Then they all become quiet again. There is nothing more to be said, though clearly each of them is desperate to say something.

By the time the bottom of the second flask of *awamori* appears, more people have turned up at the bar – no Americans though – and the volume is rising.

'Hey.' The blonde girl is coming over now, hovering by their sofa. She has an unusually intense gaze. 'I'm really sorry you had to hear all that. I hope you're OK. I just wanted to say: Masayo doesn't speak for all of us. It's a bad situation, you know. Look, I couldn't help but overhear you say you were out here looking for … *someone*. Made me think we might be in the same kinda boat … My dad's American too. Sorry, I'm getting ahead of myself, I'll leave you in peace' – she starts to back off – 'I'm Risa, by the way.'

Kit's grateful for any warmth in the chill Masayo's left. 'Wait, come and sit down – talk to us.'

Sol seems a little off, but Kit doesn't want to leave now. A local girl who doesn't hate them ... who might understand their situation ... couldn't she help them find Sol's father? Well it's surely preferable to running off after Hunter for every little thing. Risa must know far more about the place.

Two drinks turn into four and the conversation continues in a lighter vein. Risa is quite amusing about her conflicted situation, but there's so much about it that makes Kit feel Sol should be jumping about in recognition. Other than a brief 'Yeah, it's hard growing up without a father', Sol's barely engaging while Risa goes on about her family: 'Oh, they're amazing and I love them dearly, but I'm not sure they wholly approve of me. They probably wish they had a granddaughter like Masayo. My grandmothers are super traditional; they brought me up as a real Ryukyuan. They can't understand why I associate with Americans at all – no offence. But because of my dad, there's half of me that I just can't begin to understand ... and I can't leave it alone.

'When the ban was announced, my first thought was to go to the States and find him. But I don't know a single thing about him. My mother won't even tell me his name. All I know is he came to stay at their family home in Yomitan. They used to run it as a guest house and sometimes visiting GIs would stay there. My mother was their waitress and, well, you can guess what happened.

'After that, my grandmothers stopped taking paying guests, made a little Ryukyuan microcosm out there, even though they're boxed in by bases. My mother works on Kadena airbase now – they've more or less disowned her. But with no fishing, and soon to be no tourism, there are really fewer and fewer options.'

For some reason Sol seizes on the island economy talk while the paternal stuff drifts over untouched. 'What did that girl mean before,' Sol asks her, 'about the islands flooding?'

'They are everywhere, aren't they? We're suffering the effects of climate change here as you are in America. The Miyako Islands are underwater, a few villages here on this island too. We are all suffering. What can we do? Nothing will ever get done if we all just sit around preparing for the apocalypse, blaming the Japanese, the Americans. We need help from other nations. I don't know how long someone like Masayo will be able to get away with that kind of behaviour. It's dangerous. We need to get on with life!'

When, much later on, they leave, Kit feels they have made a friend. Risa's working tomorrow – she runs a cafe in town – but they've agreed to stay in touch. '*Ichariba choodee*,' she says. 'It means: once we meet and talk we are brothers and sisters. God, my grandmothers love that phrase.'

They walk back to the red-light district, the air still swampy and tropical. It is fully alive now, the nightclubs belting out American beats and groups of Japanese milling around on the pavement. Their suits suggest they've come here to Okinawa on business.

One of them has started walking on the other side of Sol.

'You're very beautiful,' Kit hears him say to her.

She laughs.

He glares at the man, youngish, with neat hair and unshowy jacket, but he does not seem to notice.

'I'm from Tokyo. You're American? ... Sex?' His eyes are wide with hope.

'Ha ha, no I'm not for sale. I'm just staying in the area.'

The man wordlessly peels off into a dim side street and disappears. Kit laments that he is so unseeable. You'd think his presence next to Sol would be enough to stop passers-by hitting on her. And if they actually thought she was a hooker, why didn't they assume that he, Kit, was her trick? It is vexing. He must cut a wholly unprepossessing figure. Had he joined the Marine Corps he might command more respect now. A uniform can be very impressive. So can deadliness. Tonight, though, Kit is grateful that his dubious life choices have led him away from the Marine Corps.

Maybe people think he's gay, like Phoenix used to say. No threat. It was one of the more devastating moments of his twenties when Sol asked him if he thought he might be. 'Well,' she went on, 'you've never had a proper girlfriend … I mean, maybe you don't even know yourself if you are …'

Kit had wanted to tell her then that he was in love with her. That's why he'd never been out with anyone for longer than a few dates, a masochist on the fringes, watching Sol draw man after unsuitable man into her imploding life. But he didn't, scared to risk their closeness. Better a friendship of frustration than nothing.

Even when she married Chase, Kit couldn't turn off his feelings. He did have relationships after that, as if he'd suddenly recognised the need to advertise himself as desirable: tested by multiple customers and awarded stars, favourable reviews and repeat purchases. One girlfriend, Lucy, lasted over a year – until she ended it without explanation. Kit felt nothing more than a greyish sort of relief. His friendship with Sol grew more intense as each new girl came on the scene. He started to hope she sensed a threat to their own relationship. You are my favourite person, she used to tell him at Dreamtime, and perhaps it was still true.

Kit began to think in a new way: if he just hung on in there as Chase fell further into the chaos of his own making, sooner or later Sol would come to her senses and leave him. Then he would tell her, and if she felt the same way nothing, no, nothing, not even *that*, would be insurmountable. They could just decide not to waste the rest of their lives, could go away somewhere and be together, live away from the prying eyes of society, back in the desert if they had to. They could … and these fantasies kept him alive.

Later, back in Hotel Matsu above the noise from the clubs, he lies down on one of the delightfully too-close beds while Sol attempts to tame the voluble bathroom facilities. She ignores the beds and him, heads straight for the chair-like arrangement of the massage person. Parts of her rise and fall as the robot inflates and sinks, the sound of ancient bellows lighting a fire.

Kit falls moodily into dark dreams of leaping whale skeletons, a marine *danse macabre*.

The American Occupation was even stranger.

More and more GIs arrived – day after day they poured in.

They stole ever more land to bulldoze, built noisy operations of death everywhere: tanks and aircraft, munitions and missiles.

We kept this house – a miracle – but they seized Seko's land at gunpoint for Kadena airbase.

We held protests there, yelled at the low-flying pilots in their B-52 bombers. They used our island to wage war on Vietnam, and American culture moved in for the soldiers' R&R: diners, pizza, bars and brothels.

Koza was segregated – streets for black marines, streets for white marines – and they fought all the time. They thought we were the primitive ones, 'savages', but they were violent, drunken, sexually incontinent – like animals.

No girl was safe.

They could get away with anything – they'd just run back to base where we could not get them.

They fathered many children.

DRAGON KING'S BATH

Wednesday.

Another day wandering Naha with Kit and Sol has fallen in love with the place. The sudden shake of small earthquakes, the temples to Americana, the sun-scattered culture clashes of this tropical island. Strange familiarity, alienating strangeness.

Kit has relaxed a little now it's just the two of them. She can understand his misgivings about Hunter, about the Americans being here at all. But Sol's aware that you can't please everyone, that some always suffer when the greater good is prioritised. At her school every pupil had to undergo a range of Virrea-sponsored nuclear experiences: surviving an atomic bomb, identifying and escaping fallout, the terrors of nuclear winter, holocaust and the total collapse of civilisation. After these no one disagreed that the USA should do everything in its power to safeguard against such disasters.

It occurs to her that Janet's hopping from one survivalist camp to another is not an overtly insane response to all this. Blessed are the preppers.

She looks at Kit sucking on a *shikwasa* juice, the orange pale against his deep Arizona tan. They are sitting in Fukushu-en, a Chinese garden celebrating Naha's friendship with the nearby city of Fuzhou. It's as if Okinawa doesn't know China is the real enemy here, though with all the Virrea warnings of imminent nuclear exchange, it's hard to deny.

Sol is drinking a local Orion beer, another American–Okinawan mash-up, and this time Kit has not questioned her. It's a relief. Some sort of acceptance on his part. It is Kit's acceptance of her fallibility that has always made her feel like she might, in fact, be saveable. At one point, hard to believe, she had thought she might be in love with him. Feels almost incestuous now.

The beer is finished all too quickly. She shakes the dregs to check.

She'd been thirteen, had run away from her then foster 'family' – the second or third already since the breakdown of Dreamtime – and fled straight to Kit. Where else could she have gone? He had smuggled her in, tried to keep her secret and hidden in his bed. He'd been a very good-looking boy, beautiful even, and she remembers his smooth and slender body, just starting to reveal its muscles. On the second night, bored with hiding out all day and hot with frustration from the touchless first night, she rolled into Kit's sleeping body and tried to kiss him awake, feeling along the angular point of his hip bone. He woke as if stung and sprang away, back up against the wall, and then he pretended to fall asleep again. She knew he was awake, could sense it in the rhythm of his breathing, the rigid way he kept to his side of the bed.

The very next day Sol was discovered by his foster parents, the same and only ones he ever had, the good pharmacists, and she assumed Kit had given her away, left some sign out because he was so appalled by her advances – because she had made sharing a bed or even a room unsustainable. He said not – well he would, wouldn't he? – he said that after she'd been discovered, he'd tried (and not for the first time) to persuade them to take her in too but they refused, just delivered her back into the merry-go-round of care. She thought maybe Kit hadn't tried so hard.

She studies him now and though he's still thin – and she knows he hates that about himself – there's a breadth and depth to him. His jawline is wider, if prone to adolescent fuzz, his eyes that same wild blue. The length of his sunny hair suits him. Yes, he's still good-looking. It's almost as if she hasn't noticed it since those thirteen-year-old lustings, the pain of his rejection. Out here, away from it all, she can see him.

Kit's right not to worry about the drinking. She feels at peace here, like she's in the right place. The manic hunger that possessed her all too recently has ebbed away and she is back in control, balancing the forces. Feeding the good wolf and starving the bad. The seasonal paths of the garden, spring to summer, autumn to winter and so on have reminded her that this is her spring. That she was lucky to survive winter. This is her second chance: the one that everyone talks about deserving.

Sol looks back at the red pagoda above a lake of lily pads and koi carp. They had thrown fish flakes in earlier: the carp swarmed in iridescent gold shoals, their o-shaped mouths gaping and bobbing. It made her think of the way she scrabbled through Hunter's bag looking for more codeine. Now she feels a kind of distance from that person, like an observer looking on calmly at a lunatic. She wonders if the people here are ever tempted to eat these sacred sea-safe fish. She wonders if she can have another beer.

The place is deserted apart from an aged Okinawan couple striking karate poses in another, more dramatic pagoda, this one above the rocks of a three-tiered waterfall tumbling from its jags. Belinda would love this place. It's just perfect for Her Recovery.

She sees Kit is buried in his Virrea again. Why does he need to open up a virtual version of the very thing they are right now inside and experiencing directly?

'I was just replying to Risa,' he says, surprised.

What is that curious look on his face? Kit has talked quite a lot today about that bar, the cats and, most particularly, Risa. Perhaps he has some sort of crush on the girl. She does not like the way that makes her feel. All sibling relationships, all friendships anticipate their own erosion when someone new comes on the scene.

She seriously doubts Risa's as useful as Kit thinks. 'Her own mother works on a base!' Yes, an Air Force base, but even so, it's not like Risa's been able to find her own goddamn father. Nor has Sol enjoyed Kit's insinuations that she and Risa are practically the same person. Sol would never be so needy, so … *desperate*. She is no one's victim. Besides, they have Hunter, an actual marine, and unlike little Risa he makes her feel safe.

Has Kit been in touch with her all day on his Virrea — all the time he's been talking to Sol?

'She was just telling me about these dragon-boat races they have here. Used to be just to honour gods and spirits. Now, with the crashing economy, some are turning them into a bit of a business. I'd like to see it — all the out-of-work fishing boats done up, turned into racers. Says her neighbour's got one.'

'I'm sure the gods and spirits are thrilled.' She's a bit young, Risa, isn't she? How old is she anyway? Probably about twenty-two. Sol eases a small sliver of *tofu-yu* from the cube before her, tofu fermented to the point of cheesiness by *awamori*. It is delicious, the inside creamy and strong, the outside fiery with alcohol.

What was she, Sol, doing at twenty-two? God knows. It's a hazy time but certainly Chase would have been on the scene. What will become of him? Maybe he's clean now too … though jails in Arizona are not renowned for it.

It is good to be free of Chase, adored and idolised for so long, but always gnawing away at her self-respect. He had money, connections, attitude and she used all three to enable her addictions. When Chase first looked her up, his frustration had been contained, blossoming up like blood from a paper cut only every so often – when they were both so intoxicated that it would be easy to dismiss the next morning. He was weathered and worldly, a glamorous adventurer; he'd already been through rehab once and thrown off its effects with ease.

He had inherited both money and his family's cavalier attitude towards spending it. Chase trusted in the universe to provide more, as it often did when he distilled opiates from it and sold them to its inhabitants – among them Phoenix and her mother, a funny thought! For a time Chase was everything Sol wanted: his middle age, paternal attitude and ready cash gave her the kind of security she had not experienced since Dreamtime ended and her peripatetic life began. On the other hand, his leanings to vice, drugs wisdom and unconventional attitude to the merits of education and employment liberated her. It simplified her conflicted existence into a single path, and there was stability in that too.

When the money couldn't keep up, Chase encouraged Sol to resume the very work he'd initially forced her to stop. She rejoined the elite escort agency of her youth and began to accompany men of standing to their various functions again, mostly dinners, the odd wedding. It was acting; it was fine. Most of the time it was fine. Chase was pleased that she was bringing home the bacon as by now they both had demanding habits to feed. But sometimes protective would become possessive. He'd turn feral, ripping her to shreds over what exactly she'd done to and for specific clients.

Then it was wrath that she wasn't up to the job, had lost so much weight, form and radiance that men no longer asked for her on their arm. Finally, it was full-time madness, except for the first few moments after he'd shot up.

But why is she thinking about Chase? Why must people live on in your head, hijacking your consciousness? It's no less affecting than if it were happening in reality. The reality of dreams is a haunting. She shudders, tries to cast off the demon, but looking at Kit smiling lazily, all the anxiety that usually shadows him vanished, she has an unwelcome flash of what her life might have been like had he returned her touch in his bed that night. All those years.

Remorse is interrupted by a buzz from her Virrea. She is aware of some small irony in the way she leaps on it, every bit as hungry for the dopamine rush of virtual attention as Kit. It's a powerful force. The written message is signed H. but the sender's profile is blank, the avatar default, as if it's not his Virrea he's using. Can marines not have devices, like prisoners? Surely they can – anyway, Hunter's not into technology, he's told her several times. He says he has news. He calls her kid, which she likes. When you turn thirty you take what you can. They are to meet at the American Village tomorrow evening. What is that, Thursday? Leaving only twenty-four hours until their ferry back to Kagoshima? Not long enough. But maybe Jonny Quiss – the real one – will be with him. Maybe they'll appear together like some mirage of American manliness, all muscle and guns. She finds herself swelling in secret places at the thought.

But it's only Wednesday afternoon. Some of the old restlessness creeps back into her bones. The ability of the opiate to knock out time, allow you just to bow out of a day or a night, is … well, she shouldn't be thinking about it.

'Do you still want to go?' Kit asks her.

'Why wouldn't I?' Sol is incredulous. 'It's why we're here isn't it?'

'I just thought after everything you heard in the bar, you might be having second thoughts, or something. I don't know.'

She views his inertia as reluctance, and his reluctance as rejection. 'Look, Kit, obviously the Okinawans have their issues with America being here. It's a complex situation and they've suffered horrific things. But you know as well as I do that our guys have to be here to stop China blowing everything to bits. There's no single story where all Americans are villains and the military's fucked. Listen to Risa!' — so she does have her uses — 'And that wasn't Hunter's take on things either. Yes I know he is US military, but he loves this place and the people here. All he's done is help us. Now he says he has news … So, I'm going to go and meet him. You don't have to.' She doesn't say so, but fake news is surely not just a problem that afflicts America. All news is suspect. How can they know the truth of what that angry girl said in the bar last night?

Sol sees Kit make that expression she knows so well, where he seems to swallow whatever emotion has been about to surface and recalibrate himself. 'Of course I want to come with you.' His tone is almost approaching brightness.

She appreciates him not saying what's on his mind. Sometimes temporary misgivings need to be blocked to allow a longer-term goal to succeed. She doesn't like to be overly analytical, one reason why Lights didn't suit her so well. To stop surfing the sea is to drown in it.

When his juice has at last departed — god, he drinks slowly — Kit suggests they see the sunset from some hot springs. They take a taxi past an airfield of Self-Defense Forces fighter jets, all bearing the red-sun insignia of the Japanese flag, to the small island of Senaga, Risa's recommendation. That cafe of hers can't be very busy. Jets overhead shake the highway, spinning white paths through the sky. What will happen to all these flying machines when they are no longer permitted to fly? There will be more modern ruins to explore: aviation cemeteries – like the old Tucson boneyard.

The island is a sacred one, Kit mansplains via Risa. Its holy places, springs and wells were destroyed by the war, the residents kicked out and the whole island commandeered as ammo storage for the US Navy. He's trying to be Hunter, perhaps. It's quite adorable.

At the onsen two receptionists look them up and down. 'Tattoos?' one asks suspiciously.

Kit has a small sun on his forearm and Sol hopes he won't feel the need to disclose it.

'Yeah, Risa just warned me not to show it,' he says on the way to the changing rooms. 'In any case, one blue sun hardly makes me the Yakuza.'

Risa, it seems, is coming too. The onsen is segregated by sex but there's nothing to prevent virtual women from going over to the men's side. She thinks of Risa's spirit, hiding out in Kit's locker, always there for a quick chat on the Virrea between hot-spring steepings. Why should she care?

Actually, Sol had thought she and Kit would go in together. She detects the same frost from the women in the hot springs that she received at the restaurant. Is it just because she's American? As it turns out, she *is* the daughter of a marine, but they can't know that. Would they feel the same about any white person, whether militarily connected or not? They are giving her the side-eye and whispering. Showering, she is aware of her ugly track marks, healed but still visible, on her arms – maybe that's it. But what woman of thirty does not carry scars of some sort? At least she's on the other side of that learning curve.

She follows another naked woman through glass sliding doors to the suddenly sodden open air. The rain is back in a big way. There are round red bathtubs for individuals ahead, then a shallow pool surrounded by rocks to the left, steam rising from its green water. On, past a frigid pond, to steps leading down to the standing bath: a large cube of fervid spring water looking out across the East China Sea to the setting sun.

The hot rain on her naked body is a drumbeat; she feels her small breasts standing to attention, saluting the sun. This part of the onsen is empty except for a woman gazing out to sea. She is resting her chin on crossed arms, her hair concealed by a white towel. Sol steps into the viscous weight and violent heat of the water and copies her pose as she feels it close around her. It is hard to breathe with the water pressing on her chest – requires more energy to inhale. There is a brief sense of panic, of some unopposable force crushing her, and for a moment she's back in Janet's stranglehold, the 'therapeutic' pseudo-womb at Lights. Sol lifts herself out of the water and the feeling floats away. She lowers herself back and surrenders to the tightness.

Claustrophobia in such expansive scenery is an unusual sensation and more Kit's domain. Has he yet plucked up the courage to ditch his towel? She grins, thinking of him watching the same awe-inspiring sunset, a single black thundercloud against the fiery oranges and reds streaming across the sky, the vast flaming yellow lowering itself into the sea. The heavy water pries her tense muscles apart and coats her scars in effervescence. Who is he thinking of though? She is suddenly, painfully aware that it may not be her. She wonders, for the first time, why Kit has remained so close to her all these years after his outright rejection of her teenage self. Maybe he does – or at least did – feel … something for her. Maybe it was not rejection but – something else. Kit is a complex man. Who knows what his reasons for doing anything are half the time? Sol has thought too often that she can read him, that he is dependable, straightforward even, but in truth he is just as odd and unpredict-able as she knows he finds her.

She feels the heat of the earth's core passing through her, the lava beneath bubbling up like gossip; it opens her scars, her fault lines, and something contained, something toxic, starts to flow away from her, fumy green ghosts of fear and fervour evaporating into the ether. With a flash of emerald light, the final glow of the sun is snuffed out and the black sea lit by a fury of stars.

Kit.

The other woman turns to face her and for a split second Sol thinks she is looking at Chrissie. She is mistaken, of course – it's just the orange hue of her hair in the starlight now she's taken the towel off. This woman is local and, in any case, Chrissie is a child. Was a child.

'Are you alright?' she asks, her thick Ryukyuan accent colouring the words. Sol feels she must see the poisonous colour of the steam rising from her into the abruptly clear sky. 'Not a good idea to stay in here too long. You need to cool off.'

Sol, suffused with noxious matter and fainting with head rush, follows her lead and leaves the bath. She watches as the woman dips a bowl in the icy plunge pool then throws the water over a chair. Sol copies her and sits down dizzily in the shock of cold.

'You're American?' asks the woman.

Sol braces for hostility, a century's resentment of the US crys-tallised against her. She, for once in her life, does not really feel like talking, just thinking her way to some kind of clarity. Of course she's not in love with Kit. Wouldn't she have noticed? But there's some kind of lead weight on her back that won't let her fly off into denial, that keeps drawing her down to an irresistible, heavy truth.

Kit.

What the hell is in this water?

The woman smiles. 'See over there? Those used to be islands. Now the sea has taken them back and turned the people into fishes. Military, are you?'

'Uh, no.' Sol speaks quietly; no one else is talking and she's getting dirty looks from other sweating chair-sitters. She tries to stand up, but something forces her back down, and then it starts, the old memory reel. She grits her teeth for its assault. She wants to trap them back in, all those Dreamtime bad things. But here is Phoenix, freed by the waters, passing through her and swirling up in eddies starwards. Here is his cleansing ceremony: the only way each child could receive his blessing, liberate him from the 'psychospiritual debris' of leading. It was a trick. Someone should have stopped him, she sees that now. Someone should have said it was wrong. Her mother knew. Knew! She was complicit. Phoenix was always full of tricks.

But Kit.

They'd had each other; nobody else mattered and together they made life in the camp bearable. Wonderful even, despite everything. Kit has always been the most important thing in the world to her. What the fuck has she been thinking all this time? Of course she is in love with him.

But the strange waters have more for her than that. They won't stop. Here it is. Little scarlet-haired Chrissie dragged off and ravaged by a coyote. Wild beasts tore her apart like a judgement sent by insulted gods: the sacrifice of a child for the transgressions of Phoenix. Why must the victims pay first? Your fault. You should have been playing with her, but you were off doing your own thing with Kit, like always. It is all present before her now, unrolling like celluloid: Phoenix announcing that he could mend Chrissie. He wouldn't let the women take her to the hospital. They were not in their right minds, he said, and it was true. It wouldn't look good. It would be the end of everything.

But as Chrissie grew worse, someone somehow sent word out. A man came to the camp. It was unlikely, the man was later quoted as saying, that the coyote had also raped the little girl. And that's when the whole thing started to unravel.

Feeling nausea rising, she stands up, saying, 'I'm sorry, I have to go—'

The woman interrupts her sharply: 'You need to be careful here, American. The god lives here, under the sea in his dragon palace. This is Ryujin's water.'

Sol flees to the nearest room, full of steam with an altar of salt. She clutches handfuls of the stuff and scrubs the shards into her skin, sloughing off the dead memories, replacing their psychic pain with the physical.

When she has finished, rinsed the salt, repeated the process until she is smooth and raw, she returns to the changing room. There is a message from Kit on her Virrea. She opens it and his Holograb speaks in mid-air: 'Sol, I'm really sorry – had to go. They saw my tattoo and kicked me out. I'm with Risa on Umikaji Terrace – in a hammock bar! – come find us when you're done.'

Is there anywhere that Risa is not? Fuming and confused, she dresses and follows her virtual map into the sudorous night, along the road towards the whitewashed Grecian village up ahead. She passes two black cats with white on their heads, like the towels upon the bathing women. She stops, still lightheaded, to watch them play-fighting in the light of the stars, rearing up on their hind legs and jabbing at each other, and she fears that they are not fighting but dancing the darkest dance, mewing in Japanese, their long tails split in two. She must be high. But she hasn't taken anything for days. She must be thirsty.

I had to get a job as a maid for an American family, when I was old enough. They were good-natured folk – I was one of the lucky ones. They helped me learn English, gave me clothes, chocolate and whatever I needed.

Their house had running water!

Haunted though.

Ghosts, yes of course! Can you really doubt it? Plenty of ghosts on this island.

I see my father all the time.

Those school friends I thought had got away – a thought that had kept me going in the camp – I see them.

They drowned when their evacuation ship, the Tsushima Maru, *was torpedoed by an American submarine.*

I see the ghosts of those children everywhere.

Where else would they be but here?

There can be no peace for them or us while our sacred island remains America's military fortress.

LITTLE AMERICA

Thursday.

Risa has shown no desire to accompany them to the American Village this evening so Kit is alone with Sol in a doily-clad taxi, this one self-driving.

Sol is wearing her red boots – for Hunter's benefit? Kit does not like them at all. She's a little on edge, though so is he, aware of the ever-shortening time until the ferry to Kagoshima tomorrow evening. They have checked out of the Naha hotel, planning either not to sleep or to stay in a hostel near the Village. Maybe those boots are simply easier to wear than carry.

'How are you feeling?' he asks her cautiously.

Sol strokes the back of her head, fluffing the spikes up and out. 'Well, I keep getting my hopes up and … This is really the last opportunity, isn't it?'

She seems to zone out, and Kit returns his attention to his Virrea and therein, Risa. It is Risa who enables him to be more a traveller, less a tourist, as Sol requires. Her virtual voice, that of a girl born and bred here, can make sense of this unfamiliar new world in which they find themselves. What he learns from Risa he can use to keep Sol safe, to allow himself not to feel so alien. To find Sol's father! She provides a sort of cultural bridge; quite generously, in his opinion, considering the American destruction here, another runaway military dad.

'It's important for the American people to see us as heroes,' Hunter had told him on the whale-bashed boat. What he meant, Kit realises now, was, 'You mustn't know about the horrible things we do in your name, let alone the things we do for our own amusement.'

On the outskirts of Naha, they slow past an expanse of car dealers and American vintage shops. Kit sees Coyote convenience stores and Uncle Sam's Used Furniture revolving as if on a cycle. Further along the highway the landscape changes to American-style diners, drive-thrus and bars, burgers, bowling and military-supply stores, interspersed with the odd pachinko parlour. Stars and Stripes all over the place. It makes him feel a little homesick. For all the instant possibilities offered by his Virrea, he has not been in touch with anyone in Tucson, but now he thinks again of his parents on the other side of the world, the archaic people-run pharmacy, the blazing desert. Out here, all that feels like home. Sunday's flight from Tokyo can't come soon enough. There's been talk – first Risa and now on the radio – of a typhoon developing south-east of the islands, in Guam, but no one is sure which way it will go – China, Japan, the Philippines. Whatever, he hopes it does not affect their flight home.

Kit makes his virtual version of Risa visual. Her holographic form pops up between his seat and Sol's and continues to chat when chatted to as they crawl along Route 58. Okinawans can drive on the left now, Risa tells Kit and Kit tells Sol – who looks slightly dead behind the eyes and less excited by his rising traveller-not-tourist status than anticipated – but until 1978 Americans made them drive on the right. It's nice not to be reliant on Hunter for this kind of local understanding. If that's what Sol's so hung up on.

There was no virtual communication at all when Kit was growing up: it was banned at Dreamtime. He'd had no idea what it was until his ten-year-old awakening, release into the real world. Phoenix used to talk about something he called 'the vigilant enemy' in their search for the eternal present.

'You'd think,' Phoenix said once, 'that the virtual world would be a friend of the Dreamtime, because both seem to offer a way out from the real world. I get it! But you'd be wrong; technology is a fabricated real world with all the same stupid minutiae in it. It tethers you to the actual and allows you to ignore the deeper, more spiritual realm.'

Kit did not understand what he meant, but he did know this: what Phoenix and all the women had wanted was to push off from the 'stupid minutiae' of the mundane. Every child at Dreamtime knew this. Transcendence was king, and bad things could happen in – or be concealed by – its service. Best to leave them all to it when you could.

Now, Kit couldn't be without virtual reality. So he didn't like his bedside trip to India ... So what? He can go to space next time – without the risk of not being able to catch the last rocket home. He can read any book on Virrea with its actual location all around him, place himself in any movie. He can start a friendship on one side of the Pacific and continue it holographically on the other. The world map has been redrawn by instant translation and the capacity to hang out virtually with people who agree with you, no longer hindered by geography. Risa's presence hanging in the ether can see what he sees, augment his reality with her information. She is as good as there.

The night they met in the bar, Risa touched on something. They were talking about ghosts and spirits, who believed in what. 'I think it's a bit like the virtual world,' Risa said, eyeing his Virrea – the same model as her own. 'The world in your device is separate from the real world, yes, but it's entwined on various levels – and it's still there even when you're not interacting with it. The spirit world is the same: it's always there, discrete but involved.' Well he could do without it, frankly.

Signs tell him they're driving through Urasoe now and on his left, towards the sea, extends an expanse of razor wire. WARNING, each gate announces grimly: THIS FACILITY PATROLLED BY MILITARY ROBOT DOG TEAMS. Behind the high wire fence of Camp Kinser that goes on and on, all Kit can see are flat white concrete-box buildings, the standard island shape, with thin, flat terracotta roofs. 'Built like that to withstand typhoons,' says Risa. Between each one is a scrubby patch of faded grass.

Sol is ostentatiously craning past Risa's hologram, trying to see too. Risa is only visual and sonic, not too intrusive surely. It's not like he's activated smell and touch and … well, sure, they, and in particular taste, would be more than creepy in this scenario. He asks Sol if she'd like to swap seats but it's as if she hasn't heard him. It occurs to him that perhaps Sol doesn't much like Risa. Well, it's not as if he likes many of Sol's friends, imminent company included. He wishes Hunter didn't make him feel quite so inadequate. Kit has made a point, in his life so far, of removing things that worry him – everything apart from Sol.

He shuts down Risa's shimmering form and switches her back to audio chat.

On through Ginowan, and sudden rain as Camp Kinser becomes Futenma airbase. Continuing north up Route 58, the razor wire switches to the opposite side of the road, anti-US protest signs studded across it: YANKEE, GO HOME! A multitude of electricity pylons and then the long, low white buildings of Camp Foster.

Between them are giant concrete courts filled with row upon row of camouflage-coloured trucks and tanks, all neatly lined up as if in a supermarket car park. A team of four marines is tinkering with one of them, their dark-green jungle cammies matching the tank: a four-headed monster. Kit can see Sol straining to view the last traces of them as trees begin to cover the wire and shield its contents.

'This is where Hunter lives, isn't it?' she asks him and he can see … what? Oh god, not that look in her eyes.

'Yes, I think he said Foster didn't he?' Kit replies casually.

Here in the heartland Sol's military fetish is clearly in evidence. If Kit had gone down that marine path, would she have seen him in a different light, desired and revered him? Perhaps even feared him slightly – was that what it was really all about? Vulnerability in the face of benevolent brute force? To know that his strength and aim and arm can be tamed by her alone … that he is animal, beastly, a dangerous trained killer at whose hands humans may die like insects. He could destroy her in an instant but never would for she is inviolate, elevated, special, his eternal love and goddess. 'This is my rifle. There are many like it but this one is mine.' He had once known all the words of the Rifleman's Creed; now the rest of it has faded.

But he knows he never had it in him, not really; he couldn't kill a kissing bug, let alone entertain the idea of murdering another human, no matter the circumstances. He would only have signed up with an eye to impressing Sol, because the Marine Corps recruiters that sought him and all the other down-and-outs in Tucson told him it was the way to earn the respect of others, that they'd toughen him up and make him invulnerable. Invincible. Because Sol had a thing about military men even before she knew her daddy was one. Or maybe she unconsciously realised he must be because Janet hated 'those world-fucking GI criminals and thugs' so much. And really, what good to do a thing he hated to win Sol's heart, when his very doing of it would have taken him away from her? Perhaps permanently, if he'd come here to the front line of the War on China.

On the left he sees malls, brand names: Gucci, Prada, Fendi. Golf supplies and beauty salons. An American wedding shop stuffed with meringue dresses. Bagels and coffee. A tattoo parlour. Here it is: small-town America. He was right – they should have come straight here and asked their own questions. Now chains such as Starbucks, the ubiquitous diner A&W and McDonald's take over, with the diamond-wire tessellations of Camp Lester on the other side. There has been no break in the sea of wire for miles.

'Look!' Sol is gesturing to a great Ferris wheel up ahead. 'That must be it!'

'We are approaching your destination,' says the car. 'You are about to enter the American Village. Get ready for a real fun time!'

'Fun times are sponsored by Virrea,' another voice interjects at terms-and-conditions speed. 'Don't forget to tag us in your Holograbbies!'

As soon as the car opens Kit's door, he can hear strains of turn-of-the-century US music and smell a damp Christmas. Strains of wet cinnamon and allspice through the rain that is now coming down in a deluge again. There's no predicting it – Virrea can't get it right, anyway. They head into the complex, keeping under cover through winding red-brick streets of pizzerias, burger bars and American shops. But it's not the America Kit knows. Here there's a milkshake on every corner. At least this theme park's free from the drugs and the gangs. No sun fugitives beating down its air-conditioned doors.

A wide circular shop calls to mind the Rust Belt, its orange wall reflecting the drenched terracotta paving stones. Full Christmas regalia hangs from its corroded metal balcony; garlands of baubled fir tree shroud a Statue of Liberty shedding tears in the torrent. There's a Star-and-Stripe-spangled rocket – or is it a nuke? Massive

Santas, a festive snowman and a couple of feisty gingerbread men look similarly depressed and dangerous, foregrounded by a palm tree. There is fake snow everywhere, and it forms an unpleasant brown mulch with the rainstorm. Must be plenty of homesick servicemen who buy into this shit; who have forgotten the reality of America and believe this mini version to be its quintessence.

Eventually they emerge at the bars and cafes of the sea wall, the wide sweep of Sunset Beach to their left, its water swelling and flexing. Sol points out a hostel that might do for later. Rain drenches a hundred happy-hour signs along the promenade and they take shelter in the first doorway. Their clothes and bags are already soaked. Sol fiddles with her Virrea and in a second they see Hunter swaggering up to them, unperturbed by the rain sheeting off his short blond hair. He looks broader than ever in white shorts and a dark blue sleeveless shirt. Stubble of a distinctly ginger hue has sprouted prolifically in the past two days.

'Hey,' he says. Hugs Sol and shakes Kit's hand, powerfully. 'We're just down here. Come and join us.'

Hunter's grin is fully stretched, revealing his strong white teeth. Kit sees Sol slip straight into character, skipping along girlishly next to the great man, her thin arm threaded through his unbroken one. Kit falls back into file behind them, the old hierarchy instantly reasserted.

The sea is lashing itself with its own tail, coming up over the walkway, and Kit feels again that he is in the presence of something ancient and raw and in no way benevolent. An eternal dragon, a kraken, a king; an army of bloodless octopodal aliens. As Kit's skin starts to tighten across him, prickling parcel wrap, Hunter leads them, dripping, into a rock bar imported straight from the US of A, where thousands of its identical siblings decorate the city streets. Replete as it is with Americans black and white, Kit now feels he could be in Arizona. Sanitised safety: the soft-metal hits from the too-loud speakers; electric guitars on the walls and the coat-your-nostrils-in-lard scent of frying meat. Meat from the meat farm, from creatures genetically modified to meet demand in a world no longer conducive to the existence of sacrificial animals.

Kit follows Hunter and Sol over to a pool table near the back of the bar where the walls are lined with old American beer ads. There's a man already there, bent over the table to take one of the last remaining shots. Is Sol asking herself if this is her father? With a satisfying crack the 8-ball slides into the pocket and, as the man straightens up, Kit can see that he is younger and slighter than Hunter but the two look quite alike. The shorn austerity of his blond hair makes Hunter's low fade and new stubble look decadent though. There's a button brightness to the man's green eyes that the slackness of his mouth belies. Kit takes in the jeans, the T-shirt displaying some esoteric album cover.

'This is Finn,' says Hunter. 'Finn Garcia.'

'Heeey.' Finn fist-bumps Sol, then Kit: 'Heeey.'

'Hey,' says Kit in a curt, businesslike tone. He is disappointed that all Hunter has dredged up after disappearing for two days is this, this youth. They are clearly a few Orions down already and Kit wants to ask how long the USMC enforced the latest alcohol ban. One week? Two? He swallows and reminds himself that enduring Hunter is a necessary evil for bringing Sol home safely. And soon. It is at home, he realises, not racing around out here pretending to be travellers, that he and Sol might have a chance. This time next week, when she's had time to get over the jet lag, he'll ask her out properly. Dinner and dancing in Tucson's finest. Start again and take it from there.

'Wanna drink?' asks Finn, sinking the black. 'He's buying.' He grins at Hunter then leans his cue stick against the wall.

Hunter smiles ruefully. 'Hardly a fair game.' Kit sees that he has taken his arm out of its sling in anticipation of playing another shot, but now he uses his meaty other to reinsert it.

Woven among the beer signs are ads for 2-4-1 shots – Redheaded Sluts, Pink Starfuckers – and cocktails, king of which must be the mighty Trash Can, glowing green like it's made of plutonium and claiming to contain the whole bar. It comes with a warning: ¥2,500 PUKE CLEAN-UP FEE. Beyond, there's a terrace wallpapered in politer notices: 'Dear Customers, Do not spit or throw anything else over the wall. Please use the garbage bins inside. Offenders will be penalized and asked to leave the premises. Thank you for your understanding. Bar Management.'

Kit sees Sol watching him and drops his eyes. 'I'll help you carry the drinks,' he tells Finn, but a robot waitress with pneumatic tits is already zooming pool-table-side.

'How can I help you boys today?' she asks with an improbably large baring of teeth. 'Same again? And for your guests?'

It is a matter of seconds before she zooms back with a tray of Orions, some nuts, something unidentifiable on toast. 'It's Happy Hour! Everyone gets a free appetizer in Happy Hour, silly.' She strokes Kit's arm lustily before whizzing back behind the bar. Sol looks daggers at him. He will never understand her, never thread his way through the psychic maze of small things that thrill her or fill her with despair. She is a language he has learned since infancy but he'll always find the grammar fucking impenetrable.

We fought hard for Okinawa to be returned to Japan, our first invader, thinking that it would at least liberate us from the bases.

But Tokyo tricked us.

The Americans handed us over but Japan let them remain as an occupying force.

In fact, even more GIs came, the ones the Japanese didn't want on their mainland.

And so the bad behaviour of the military continued to make our lives a misery.

Our women lived in fear.

Our men were killed trying to protect them.

Japan was pleased to have us back: the old colony and dumping ground.

'Pig eaters' they called us.

Even now the Americans teach their uncivilised soldiers that we, with all our proud royal history, are the rednecks of Japan.

THE TALE OF JONNY

Sol's impatience is pulsing in a temple vein. She can't see what possible help this guy Finn can be, and Hunter has offered no explanation for his presence. Time, as Kit has been insisting all day, indeed all week, is running out. At least Hunter is Jonny's generation, a potential contemporary. This boy is younger than her, and that means he's probably useless.

They've already discussed the typhoon that's brewing ('Gonna be a humdinger!') and Finn's currently going on and on about the many and varied ghosts here in Okinawa. 'They had to tear down a whole barracks on our base, Foster,' he's saying. 'Nobody would stay there. There was all this, like, *laughter* coming out of nowhere, voices when there was no one there, doors banging, windows rattling, you name it.' He looks absolutely delighted about it.

Sol says nothing, hoping that without oxygen Finn's one-man show will fizzle out. But he is only warming to his theme. 'Then there's Gate 3 at Hansen, that's haunted as fuck too. Everybody knows it, no one'll go near it ... They had to shut that down as well. They say there's still a samurai haunts Foster – I've never seen him myself but I know ten people who'll put hand on heart and swear on the Holy Bible that they have. And Foster's nothing to Futenma. Nobody wants to go there. They disturbed all those local graves building the base, didn't they?'

'They did? Jesus – what …' Kit begins and trails off, creating a gap for Sol to interrupt: 'So you're in the marines as well, then?'

'Yes, ma'am.' Finn salutes her.

'Hunter said you had some news about my dad?' She looks to Hunter for help and he nods faintly towards his own pocket. A strip of pills poking its sweet red candy above the parapet. Fuck, he's good.

'Yeah, sure,' Finn admits. 'Well, not exactly news – I never met the guy but I've heard of a Jonny, Jonny er – think I know where he could be now.'

A fluttering in her eardrum beats the bar into momentary silence. This is it. 'Where?' she chokes.

'Well, before I came to Foster, I was at Camp Schwab, up north by the new air station we built *on the actual sea* … it's awesome, man—' Oh god, he's going into one of his stories again. She flicks her cigarette so hard it snaps and Finn jumps to attention. 'Anyway, when I was there the boys would tell stories about this guy called Jonny. He was like a legend to them, but – er – a real one, not a ghost.' What? 'Not Quiss though, but not far off. They called him Jonny – pardon my language, ma'am – Quim, because, I figure, er – he had such a way with the ladies?'

Sol sees Kit wince. But really, so what if her daddy is something of a stud? It's not a crime is it? 'Please – go on.'

'Well, OK, this is the thing, there was some scandal, yeah? But we're talking, like, a while ago, I don't know when exactly … There was this girl, an Oki girl, from the strip club opposite the base. Jonny had a thing for her. He did for a lot of the girls, apparently. One time he took her off into the woods – it's all forest up there, in the north, you know; we got a jungle training camp and shit up there, it's easy to get lost, I mean – and, well, you know, he showed her a good time. But something happened – there was an accident …'

'Shit. What do you mean?'

'I don't know exactly. Something went wrong. The Oki girl er – well, she *passed away* somehow. So Jonny couldn't stay, you know? Even though it wasn't his fault. Military were able to save him from being tried by the local courts but they couldn't let him stay either.'

'Shit,' Sol says again.

'Yeah,' says Hunter. 'I thought I'd heard the name from somewhere but Finn reminded me where exactly.' His Deep South accent seems not so pronounced today. Maybe it just stands out less here in 'Little America'.

'I called a couple of the old guys from Schwab, been around longer than I have. Said he'd gone off to Ishigaki, run off with another local Oki girl, Yuna something-or-other, was running a hotel with her and, they think, married her too.'

'Ishigaki?' What Sol really wants to ask is why hadn't her father, disgraced and deported, returned to her, the tiny daughter he'd left behind, and her mother? Maybe he tried, she thinks with sudden horror. Maybe he couldn't find her, cut off from the world as she was in the Dreamtime camp, or later, in and out of care. But the cheques found Janet …

'It's another of these islands, 'bout two hundred and fifty miles south-west of here.' Very reassuring, the way Hunter just knows stuff, takes control. He's a real grown-up.

Finn tugs at his T-shirt. 'The guys at Schwab say he changed his name; had to start again or it wouldn't have been safe for him to stay on these islands.'

'But he'd fallen in love with the way of life down here. And the women. Didn't wanna leave. 'S understandable,' says Hunter with feeling.

'Well, do you know what his name is now?' Sol demands. 'If he's running a hotel it must be pretty easy to track him down.' She can sense Kit's silent yet growing alarm hanging in the air, ferry-shaped.

'We've got a name and the hotel!'

'Oh my god! Seriously?' She accepts a Pink Starfucker from the zooming tray-bearing waitress. Sidles closer to Hunter's pocket.

'Hotel's called Cat Island, proprietors a Mr and Mrs Jay Carter.'

Another Carter. Maybe that's why she was drawn to that old goat at Lights. Her unconscious had been laying clues for her. Belinda told her that could happen and so it had, right under Belinda's rhinoplastied nose. And now, finally, something tangible after all these false starts, things not being what they seemed. The end of the line. 'How easy is it to get there? I want to go as soon as possible.'

'We'll sort you out, baby,' says Hunter and she trusts it's true.

Kit finally succeeds in interrupting, his face a peculiar colour. 'Sol, can I talk to you for a second?' He picks up his rucksack decisively.

She follows him outside where spiralling rips of rain are still whipping up the sea. They stand under the awning of the bar, watching it in silence. Sol takes out her Uruma seahorse pack and lights another cigarette.

'Sol, this has got to end here,' Kit begins. 'We've come a good way, given it our best, but this is serious now … We have to catch the ferry tomorrow night or we'll miss our flight home. This is it; there just isn't any more time. We simply can't travel another day further away from Tokyo, following a whim.'

'Are you joking? We know where he is now! He's in reach, at last.'

'So take a Virrea trip to the hotel, speak to the guy, build a relationship online … This is what virtual reality is for.'

'I will, I will, but come on Kit, you saw the trouble that got me into with the Tokyo asshole. Come on, this is the final stage of the journey – we've come this far ... I don't know how you can just give up when we're so close I can fucking taste it. You're right that "this is it": this is my last shot at actually meeting my dad.'

Kit grimaces. A weakening? She presses on: 'And look, it's only Thursday. We'll get a local flight back from Ishigaki to Tokyo on Saturday or even Sunday morning if the plane home's not till the evening. Even if we miss the flight it's not the end of the world. There's bound to be another before the year ends, and I should think beyond the so-called ban too – or, if not, we can get home slowly, by sea and train or horse and cart or whatever. Or, we can just not go home. You can, if you want. I could stay.'

'Sol, this man, the one they're saying's your father – he killed a girl! Doesn't that mean something to you?'

'What! Of course he didn't kill her; she died accidentally, as a consequence—'

'As a consequence of what ... frisky consensual sex? Like that girl we heard about in the bar the other night, the one who was on her way home from school? Open your eyes.'

'Kit, you're being crazy. And Finn said it wasn't his fault, whatever it was that happened. Look, stuff happens – the girl worked in a strip club. Things go wrong with kinky experiments all the time. We can't know exactly what went on, but it probably was an accident, don't you think? We won't know the truth until we find him and get his side of the story. But hey, he's now living in wedded bliss running a hotel on an island of cats. Doesn't sound very murdery, does it? I mean, clearly he's mellowed ...'

'I'm not going.' Kit has literally dug his heels in, toes lifted from the wet pavement. 'And I'm begging you not to. Sol, seriously, please ...'

He's staring at her with such furious intensity she thinks he's about to kiss her. And then she knows with sudden clarity that Kit is the only one among them making any sense. He is right. This journey is over: how could she be thinking of pursuing her father and all his mess further into that angry sea? The world is preparing to grind travel to a halt, throw up the chips of its people, let them fall where they may and make the goddamn best of it.

She wishes Kit would kiss her. She nods and steps closer to him.

'You're right,' she opens her mouth to say, but Kit draws back as if she has paid no attention to his argument and retaliates, 'It's just not safe. And what about the typhoon? Risa says it'll probably hit Okinawa, then China—'

Ah, yes: Risa. Her claws and nostrils flare.

'It makes no sense to travel further out with a massive tropical cyclone on the way,' Kit continues. 'We need to get back to Tokyo as soon as we can.'

'Fine, I'll go without you. Probably be safer in Ishigaki anyway, if the typhoon's heading here.'

'You're not going! I won't let you!'

'Oh fuck off, Kit. How're you going to stop me? You know, you needn't have come on this trip at all. You've only ever had your eye on' – she hesitates – 'going home. Hunter said he could—'

'Sure, why not? Why not travel into the middle of fucking nowhere with someone you've only just met? Sol, there are three days before our flight leaves. The only one we have, the only one we can count on catching before flying is no longer possible. Three days. You must understand that?'

'You're the one who's so concerned with getting home. Maybe my home is with my father.'

'Yeah, he does sound like a really great guy. Definitely worth the trouble. I'm sure you, he and your massive marine pet will be incredibly happy together.'

'Go home, Kit.' Sol turns back to the bar and walks towards Finn and Hunter.

He goes. She doesn't know where and she tries not to care. But she notes that he has taken his rucksack with him, out into the rain. So that's it; she's on her own now. It's probably better that way. The job of finding her evidently flawed and possibly criminal father is really hers alone; for what is she if not flawed and criminal? It is proof of their shared blood.

Sol goes straight to Hunter who takes care of her as she knew he would. They play a few more games of pool with Finn, sink a few more Orions, the sun long set over the treacherous sea. The rain is still torrential, but inside the cocoon of the bar and the beer Sol is barely aware of the drumming thunder, roiling waves. There's no sign of any curfew or drinking ban – the bar is filled with servicemen and women growing ever louder, some starting to dance and touch. A few drunk girls cling to bar stools, spread their legs and shake their asses.

At one point, Hunter takes Sol downstairs to a closed part of the bar. 'I brought the party,' he says, grinning as he leans forward to kiss her, and she realises there is something on his tongue: a new shape of pill. Dizzy in her red heels, she sinks back against the wall behind her and, longing to lose herself, kisses him back. His enormity around her makes her fragile, his authority makes her passive; but somehow, now, it is Kit whom she is unable to eradicate behind her closed eyes. Kit's gone, though. To meet Risa and complain about her, Sol, presumably, or directly to the ferry port.

New jags of heat shard through the old familiar warmth of the first pills. Softens the hard places as she catches her breath. This ain't codeine. Welcome home.

'Don't worry,' Hunter says later. 'I'll take you to Ishigaki myself.'

'That's really sweet of you, but aren't you, you know, busy?

Just got back from Tokyo and everything? You said you had to be back on base.'

'Yeah, it's a long story. But basically I have business there too – it's part of my work to keep an eye on American affairs across the islands.' He taps the side of his nose for intrigue, winks in case that were not enough. 'We need to go soon though, before the typhoon. Kit gone, has he?'

'Yes.' Sol keeps her face impassive. 'It'd just be us.' She sees Finn give Hunter a not-so-subtle nudge of suggestion and mutter something like, now's your chance, dude. She finds this friendship puzzling. 'Do you think there'll be any space left on the flights?'

'No, shouldn't think so, but the boats'll be going for another day or so before the typhoon gets serious.'

Sol thinks of the black water tides and feels no fear. If the boats are still going. Besides, who could ever be scared with a trained fighter looking after them? In any case, she'll probably see Kit at the ferry port.

'Not a ferry – I know a guy who'll give us a ride in his private boat early tomorrow,' says Hunter. 'When the weather'll be calmer.'

'No point going to bed then,' says Finn, winking at her. 'Go on then,' he says to Hunter.

'I need to pick up some stuff from Foster, OK?' says Hunter. 'You happy to hang out with Finn and the boys for a bit?'

She is and she does, or at least she must have done … but it all becomes a little hazy at this point. She remembers going to another bar; shots of habu sake, seeing the bottle with a poisonous pit viper coiled inside. She remembers lemon-drop shots, and more pills and a different pool table, different vintage ads on the walls giving her a sudden confusion that she was already back in Tucson, or perhaps had never left. No Kit though. At some point, no Virrea either, no Finn and no Hunter.

Then: Hunter re-emerging, carrying the bag he'd had in Tokyo, a long scratch down one side of his face, red and inflamed.

'My wife,' he explains. 'She's been waiting for me all night. Made dinner, y'see.'

Okinawa did not always look like this, all tarmac and concrete. The Japanese construction companies bulldozed what the Americans hadn't.

Even the mountains! The home of gods. Can you imagine?

The mainlanders kept us poor, prices high, and moved in their own businesses to destroy ours.

They let the Americans bring their poisons to our beautiful island: mustard gas, VX, lewisite, Agent Orange.

There was a sarin leak near this very house.

In the sixties the world was looking up at the moon.

Not us.

We were looking at the Pentagon's toxic arsenal.

They dumped tons of that stuff in our poor choking oceans.

The stupidity of these people! You know how it leaked in the first place? They made a new, cheaper sarin — and its acidity ate through the walls of the rockets.

Greed, lack of upkeep, disrepair — the same reasons we have radioactive waste all over the place now.

PHOENIX RISING

Saturday.

Kit had never intended to leave Sol that night. If she'd insisted, as he sort of knew she would, that she travel on, he would of course have followed her. He had simply gone for a walk in the rain, trying to cool his frustration and ignoble urge to shake her until she rattled. He'd wanted, he reasons, to make the strength of his feelings absolutely clear, in case Sol was in any doubt. Had hoped that when he was truly and transparently concerned, she'd listen to him. Almost as if he didn't know her at all. Idiot! And now it's too late.

Kit had only walked along the seafront away from the Village, dripping rain and sweat. He marched down a palm-tree-lined resort path, dodging the odd golf buggy ferrying fellow Americans to their entertainment. Some of them were sitting on steps leading down to the sea, drinking and talking, unbothered by the rain, which did eventually stop, and the cresting waves, which did not. He walked on around the harbour curve and came on to the blue, white and terracotta paved seawall, fighter jets on night-time drills occasionally terrifying him. His pulse began to beat less violently when the weather withdrew its forces; he'd been about to turn round and come back when he saw, to his surprise, the elfin, spiky-haired silhouette of Sol up ahead. He carried on up the path, tapped her on the shoulder – but the girl that turned round had bright red hair, he could now see up close, and was not Sol.

'Can I help you?' she asked. Her childish voice reminded him of someone. Chrissie? But it was just the red hair, a trick of the light.

'Uh, no, sorry, I thought you were … you look like a person I—'

'Who's that then?'

'My friend – but she's in a bar in the Village and I should be getting back.' Though Kit found he couldn't get away from her. She kept asking questions, spinning out a conversation he couldn't exit without being rude.

Finally he started to walk back the way he'd come, with the girl tagging along beside him, and at some point she drifted into the background.

He felt he couldn't have been more than an hour; he hadn't walked that far, and he knew Sol would be in the bar for the long haul, as was her way. But he'd lost track of time, clearly: the clock said hours had passed. Okinawa playing tricks on him.

By the time he reached the bar on the waterfront, it was too late: Sol had gone.

He shouldn't have taken his bag with him, he realises, now seeing himself through Sol's desertion fantasies. Almost anything can be misconstrued as abandonment. The robot barmaid confirmed that she had left 'hours ago', and added, 'This yours?' To his horror, she was holding Sol's Virrea. He stupidly tried to contact it anyway, watching the thing illuminate soundlessly, its receiver elsewhere. He went from bar to bar, couldn't find her. Tried to call up Hunter through the search engines – Kit had stubbornly refused to take his details in the belief that their engagement would be brief and perfunctory – but he seemed to be invisible online. Kit could not find him listed anywhere.

Had Sol gone back to Naha, to the ferry port? Or was it possible to take a boat from here? He knew where she wanted to go – Ishigaki. So perhaps he should have tried to get there himself before it was all too late. Trusted that she really was that impetuous. But in his frenzy he kept looking locally. He thought she might have taken a bed in the hostel they'd seen by Sunset Beach, passed out there not realising she'd lost her device. In the morning, she'd go back to the bar to reclaim it and he would be waiting. But the receptionist wouldn't tell him if there was anyone of her name there and the back and forth proceeded until Kit, exhausted, took a private room – all the dorms were full.

There was no sign of her around the hostel or the Village in the morning. He took a taxi back to Naha, to Hotel Matsu, where they hadn't seen her either, and then to the ferry port where he discovered that all routes had been cancelled. Typhoon Fenghuang was approaching much more quickly than anticipated, gathering speed, force and headlines as it went, now upgraded to category 5 'super typhoon' status. No one could move until it passed. The ferry to Tokyo had been cancelled, not that he'd ever have gone without Sol, and they'd miss their flights home. Who knew if there would be another? He hung on to the idea that the violent weather might disrupt those flights and then the airline would owe them a replacement.

Why had Sol not found a way to contact him? She must know how worried he'd be. Not knowing what else to do, Kit had called on Risa. People were leaving Naha, she informed him – it was going to be 'really bad'. Some had been evacuated, others were choosing to leave while they had the chance, heading north before tomorrow evening when the storm would pass directly over the island's southern tip, hitting Naminoue. Kit remembered the shock of Sol's nudity in the turquoise bay, his own shyness. The shrine for safe sea passage.

'You can come and stay with me,' said Risa. 'I'm going to sit this one out with my grandmothers in Yomitan.'

She had picked him up in her little red Toyota and drove the two of them back up Route 58. Kit insisted on stopping at the American Village again, looking around in vain for any sign of Sol or the man he was now viewing, perhaps unfairly, as her abductor − Hunter. All the bars along the seafront were shut up, waiting out the storm surges, but further up from the coast some places were open, the stray cats from the seafront gathering to shelter there. No one had seen Sol, they confirmed when Kit showed around a Holo on his Virrea. He realised that all the images on his device were of Sol.

They continued north along the coast by the vast airbase, Kadena − 'That's where my mom is mostly now,' said Risa − then turned off the highway past a great vermilion shrine gate that, it turned out, was not actually a shrine at all, but Torii military base. From there an abrupt rural metamorphosis as they entered Yomitan. Swathes of soaring sugar cane lined the narrow road and fields of chrysanthemum and purple sweet potato. The air was thick with insects and the roadsides with womb-like graves, as if this were the only space left on the island to accommodate them.

'Well yeah, mostly we built the tombs before you built the roads,' Risa explained. 'Look, I have to warn you that my grandmothers are not America's greatest fans. But I think it will be OK! I've told them about you, and they understand the danger. It's much safer for you to be up in Yomitan with us.'

And now he is here and Sol is where?

—

Risa's grandmothers' house is a good size, able to contain four generations of women with room to spare. It is a mixture of old and new, topped with the traditional Ryukyuan tiles – a gently sloping red pyramid roof with demon-repelling *shisa* on it. The black wall in front of the door also helps to keep the bad spirits away, he discovers. Inside, it's quite modern. Though airy, it's divided up into separate rooms and its walls are solid concrete, the whole building closable against the darkening elements. Risa explains to him how the coral walls outside act as a windbreak, the shape of the roof guiding even the strongest winds to skirt the top of the house.

Kit picks up a perfect blue jewel from a shelf of gnarled wood in front of him. It feels satisfying to hold, cool in his hand.

'That's sea glass,' says Risa. 'Actual glass, sculpted by the sea. Human waste battered into something lovely.'

Up early, they're doing a little light typhoon preparation before breakfast: placing the ornaments of the sea in boxes, placing the boxes in larger boxes, pinning everything down.

'It's beautiful.' Kit thinks of the love hotel in Tokyo, the green shoots penetrating the walls, nature taking back what belongs to her. Sol.

The grandmothers live above Toya port. Once a small fisherman's wharf, now it houses the racing *sabanis* Risa had mentioned: traditional fishing boats bright with painted images, decorated to resemble dragon boats. This new commercial racing is unlikely to appease the great sea dragon, Ryujin, but it brings in the money, she says. And for a people who belong to the sea, any excuse to be out on it counts.

The road is crowded with other houses, graves and small gardens busy with yellow tropical flowers. Though set back from the seafront and much higher up, all the tsunami signs, evacuation routes and the audible, visible waves themselves let Kit know that he is in the sea's territory. Last night from his futon was a star-dark blackness he'd not met since Dreamtime. No light and all those tombs, the menacing sea, no Sol. He did not sleep much and, when he did, his dreams were wakening panics. He thought of Finn's ghosts, the roughed-up graves on Futenma airbase. Of Chrissie and the original sin his life was sown in. When the sun came up he yelled out in fright to see a green dinosaur spread-eagled on the wall by his nose. A fat lizard, he realised, as it did its high-speed waddle out of sight. Already today he has seen beetles, hornets, a praying mantis. This is a different Okinawa.

'This is pretty too – but deadly.' Risa points to one of the shells next to the sea glass. Kit recognises the convoluted patterns of the brown and white cone shell from Naminoue beach, intricate as a Gila monster's. 'This is the most lethal of all the cone shells. People call it the "cigarette snail" because if it stings you, you have time to smoke precisely one cigarette – and then you die. Ha ha! There are thousands of them on the shore down there; you can pick them up in the coral rock pools when the tide goes out. Don't touch the live ones! Look for a thin orange tongue hanging out, that's the creature.'

He thinks he'll pass on that one, thanks. The things that live in the sea. It doesn't bear thinking about.

They keep the radio on as they move through the rooms, pausing now and then to pay attention to it. Kit recognises it as a radio since they'd had one at Dreamtime, the extent of technology that Phoenix allowed there and mostly for his sole use. Hearing the local news read aloud, accessed by translation earpiece, feels different from watching the international news, dominated by America. Mostly Virreal ads actually. This is a much duller beast, less hysterical, less personality driven.

Super-typhoon Fenghuang, the radio regrets, has already caused several deaths in the Marianas, including one on a US firing range:

a local woman working in a burger bar was stabbed by the glass of an imploding window. There is talk of 150-mile-per-hour winds, storm surges and flooding. No news of Ishigaki-bound ferry disasters, or local aircraft in trouble (had Sol somehow managed to get on a flight). There has still been no word at all. If she's with Hunter, could she not have borrowed his Virrea to contact him? Let him know she's safe, at least. Maybe the fact that she hasn't means she is not safe.

Kit's feeling of entrapment in his own skin, tricked by his drawbridge eyes and separated from the world, has expanded to a general sense of sea-bound incarceration here on this Sol-less foreign island. He is utterly powerless to help her. It is as it was when Dreamtime was broken up, his mother led away. All the mothers. But then at least he and Sol stayed together in care, and they clung together as they had always done. Anything, even the group home, was bearable with each other. When they were separated and sent to different families, he thought he would never see her again, and his own body grew hostile and forbidding, imprisoning him from a world that held her. He felt as responsible for that split as he does for this one.

'So Ishigaki's relatively safe, is it?' He keeps asking Risa for reassurance. He can't see how that island's sufficiently removed from the current path of the typhoon, which is meant to end up striking China's east coast. Isn't Ishigaki directly on the way?

'Again, it's just going to pass near by. But you know, nothing's certain. It could suddenly change direction.'

Kit prays Sol is safely inside somewhere. Her behaviour has been so erratic since they came here he doesn't know if she can be relied upon to look after herself. He hopes that she is enjoying marine privilege. Risa's grandmothers clearly think Kit should be. 'I'm sorry, I just don't understand why the military aren't taking care of you?' asked Hana when he arrived.

'I'm afraid I don't know any Americans here to ask,' Kit admitted uncomfortably. 'Risa very kindly—'

'Well, they have a certain protocol, you know: they take care of their own. They're even "taking care" of my own, my daughter – or they need servants while they're locked down in base.' Hana looks at least two decades younger than her sixty-nine years, as does her mother, Umitu, astonishingly unlined at ninety-eight. Pretty agile too. Kit feels older than both of them.

Umitu speaks English and Hana seems to understand it, but interpreting Hana requires a translation piece. Occasionally she switches from Japanese to Okinawan so he and the translator can't understand her at all. Risa tells Kit not to worry: Hana gets that having him there is an opportunity – the last chance she has to educate an ignorant American before travel ceases and it's too late to communicate anything. As if the internet is a sheltering sky: beyond it, a chaos of truth.

'Fenghuang.' Kit rolls the name of the typhoon around his mouth, biting down on it, trying to own its odd familiarity. 'What does it mean?'

'It's Chinese,' says Risa. 'It means phoenix. I think you have phoenixes in the West, yes?'

'Yes.' The blood in his head pulses harder. That name. Phoenix rising out of the ashes even here, back again to fuck things up.

'Well, the Chinese phoenix is different. It has the head of a golden pheasant, body of a duck, peacock's tail, swallow's wings, a parrot's mouth and the legs of a crane.' Chimeric monster, that fits. 'They're meant to be symbols of virtue and grace, so don't look so miserable, man. It's all going to be fine.'

Hana is cooking as they pack up the dark blue bottles of the kitchen – arcana Risa translates as 'mugwort for floor', 'sakuna paste', 'hippazu tincture'.

'Herbs we use for different things,' explains Umitu kindly. '*Sakuna* means "long-life herb". *Hippazu* is local pepper. We try to live in harmony with nature here. The stream at the bottom of the garden was being choked by our chemical detergents, so we make our own now, for the house and for cleaning ourselves. Most of the herbs we grow in the garden.'

Through the kitchen window he can see the sea thrash and menace the land. 'Are we actually safe here?' he feels compelled to ask Risa. 'Phoenix is coming for the south-west corner of Okinawa, no? Isn't that where we still are, and now right on the coast?' On the other side of the island, he notes his Virrea map with palpitations, is nothing: just a yawning oblivion of sea for thousands of miles. A blue blank space.

'You're never too far from the coast on Okinawa, but we're a good way north of Naha here. We'll feel it – I mean, you can now, can't you? – but Naminoue's going to feel it more.'

'Yes, don't worry!' says Umitu. 'I've seen a thousand typhoons in my lifetime. Okinawa has seen a thousand things worse than this. It will blow over soon enough.' She pats Kit on the back as he thinks of its flooded villages, whole islands underwater. 'He's a nervous one,' she says more quietly, and perhaps she thinks inaudibly, to Risa. 'A nervous American. Can you imagine ...' She goes in to the dining room chuckling to herself and they follow her.

Hana brings in juice, miso soup and a conflicted expression. She waves off Kit's attempts to help and gestures at the low table where Umitu is already sitting cross-legged. He takes a sip of the same sour–sweet *shikwasa* he'd drunk with Sol in the Chinese garden, as Hana scurries in and out of the kitchen to deliver a vast array of tiny, fragrant dishes on crimson and turquoise lacquerware. He has no idea what anything is, though he recognises the odd carrot, purple sweet potato, the ubiquitous *mozuku* seaweed. When Umitu points to each ingredient in turn, Kit is no better informed. The names of the many leafy local plants are just not familiar.

'Wow, look at all this.' He is a little overwhelmed; there must be thirty dishes. 'Is this all … breakfast?'

'Yes,' replies Hana crisply. 'This is not America. It's of the greatest importance to know that our loved ones are well nourished. Our cooking here is *nuchi gusui* – the medicine of life – and we take pride in it.'

Risa looks up at her grandmother through her too-long blonde fringe, her eyelashes catching. She smiles encouragingly at Kit. He doesn't know why she has her fringe so long. Mustn't it be annoying having it in her eyes like that? Is it fashion or neglect?

He reaches gingerly for a small bowl of what looks like freshly mown grass.

'*Sakuna*,' says Umitu with approval. 'You eat one leaf, you make your life one day longer. Pour a little soy sauce on it.'

It does not taste unlike minty grass, but the thought of his extra day cheers him on. Proceeding through the tastes and textures of each small dish, he realises that the grass was the least delicious on a mounting chain of goodness. He feels he is eating a whole garden, a forest, a stream, a bit of sea, a bit of mountain. Here a giant green leaf in some sort of cold broth – boiled bird's-nest fern, he is told a second time – there something grated, something pickled, bitter-sweet, pungent … He falls into a rhythm as new flavours continue to emerge.

Hana's right: this couldn't be more different from the breakfast buffet at the Tucson Grand. The smell of fat and sugar rising from every metal vat, obese customers coming back again and again, piling up plates of waffles and doughnuts and pancakes, deter-mined to get their money's worth. The bottomless coffee flasks. The inertia. So much fuel for so little exertion. And the waste! In mainland Japan, Risa tells him, customers are charged extra if they do not eat what they have taken from the buffet. In this manner, gluttony is punished.

Hana seems surprised he's enjoying it. 'Umitu taught me these things when I was little.'

'Yes,' Umitu agrees. 'We used to be famous for this medicine breakfast when we ran the place as a guesthouse. Americans never got on with it though.'

The ghost of Risa's father shuffles the air. A window blows shut.

'Listen!' Umitu raises her hands in glee as she passes them in the garden that afternoon. She shields herself from the gale, approaching the stream at the garden's edge.

All Kit can hear is the sound of the wind. Or the waves, further away. The garden is beset by swarms of furry tiger-like dragonflies, huge for their species, as were the eagle-like bats Kit saw swoop over the sea last night. The dragonflies usually come earlier, in September, Risa tells him. They bring the typhoons.

'It's so peaceful,' Umitu whispers.

Risa shrugs. 'Usually the noise from Kadena is deafening,' she says. 'Endless roaring of engine jets – all through the day and night. My poor mother.'

'Won't the flight ban affect that though?'

'Oh yeah, I'm sure they'll all just pack up and go home. Wait for China to move in.' She laughs, checking a *gajimaru* tree for any branches that might fly free from its trunk of entwined aerial roots.

'In that case, I guess you might still have a chance of coming across your dad here.'

'Like Sol, you mean? No, I've checked every base, like *every* base, asking around with the only information I'm ever going to know: that the guy stayed here in this Yomitan house, that he met my mother, and that I look like this – do I remind you of anyone? I even went to Japan and asked in the last remaining American set-ups there. And I hate the mainland – it's too hectic, too rigid.'

Kit thinks back to his time in Tokyo. He noticed the hectic, certainly, but not so much the rigid. His whole experience of time and place seems fluid and shifting, even more so in memory. He is about to tell Risa about his strange experience with Sol there; her openness invites confession. But he thinks twice and stops himself. 'You must be able to get a name,' he says. 'Something to go on …'

'He gave my mom a fake name.' Then Risa brings Sol up anyway, peering covertly at him through her bleached fringe as she checks another tree. 'So, you don't much like this guy that Sol's gone off with?' is the question she settles on. Kit finds his eyes drawn to the way her mouth moves, as the length of her fringe hides a great deal of her expression and her manner and voice do not give much away either. To him, at least.

'I don't even know if she's with him, to be honest. He's alright, I guess, just a bit, uh, well, you know. He's very sure of himself.'

Risa fidgets with her coral necklace.

Stealthily, as the sky has been dark all day, night closes in. Dinner, heavy on the bitter melon, light on the Spam, has been eaten. Crates of bottled water have been stowed in the bathtub – 'Don't drink from the tap! Kadena's poisoned the supply again' – and there are various torches, spare batteries, candles and kerosene in the bedrooms, should the electricity go. Storeroom supplies have been assessed and found satisfactory. In any case, Risa says, there's a store down the road that the owner never shuts, no matter how bad a typhoon gets. 'He's a bit nuts.'

Finally, they close the windows and their shutters, and lock the door against the oncoming storm. The radio remains on.

They don't know the deadliness of that stuff.

They forget.

They get used to it.

That time they nearly blew up the whole world?

Just a false order to set off the nukes. We'll be ended by a fat-thumbed bureaucratic mistake.

But we don't know the half of what goes on, you know.

I had my special birthday last year: in Ryukyu at ninety-seven you return to childhood.

And it is true, I see it all happening again: ever more military, more bases, more chemicals and waste spreading out across our islands — to stand up to China, or so they claim.

America doesn't have to disclose a thing. Even contamination.

We're not allowed to check.

We can only tell what's going on when the animals start dying.

Or we do.

On Ishigaki people get sick.

On Iriomote people disappear.

THE TALE OF UMITU

Sunday.

Sometimes, Kit has heard, people go to the sea after a hurricane, curious to see the high waves. The strong winds have ceased; the fear lifts. But this is the typhoon's greatest trick: the power of the sea dragon is still there, just waiting to snatch its prey high up and far out.

On the island of Ishigaki, however, the dragon was too impatient to lurk in the deep and wait for these intrepid scraps. He shifted his shape and came up on to land like a crocodile, rearing on his hind legs in great waves forty metres high that swept over the island. They destroyed everything in their path. The typhoon had changed course in the night to hit Ishigaki full on the nose.

In Okinawa, the winds still roar around the concrete house in Yomitan, shake the leathery leaves of the *gajimaru* tree and whistle over the roof. One of the *shisa* – the one with its mouth open to scare spirits who'd do the house harm – is lifted clean off the tiles and sent spinning to smash below. Akira, the cream-bodied, brown-bobtailed cat, hisses at Kit and runs into the kitchen, seeking refuge.

Hana confesses she found an oarfish washed up on the beach last week. Everyone knows it means fault action when the serpentine fish of the deep sea – the servant of the great sea dragon – is belched up into the shallows. It is this ill omen that makes Umitu, at last, fearful.

'Shit,' says Risa, which had been Kit's repeated response as they listened to a local newsreader break the morning news of Ishigaki's devastation. How the islanders thought the typhoon would skirt around them; how they awaited a storm, yes, they expected to feel it, yes, but not *this* … A direct hit without warning in the night, no time to escape to higher ground …

Shit. The electrics have gone.

Kit feels only disbelief, as if he is fluttering on the very edge of reality. They're meant to be flying home today. It's Christmas Eve tomorrow.

He had gone to sleep the night before unnerved by the whine of swarming winds but consoled by the notion that Sol was better off away from Okinawa. He'd tried to contact the hotel the day before, remembering its name had something to do with cats and able to search online for it. The profile and handle he found – @catisland.j – met with no response, and when he tries again now, aware he will need, but not be able, to charge his Virrea soon enough, he finds his signal is down, as is the wireless connection.

His numbness is drifting into frustration. What if Sol is still in Okinawa after all, without her Virrea? Maybe she did come back to the bar in the American Village to look for it. He shouldn't have taken it! But no, he's going round in circles. He came back to the bar to check. No one had seen her there. He tried every social-media channel, every search engine, every connected word he could think of to locate Hunter – military, Okinawa, marine, etc. – but absolutely nothing came up. It's as if he does not exist. Come to think of it, Kit has never seen Hunter use a Virrea, though didn't he contact

Sol on one once? Is it even possible that he doesn't have one or any online presence? Virrea or no, Sol is at least, he has to admit, in the company of a hero type, brutish and strong, who can protect her. Who better to be with in the midst of an environmental disaster than a US marine?

It's dark as night, or almost, outside now, though it's the middle of the day. The storm has accelerated with more force than anyone, least of all those responsible for tracking its movements, had predicted. Umitu bustles about lighting candles and fiddling with the kerosene stove to boil the bottled water, despite already asking if the others mind their matcha tea cold. No one is objecting, obviously, but she keeps asking.

Kit is trying unsuccessfully to charge up the solar panel on his Virrea with a candle flame. He can sense the thing dying even as he scrabbles for Ishigaki news that will not come. As if the plastic skin of the device is trapping the information inside, like his own shell, bursting with self. Sand is stuffing up his nose, access denied to the world outside himself; he starts to feel as if he can't take in enough breath to stay alive.

Risa sees him struggling to expand the locked muscles in his chest and asks him if he's OK. He tries to explain the familiar gasping pain, like there's something sitting on top of him.

'Ah, I know that one,' she says. 'It's just the *kijimuna* playing tricks on you – that's one of their all-time favourite tricks.'

He laughs slightly, immediately feels the chest tension ease. 'What the hell is a *kijimuna*?'

'Oh, they're mischievous little things – like fairies, short with bright red hair. They're tree spirits, sprites of the *gajimaru* tree specifically ... that banyan we were tidying up earlier? Bound to be riddled with them. They're always up to something, and they particularly like to lie on humans so they can't breathe.'

'This explains so much!'

'Yeah, you can push them off. Or you can, er, release wind. They don't like that at all.'

'I see. Sage advice.' He laughs again and feels a little better.

'They usually come down from the trees at night but I reckon this one grew confused in the dark of the typhoon.'

'This is not the first mad thing to happen to me on this journey, you know. That night in the American Village, when I left the bar so I could get some space? This random girl came up to me and started chatting – and listen, you know what? She did have scarlet hair … and suddenly hours had passed. By the time I got back, Sol had already left.'

Risa looks at him and her expression is inscrutable. 'Just fling an octopus next time you see one. Man, they really hate that.'

'Well, thanks. This is what you don't learn growing up in the desert.'

'No worries. So, what's going on with you and Sol? She's your girlfriend?'

'No. No. It's, uh … complicated, I guess.'

'Oh yeah?'

'Well, we sort of grew up together. Known each other all our lives. I suppose I've always had a bit of a thing about her but Sol's – how can I put this – she's completely wild. She's made some bad decisions in her life, you know?'

'Sure. Haven't we all?'

'Hmmm. Yeah, I'm guessing not like hers.' Kit hesitates, but Risa continues to look at him impassively. 'So, anyway she got into drugs, married a total shithead, did all sorts of dodgy things for money … and I hung around and picked up the pieces where I could. I keep her safe, or I did until now.' Nausea rises.

'Doesn't sound like much of a life for you.'

'She's my best friend. We've been through a lot. A lot of stuff no one else could understand – our upbringing, you know. It was pretty weird.'

Risa looks away. She must have found what she was searching for in his face. 'And does she know you're in love with her?'

Kit's kneejerk reflex is to deny it; he opens his mouth to do so but somehow, here at the ends of the earth with apocalyptic winds rattling the shutters, he cannot.

'Well, something did happen between us in Tokyo actually. I don't remember what I said exactly but she would've got the message, yes. It was funny though, in the morning she'd vanished and when I found her, she was with Hunter. She said she'd been with him all night. I suppose she didn't want to acknowledge what we'd done.'

'It wasn't her, you stupid boy,' cries Umitu, who it transpires has been eavesdropping keenly. 'Don't you know anything? It was a fox!'

Kit is taken aback by the confrontational style of the formerly demure old woman who is practically hopping with conviction. 'Uh –' He doesn't know how to answer this. 'Yeah, I mean, I did see that it was Sol. We talked. We, uh, you know … We found this ruined love hotel in Dogenzaka.'

'Fox, fox, fox,' Umitu squeals, ignoring Risa's pleas to please calm down. 'How many tails did she have, nine?'

Kit says nothing, but a shadow of a memory is beginning to prickle, buried deep in his mind. There was a fox.

'The mainland is full of them!' she says. 'Shapeshifting rascals. Any woman you meet after dusk could be a *kitsune*. Did they not teach you that at school?'

'They did not,' he confirms.

'And in the ruins too. Who knows what else was skulking there? You have to be careful in Japan. It is not like other places. Here too in Okinawa. Strange things happen. At least you're safe from those demon foxes here though. They don't come past Kagoshima. Plenty of other tricksters, let me tell you. I met a shapeshifting snake out in the garden there only last week. It was Seko, my late husband!'

On that note, Umitu has to go and lie down.

Kit makes a mental memo to check the house for snakes before bed, a useful Dreamtime habit. 'You don't really believe in this stuff, do you?' he asks Risa. 'I mean, I know you said in the bar about ghosts being like Virrea or whatever … but you were joking just now, weren't you, about the flame-haired fairies and foxes and all the rest of it?'

'Well … sure.' She takes a sip of tea and looks mildly uncomfortable. 'But, you know, I grew up on this island, with its spirits and stories and grandmothers who wanted me to understand. Children don't really need it explaining, though, that there's another world that's just as real as this one we call reality. I've always felt it. It's just that it can't be pinned down to any point on our spectrums of time or space. An in-between place. And Umitu is right: strange things do happen here.'

'That's really weird,' Kit ventures. He has mostly managed to dismiss the teachings of Phoenix – and the bad dreams they still evoke – as the ravings of a criminal lunatic. If you want to lure people to a commune and have them do your horrible bidding, you have to have a crazy belief system they can get involved with. He does not like to hear the same kind of ideas expressed by someone sane.

'Weird is standard. Terrible things have happened on this island and so maybe it's like our history is still alive in the present. It muddles the timeline when the past can't die.'

'Do you mean ghosts on the bases, that sort of thing? That guy I told you about, the one in the American Village, Finn, he was talking about—'

Umitu, evidently too piqued by fox seduction for a nap, returns to sit with them, perhaps sensing a new audience for the old stories. 'Yes, of course – Okinawa is full of them. Bad memories made manifest.' Kit sees how she lowers herself on to the tatami mat with almost the same ease as Risa, despite the many decades between them. 'Our island is built on sadness, terror and loss. Like so many islands in the Pacific: peaceful people living in harmony with the land of their ancestors, the spirits of animals, the sea … replaced by barbed wire, pollution and violence. Life swapped for death. You want to know about Okinawa? I'll tell you. I'll tell you everything and then you go home and tell your country, how's that?'

Kit agrees. He wants to understand. He has nowhere else to be.

'You know,' Umitu begins, 'I lost my father in the war. We all did. We in Okinawa had never seen anything like it when war came to us …'

She's settling into a soliloquy, one that feels long rehearsed and often repeated. Older generations always want to tell their war stories, don't they? It's a symptom of their trauma, the compulsive need to convey it. They tell Kit it's to prevent such things happening again, but there's more to it than that. Committing it to narrative form is an attempt to contain it.

Umitu seems far away as she continues.

Blitzed by the wind, tiny parts of leaves are plastering up the windows, turning them into green mosaics. It's like another layer of sweltering insulation. Kit longs to open one.

Umitu has stopped. She looks exhausted by her recollections, the dreadful understanding that things have only got worse.

Risa moves over and puts an arm around her.

Kit does not know what to say.

He does not understand why they hear nothing of the suffering of Okinawa back home. It's trapped in a time warp, the Second World War still alive. He cannot imagine surviving day by day in caves, hiding from the enemy. Perhaps he would have been stationed here if he'd walked the military road. Perhaps he would have been in Camp Foster or Schwab or Futenma airbase, and he'd never have met the civilians, heard the other side of the story. He would have eaten pizza and taco rice, hung out with others like himself in the American areas where he felt at home. Dismissed the daily protests as the work of a primitive people who don't know what's good for them. Risa told him there had been over a hundred thousand protesters on the street after the last child rape and murder. Thousands still sitting up at the new base built out of the sea, which killed the last of the sacred dugongs. Why has he not heard about any of this?

Umitu nods grimly, unbothered by the massing green foliage on the glass. It is as if she can read his mind. 'Well,' she replies to the question he did not ask aloud, 'America controls the media, we all understand that, don't we? And the media controls the story. The Land of the Free is right inside that dead little device of yours, the one you find so liberating, Risa, when it's alive and spying on you … It's listening to every word you say, everything you wish for, and there are people ready to pounce on you, pick you up and send you far away if they disagree. And in return it gives you virtual reality, what it wants you to see and none of the things it does not. CIA's little helper.'

Kit has heard this kind of view before, dismissed it as the general preserve of much older people who knew a different world. Now he's not so sure. He tries to calm Umitu down, to gently steer her back to her story, where she seems almost comfortable in her resignation. There is familiarity in the narrative, no matter how painful.

Umitu's eyes are closed but she says wearily, 'I don't know how it can ever change. We are dependent on the bases economically, you see. And if tourism is to die now that people can't travel – well, what hope can there be of getting rid of them? Even if they do give the land back, it will be so filthy we won't be able to do anything with it. Yomitan is already saturated with their arsenic.'

And 'people get sick' on Ishigaki. What the fuck does that mean? He needs to ask, but she looks exhausted.

They have fallen into a late-night trance when a deeper rumble cuts through the monotonous scream of the sky, a threat that shocks them all to sudden life again. And then an enormous crack and wrench: the house is shaking, Kit is flung back against the wall by the force of it; Risa is grabbing him and Kit's back on the boat, out in the deep, rammed by sea giants. What the hell is it? An earthquake? He drops to the floor as he's been taught, taking Risa with him.

He dares to look up as furious winds rush in. The *gajimaru* tree has broken through the shutters and the green glass window. It is waving its branches like a kraken through the wound.

CAT ISLAND

Saturday.

When they arrive, the sky is dark with storm clouds. No way should they have been out on the sea in these conditions; no commercial ferry service would have taken them. The speedboat was rising up a vertiginous wave when she came to in a swell of nausea. She found herself curled into him, drugged and drowsing the journey away with her head on his chest, his good hand in her hair. It is only at the port that reality penetrates the haze: Kit has not come with her and, what is more, her Virrea is missing; she can't even contact him. Abject powerlessness without her device – like being back at Lights. She tells herself that Kit will remember the details of her conversation with Finn – though she hardly does. He will know where she is heading and come to find her there. Or there will be devices at the hotel. Her travel companion – unthinkably! – is Virrea free.

She has a curious sensation of being naked, as in a dream of unwitting bareness in a bank, a school, a supermarket. It's a trick of the mind, sure, but there's a physical queasiness that pervades beyond the boat too. She has not felt quite herself since hitting the beach in Naha, and occasional dire thoughts of the sea's alleged toxicity well up with the sickness. Just as likely to be mild withdrawal though and that's far easier to deal with, particularly as her escort's little luggage is heavy on the magic pills.

Immediately behind Ishigaki port is an uninspiring grid of bars and restaurants – all closed, for it is daytime despite the thunderous dark. There is no one around; everyone has packed themselves away for what is coming. But she notices a trio of war-torn cats, one white, one black, one tabby, arranged as if in conference outside a red-lanterned *izakaya*. Two have an ear missing; one is toothless; all three have damaged tails. When one sniffs the air and sets off purposefully towards the docks, the other two fall into line behind it.

'Shall we follow them?' Sol is already doing so.

Hunter shrugs. 'They know their own.'

The cats trip-trap over the long blue bridge that extends across open sea to a small bejungled island. Here they split and scamper into the forested paths ahead. All around them other cats of all persuasions filter through the undergrowth, going about their business, sniffing the air with tails erect to chart the progress of the oncoming squall.

'This is Cat Island, then?' she asks.

'Whatever gave you that idea?' Hunter's grin makes her feel better about everything. The island is man-made, he explains, like the ones the Chinese conjure out of the South China Sea for their military bases. But this one had lain idle and so the cats moved in and made it their own. The feral occupants seem genial enough, but it's clearly their territory. Sol gets the feeling that trespassers, though tolerated, are not encouraged.

She stops short at a dart of beaded black and red in the undergrowth, her desert brain flashing the Gila-monster alarm.

'Don't worry,' Hunter tells her. 'Sounds like an odd-tooth snake, get them all over here. Won't do you any harm. C'mon.'

The cats are mostly heading for the southern side of the island, and Hunter agrees that this is where the hotel must be located despite no Virreal research or reference.

'Have you been here before?' Sol asks, but he shakes his head, swerves to avoid a Japanese bobtail that has stopped abruptly to wash a leg.

The conga line of cats draws others from the undergrowth as the procession creeps south. Buildings start to appear on the far shore, along with storm-dimmed sand and sea, dirty blues raking and biting the grains.

A vast bronze cat confronts them where the rainforest gives way to a series of Grecian pillars, dancing cat demons engraved upon them. These carve the way to the thatched roof of a hut that must act as reception. Did her father sculpt this vision of feline reverence? It's hard to believe. Sol's heart flies out of her body when she sees a sign declaring the hotel, and indeed the whole island, to be a no-Virrea zone. How will she contact Kit? She is desperate to let him know that she is safe. To know that he is. Maybe he's back in Tokyo already, out of harm's way. She should pretend that, for now.

'But ... how do people book?' Sol asks the girl with broad eyes on the desk. She is wearing a name badge that says 'Anita' on it and her face is ... Sol can't think of the word. Precise, she settles on. A Ryukyuan looker with a California accent.

'Ah, they don't, usually. People tend to just come and go in a place like this,' Anita replies.

This casual beach-shack vibe makes no sense to Sol. The place is full of luxury – private villas, bosky gardens of tropical leaf and flower, its own beach, furnishings of teak and bone. It no doubt costs a fortune. With that in mind, she makes her enquiries, using all the names for her father she's encountered so far. 'And his wife, a Mrs Carter ...' she adds. 'Yuna, was it?'

The girl blinks her surprise.

'Are they here now?' Sol presses. 'Can I speak to them?'

Anita drops her eyes. 'No one has seen Mrs Carter for a long time now.'

'What about my father then?'

'You've no idea the journey this woman's been on, looking for him,' Hunter joins in, sounding almost waspy, his drawl of the Deep South departed. Sol glances at him gratefully.

'Mr Carter is no longer here either.'

'Well, where are they?' she demands. 'Is this their hotel or isn't it?' She feels her face flush, hand itching in the pocket of her blue tunic for a pill. She can't bear to think she's hit another dead end, and what that really means: that she's screwed Kit over for nothing.

'I'm afraid Mrs Carter disappeared some years ago. She went to visit family in Iriomote and never came back, then Mr Carter went to Iriomote to look for his wife and he also vanished. He hasn't been to Cat Island in at least seven years. I've been here the whole time, so I'd know – I'm the manager, you see. He does still own the hotel though, in name at least ...'

'Great. Fucking great,' cries Sol.

'I'm sorry,' says Anita, looking profoundly so, as if imparting this information wounds her deeply. 'We are on the front line here; with the Chinese just over there on the Senkaku Islands, people who go wandering tend to get into trouble. The new American base here has made Ishigaki a target.'

Furious with disappointment, Sol continues, 'So it's off to the next island now, right?'

The girl nods nervously at Sol, and then at the seething sea. 'Look,' she says, 'you're here now and you are the proprietor's daughter. It's not safe to leave at the moment and I'm sure Mr Carter would be extremely upset if he found that we'd turned you away. The typhoon is going to pass by us this evening. You can stay in one of our empty villas for a nominal fee if you don't mind sharing it with some of the cats.'

Hunter, who to Sol's surprise introduces himself as Finn – part of the spying thing he keeps alluding to? – says there is no point in setting off immediately. No ferry will take them to Iriomote in weather like this. They should take up Anita's very generous offer, shouldn't they? No, it is of no great importance that he's allergic to cats.

Sol feels herself swaying as they stand there. The girl eyes her warily again and then sets off, beckoning for them to follow. She leads them – heads down and muscles braced against the strong winds – through the tropical garden, houses dotted distantly along winding sea-bound paths. Every villa is in traditional Ryukyuan style, such as, had Sol only known it, currently houses Kit in Yomitan. *Shisa* lions pose, prickle-backed upon their red-tiled roofs, and a small demon-repelling wall stands before each entrance.

'OK then … break it to me. Iriomote?' Sol's voice is thick and echoey in her head as they walk in the bluster of restless *gajimaru* trees.

Hunter pauses. 'Well, I've only been there on Virrea but—'

'But you're not on Virrea are you?'

'Yeah, that's a fairly recent decision. So, listen: Iriomote's all thick jungle and mangrove swamps. It's completely wild and not easily habitable: Japan's final frontier. Our boys had to set up another training camp there in 2025 – because of the Chinese – and most of the island's closed off for military activities now. I think there are still a few people living there, around the edge where there's a road. God knows what your father's still doing there, if that's even where he is at all.'

'The woman he married, she was from here was she?' asks Sol.

'She was from Naha,' says Anita raising an immaculate eyebrow. She looks as if she's about to elaborate but then falls silent as they reach two turquoise *shisa* on pillars: the entrance to a villa.

The girl opens the door with a small buzz of her hand and, in that instant, Sol realises that she is a robot.

She looks at Hunter to see if he's noticed too and he winks at her, smiling. But there must be real people working here as well, she thinks. People whom Jonny – or Jay, or whatever the hell name he's currently chosen – might have confided in, who would know where he is, or where his wife is. He may not have talked to the managerial robot about personal things … That girl is seriously sophisticated though. Sol hasn't come across such a convincing android yet – and it is disconcerting.

The house is extraordinary. All one room and on one level, it opens straight on to the beach. The wide sea-facing side is all glass, giving the effect of being on a boat out to sea, a state which feels apt to Sol. She giggles. The only way she'd been able to cope with waking sick on the sea was to get higher, and it seems she still is a little. There is a bathtub on the sandy veranda that, they are told, draws up hot spring water from deep below the earth's surface. A plastic Christmas tree stands in the corner.

'Your cats will be along shortly. Please let them in when they ask. The bar and fridge are already stocked' – Anita gestures to the small kitchen area – 'so you'll have provisions for the storm tonight, and it should all be over by morning. Room service will be operating until nine this evening if you need anything else.' She turns to leave, opening the heavy door that has swung shut. 'Oh look, they're here already.' Five cats meander around and through the girl's legs, rubbing their whiskers on her automaton flesh as they pass.

Sol bends down to greet them: a stripy tiger, two pretty calico bobtails, a tiny black kitten with white socks and a ginger tom that immediately starts spraying everywhere. They acknowledge her briefly before dispersing with authority to different hotspots around the house – the tiger to an armchair, the calicos to the bed. One calico has bright blue eyes, the other has one blue and one gold. The kitten scales a curtain, and the ginger tom, sprayed out, gazes wistfully out to sea through the wide glass panes.

Anita, indicating a stock of cat biscuits and an automatic litter tray, departs.

Hunter goes straight to the mahogany drinks cabinet, whistles as he sees the full bar within. The fridge is full of cold wrapped offerings that look like buffet leftovers. There is what appears to be a lifetime's supply of Oreo cookies and a pile of Spam cans in the cupboards of the little kitchenette, along with some rice and taco seasoning, a baffling variety of instant noodles and some curiously flavoured chips. Orion beer is stashed variously around the villa.

'Spam 'n Oreo, American gods,' exclaims Hunter. 'Who could ask for more?' He fixes the drinks – cocktails of rum and fruit juices, for a beachy feel – and tries to open the sliding pane of glass at the front. 'I think she must have locked it already. Probably shouldn't be out there anyway to be honest.'

They sit down on the tatami mats, feline ringed, and look through the glass as the angry tide creeps closer and the waves rise higher, each one feeling like it might crash over them and sweep them away, house, cats and all.

'This feels like the least safe place imaginable to wait out a typhoon,' says Sol, but she does not really feel unsafe, opiate warmth blossoming over her skin. 'We're practically in the sea.'

Hunter puts his good arm round her. 'Remember that big

tsunami a few years back? Well, y'know, it was the people out in the sea that survived.'

'That's enormously comforting.' She smiles despite herself. 'Hunter, do you think we're really any closer to finding him? My father?' She's not sure how long she has before the plane home – not long, she imagines, the days of the week blurring into one without her Virrea – but it's reassuring to know that the flight's there, waiting for her. If there's nothing here for her she can still get back: Hunter will pull military strings, whatever it takes. Kit will probably be thinking – hoping, perhaps, if she's lucky – that he'll see her there, at the airport. It's the only plan the two of them have in the absence of communication.

'I think we're very close, baby,' Hunter answers, kissing her hair.

'I was thinking there must be someone working here who's in touch with my dear old pop, someone who knows exactly where he is. If he owns this place and is still taking the proceeds, he must be in contact with someone, don't you think? Or his wife might?'

'Ah yes, the Oki girl he brought with him when he left the island … Sounds to me like she's split.'

'How're you going to keep in touch with *your* wife?' Sol asks slyly, not looking directly at him, 'when you don't have any kind of device?'

'Oh, we're not that close any more to be honest. I met her in a club; she was a dancer there. We stayed together because of the kid, mostly, but we've been all but separated for the past few years.'

'You have a child?'

'One. A boy, Lennie. He's seventeen – already started in the marines. But y'know, I'm away a lot, my recon work and so on.'

There is a silence. The sound of one calico grooming the other with abrasive tongue fills it.

Hunter takes his shirt off.

'So hot,' he murmurs, moving his hand down her body, stroking her waist, her hip.

The skin shivers beneath his touch and she shrinks away.

Why didn't the robot girl ask if they wanted a twin room, or separate rooms?

They look generations apart.

He's a father, she thinks.

He could be my father.

The thought is gently comforting as he presses her back against the bridal bed, its sheets covered in a heart of dried petals.

At Dreamtime, they would pick desert wildflowers for the cleansing of Phoenix.

Does she want this?

Hunter pins back her arms in one great hand and pushes her down on the bed.

The crushed flowers release a sickening odour.

Does it matter?

He holds her there.

His strength is absolute.

Her eyes fix on a turquoise and silver panel, a crane taking off.

They bob up and down on the static image.

When she next awakes, her face stuck to Hunter's thick chest hair, the world in darkness is exploding, walls of water crashing all around her, submerging the house. The glass sheet rattles and the cats howl. The power dies, air lightless and heavy with dull heat almost instantly as the aircon clunks off. There is no running water, Sol discovers, and the electronic lavatories have powered down. It is lucky, then, that plastic water bottles have resisted all attempts to ban them.

'What the fuck is happening?' It feels like the world is ending.

'I guess this is just the typhoon passing by,' says Hunter. 'Things can get pretty rough but yeah, I agree, it's a lot.'

Sol is still unable to go and look for non-robot staff as the doors and windows are locked until further notice. For your own safety, a tannoy announces from time to time, the voice that of the girl from earlier. Is there no one else? Outside the aftermath rages on, flood waters liquefying the sand and making the garden grass a marsh, even though the sky is clear and eerily still. And so the cats stay indoors with the humans that shelter them, even as water drips through the Ryukyuan roof.

The heavy chalk thickness of the sky has robbed Sol of her wits. She is exhausted beneath its weight, all energy snatched up into the storm. She falls in and out of sleep, waking the same white limbo as dreaming. There are moments of sudden stillness when it feels as if all the air has been sucked out of the room, bouts of low pressure. Time ceases to have meaning, except when the white is replaced by black and vice versa. This can't be one typhoon but many, a ceaseless death-march siege. Maybe this is now reality.

They lie on the huge honeymoon bed, trapped inside their peerless beach house with nothing to do but fuck. Hunter can be a deft and brutal lover; his moments of gentleness when they come, as they do now, feel impossibly volatile, like an ogre cradling a songbird. Sol is aware he could snap her in two with one crunch of his good hand and there is some thrill in this, some sense of safety even, so long as he remains on her side. His strength can be her weapon.

When Sol has finished, shuddering in the sweaty grasp of Hunter's boulder-like thighs, he falls asleep, muscle and tattoo rising and falling like the waves. Feeling nauseated again, she helps herself to another pill. She likes the sense of solipsism, slipping into her own dreaminess unaccompanied. Sometimes.

The techniques she picked up at Lights to get her off the stuff are now most effective at letting her take it up again. Calm, acceptance, perseverance; useful qualities when drifting back into the den of the sick. All she has to do is listen: the siren song will do the rest. She sees her red boots standing up in the corner of the room. Hunter is generous.

She snuggles into him, his cast right arm hanging stiffly around her, sling slipping off. Sol creeps one hand gently towards his and then stops suddenly as she comes up against something strange and prickly. Adjusting herself to look more closely, she finds that the hand peeking out of the cast has ... *something* attached to it: hair. It is growing out of his palm, like fur.

Hunter wakes up at the movement, looks hard at her and sees her revulsion. He looks at the hand and sees what she has seen. His eyes flash and then a film descends upon them. 'It's crazy gross, ain't it?' he says casually. 'Why d'ya think I keep it covered up!'

'What the hell is that?' She is unable to stop her voice wavering a little. The criminally insane grow fur on their palms, Phoenix used to say.

'That's what happens when you keep your skin away from the air like I've been doing. Seriously. It hothouses the hair like a motherfucker.'

Sol laughs.

'Like a tropical plant,' he goes on. 'It's outta control, man.' He passes her a cigarette.

It's odd, she thinks, that Hunter's chest hair should be grey and shaggy but this new palm hair is red and virile. His stubble too has become a beard of copper wire.

Sol is uncertain how long they have been in here, living out of the minibar. It feels like a couple of days since the tannoy last boomed into action, the cats howling in response. Keep calm, Anita had told them then. Ishigaki has taken a direct hit from Fenghuang; the island is in a state of emergency. Cat Island, despite appearances, has escaped the gravity of the storm surges that engulfed Ishigaki's north, killing hundreds, sweeping away houses and leading to flooding and landslides. Damage here is thought to be superficial, but the situation remains precarious. They must remain indoors.

They have heard only this one voice across the winds, though they once saw a waiter braving the weather to bring them further supplies. Real or robot, he was lifted into the air and sent spinning out to sea.

The cats cry at the glass, but Sol cannot let them out. The litter tray can't do its job without power; they must just hope the doors will be opened soon. Tired of their biscuits, the cats eye up the humans' purple-sweet-potato chips. The tiger and the tom have seduced the two bobtails and even the kitten wants in on the action. Their yowls blend into the cries of indistinct beasts she conjures in her sleep-daze.

Sol and Hunter have fallen easily into a kind of lowlife routine, cycling the hours with drinks and pills and sex and sleep. Just the two of them and their five-cat family within the confines of these walls. She is in the void and there is safety in that. Here she may embrace stasis; Hunter's medicine brings a contentment in inertia.

She wishes it were Kit in here with her.

Hunter has ceased to hide his hand in the sling, and now just lets it poke out. The orange fur seems to be sprouting more thickly – from his upper arm now too where it emerges from the sling. Sometimes it is all Sol can see.

'Think I'm ready to take the cast off,' Hunter announces at some point.

'Don't you need a hospital to do that?'

He looks horrified at the prospect, then recovers himself. 'Have you seen outside?' he asks, gesturing to the biblical scene beyond the glass.

She wonders if there are others here, similarly trapped in their rooms, beset by cats and junk snacks. No word on the tannoy for ages now, and the swelling heat inside the locked doors and windows without aircon is suffocating. She is fearful, and yet she feels that the cats, grateful for safe harbour, are somehow protecting them. She hopes someone is protecting Kit, wherever he is.

LOST IN TRANSLATION

Kit realises he has been staring at Risa's mouth again, at the v-shaped indent in the centre of her upper lip and the way it dances and changes shape. It reminds him of Sol's.

He dreamed about Sol throughout last night, only to see near morning that it had not been Sol all along. It was Chrissie, dying over again, gashes and scratches and hanging-off limbs. The details of that day continue to shimmer and twist, overlaid by layers of stories. What is memory, what dream, what haunting? Who is to blame? When he woke in one of the communal sleeping areas, shaken by the near constant rumblings of earthquake, it was Christmas Day.

They have fled their shattered house for shelter in this neighbouring one. Neither the man nor the two women who live here speak English; they resolutely ignore the American, and Kit can't translate it when they speak, as they are doing, in Okinawan. Nevertheless, he is able to detect some information simply by watching: the man Také is insane. And he is likely his only ticket out of here.

There's a sense of age to Také that has eluded even the very old women Kit has met here. Though weathered, his hair is still thick and dark, and his frustration has an energy that mirrors Kit's own. 'Ishigaki,' he keeps exclaiming wildly and often, throwing his hands up, making for the door only to be restrained by the now five women available. He punctuates nearly every unintelligible sentence with a chuckle. Whether it's nervous, manic or simply expressive, Kit can't decide.

'What's the deal with that guy?' he asks Risa. He can feel a pulse throbbing in his temples, in his stomach. The lack of news is maddening, networks down across the devices that still have any power. Of course their flight will be long gone, but he needs to talk to the airline, his parents, *someone*.

Risa's cagey. Eventually: 'His daughter's missing. She went to Ishigaki a month ago – he still hasn't heard from her and doesn't know why. He was worried before the typhoon, was going to sail to the island, find his daughter and bring her home. Now he's even more worried. Také can't go anywhere in this, but he keeps threatening.'

'What, sail there himself?'

'Yes, he's a fisherman. Or at least, he used to be. He's the guy I told you about with the racing *sabani*.'

'Risa, I need to go too. I have to go with him. The typhoon is over: we must go as soon as we possibly can.'

Risa doesn't see it that way. 'You don't have to and it's not safe!' The v-shaped dip disappears altogether as she purses her lips. When she releases them they are engorged with blood from biting, a non-sexual sex flush. 'And don't you know we're in the middle of a national crisis here? Who knows what has become of Ishigaki – you see what has happened here ... Our house is all but ruins! Sol chose to go despite your warnings. She left you. She may be dead for all you know.'

Kit flinches.

Risa has not finished. The flush has reached her cheeks. 'I think she's using you, Kit. I think she's been using you – and everyone around her – her whole life.'

He is not sure what he can say to this. The sensation of exploding outwards is back – into the rigid walls of a body that will not give. He settles, lamely he feels, on, 'There are things you don't understand.'

'What don't I understand? I think I see the situation with perfect clarity. You're too far in it to see anything yourself. She's an addict, a user of substances and people. You're blinded. You're a victim.'

'Sol is damaged,' he says carefully. 'That much is true. But so am I. She was born addicted to opiates, you know that? Even as a baby she knew craving, an emptiness that can never be filled. Lying next to a pill-popping mother who knew the same thing.'

'Everyone knows sadness, Kit. It's how you deal with it that counts.'

'She's had a hell of a lot more than most. We grew up in a—' He hesitates, swallows, ploughs on, the time for deception, even of himself, over – 'in a fucking cult. The man who was meant to be looking after us all … he didn't. He made us do things to him no child should ever have to do. Sol and I are the same. We protect each other in the only ways we know how.'

'She protects you by taking drugs and getting drunk, by seducing men old enough to be her father, by running off into danger and emotionally blackmailing you to follow her, by—'

'That is how she protects me. She saves me from becoming trapped in myself, paralysed by inertia – fear of movement … fear of life. She makes me feel alive. She makes me live my life – instead of hiding away, just existing day to day.'

'Some kind of life. Your need to love that woman is the poison in you. And for what it's worth, I think you're crazy.'

Kit tries again. 'Better crazy than dead inside. Sol is a lunatic, I know, but she deserves love, doesn't she? Compassion?'

Risa is not interested. She ignores him. Eventually she speaks, her face still impassive. 'Maybe you'll stay for me. Maybe I need you.'

He remains quiet. Still and small, lost in the weatherless vacuum of Yomitan. Fearful of not finding Sol, his antidote, his cure for life. No, the cure for life is death.

What is left in these terrifying conditions, when soon everyone will be static and locked within their land borders, the sea unnavigable, the sky untravellable, energy stuttering to torpor in the face of the electric swells of the earth ... What is left, for god's sake, is Sol. His love for her, his protection of her is the very thing that sustains him.

He must say something. 'Risa, I'm really sorry, I can't stay. I have to find her.'

'You know, I've been wondering this whole time if my dad's like you. I was kind of hoping he might be.' Risa puts down the green tea she's been drinking – cold again as the power is still down – and it is as if she has put Kit down as well. The emotion departs from her voice, the flush from her face, and her composure returns. A Virrea restored to factory settings. 'I guess all Americans let you down.'

No games, no tricks. It's better to be straight with her, isn't it?

Risa's walking away but there's nowhere to hide in this open-plan house. He can see Také pacing up ahead. She turns back: 'Kit, Také's going to go, whatever we say; his wife and sister can't stop him forever. But why would a Ryukyuan fisherman do you any favours? He can't even bring himself to look at you.'

A light appears overhead. The power is back on. Umitu goes immediately to the kitchen to retrieve the kettle, the radio.

The news is bleak. Some islands are entirely underwater, reclaimed by the sea.

'Ha,' she snorts. 'As if they weren't already. You can't blame the typhoon for everything.'

Ishigaki is partially submerged: the description causes Také to start pacing again. Not only is there widescale destruction but also an outbreak of some new disease.

'Again!' Umitu exclaims. 'Didn't I say? God knows what they're doing down there.'

There are warnings of further disaster from the burst sewage pipes and filthy flood water sloshing about, stagnant. Ishigaki is too close for comfort to the polluted deep-sea mining sites. It's a humanitarian crisis and there are no flights except for those small planes taking aid to Ishigaki and evacuating people. No mention of Cat Island, but maybe that's a good thing. Hope remains. Kit tries the hotel on his Virrea again. It's as if it doesn't exist.

'You don't even know if she's there,' Risa begins to protest again. 'Is it really worth risking your life for?'

But he does know. He can feel it now. He has to get Také alone.

The next night, it is Také who comes to him.

Kit is deep in dream, back in Tucson where the airplane boneyard is spreading over the city, over the whole desert. Dead cars scatter where they fall, abandoned, and he and Sol are dodging them, flying hand in hand around them, trying to get out ... out to where?

A light tap on his shoulder and the man is standing above him, one finger pressed to his lips. Také retreats to the doorway of the mat-covered area Kit shares with Risa, Umitu and Hana, and he waits. Kit is up, silently padding towards him even through the surreality of the boneyard, an old man reaching for his hand instead of Sol.

He looks back at Risa in the darkest predawn, sees no flash of open eye, as Také moves cat-like through the quiet house. He wants to wake her, to thank her, to say that though he is creeping out of her house, fleeing by stealth in the night, he is not leaving her as her father did. But isn't he? She would only try to stop them.

Kit's bag is waiting for him by the door and once he's there Také, invisibly, is already on the other side of it, walking down the sea road past the wreckage of Risa's house. Kit closes the door ever so carefully, startles at its inevitable click and scampers after him. Také seems a younger man in motion, his back straighter, his gait more secure.

As he draws level Také gestures for Kit to put his ear and tongue pieces in. 'It's time,' he says then, ditching Okinawan for translatable Japanese. 'It's safe to sail now. You and me, we're both looking for someone. If you help me, I'll help you. How about it? I need an American with me to talk to the marines – they'll never let me through otherwise. You'll see. I'll explain on the way.'

Kit is nervously looking over his shoulder, expecting the five women to come racing out to stop the old man. Should he be stopping him? '*Is* it safe? Of course I'll help you any way I can.'

'The storm is over now.' The streets of Yomitan are alive with the night cries of reptiles, the dawn caws of birds. A swell of red light is just starting to break the horizon. 'Too late already,' he mutters. 'We must hurry.'

Down and down they go until Toya port appears, a multitude of boats. They weave around them and then Také stops, standing proudly before one. He pats the boat's flank: 'Here she is.'

Kit takes in the furled red sail, red oars, red dragon painted on cedar wood. *This* is the racing *sabani*? He can't mean this … it's more like a canoe. No match, surely, for the open sea.

But Také nods encouragingly. 'Trust me, she couldn't be safer. I made this *sabani* myself, you know.'

That, and the proximity of wild water once again, diminishes Kit's confidence all the further. He longs for clinical Arizona, where nature is contained, commodified and turned into theme parks. He inspects the fastenings pinning the creaking boat together: wooden dovetail keys secured with bamboo nails – like a piece of household furniture, not a sea-going vessel. It's a joke, a trick, a way to punish the American for the sins of his fathers, his brothers.

Or, what Sol would say: a man of the sea must know what he's talking about. Now is the time to trust.

'Are you coming or not?'

IN A DARK TIME

Hunter is an animal in the sack, Sol thinks grimly as he mounts her yet again. Her vision splinters into a thousand segments of the colour wheel and small droplets of sweat coat the skin of her thin frame.

She has come almost to enjoy the reddish furriness of Hunter's emergent paw, scratchy yet soft, like an old mauled teddy bear. It is more mobile too, not incarcerated in the sling, which has been entirely abandoned now that its secrets have been revealed. Sol helped him cut off the cast. She wonders if it was there simply to conceal his sprouting hand and arm, and not the cause of its hairiness, as he had suggested.

Anita the android lives. She comes to see them, freshly charged from some emergency generator that still fails to electrify anything in their beach house. She brings fresh supplies of purple-sweet-potato chips and beer for the humans, some drowned mice for the cats, a bucket for the leaks and a plastic bag for the cat droppings.

'We didn't know there were any mice left on this island,' Anita says brightly, 'given the number of cats competing for food here, but the storm sent them scurrying from the gutters.' She looks with concern at Sol's damp brow. 'Are you ill?' she asks.

Sol shakes her head. 'It's just so hot in here.' But her mind is swimming and she feels unusual in all the worst ways. Everyone fears these fluey warnings now; robots in America have been programmed to spot them too, the better to enforce an immediate quarantine should yet another mutated virus threaten humanity. She is high; that has consequences. Can one expect to feel great when surfing the opiate seas? Yes, she remembers. Peak unadulterated wellness at the crest of every wave.

'There's something going round. You need to be careful here.' Anita switches off the automatic lock so they may open the sliding doors to the beach. The cats can leave to paddle in the static pools of water outside. Mostly, though, they stay. The air is as listless as the puddles, the sea as the land; all utterly numb.

And Sol is too.

Before she goes, Anita tells them that the US military are doing the rescue rounds. This ruptures Hunter's unsulliable calm: they should go now; they plan to get to Iriomote as soon as they can. But, he slows himself down, thinking aloud: seeing as this place has been left pretty much intact, it is unlikely the boys will come to Cat Island.

'What does it matter?' says Sol. 'They'll help us.'

'You're not well,' he tells her. He wouldn't be jumping on her every second if he thought whatever she had was contagious though. 'We'll wait here until you're able to travel. Hey Anita, we're really glad you're OK. Wanna stay here and have some fun with us?'

Hunter flips Sol over so she is on top of him. He tries to make her sit up as he grows faster and more urgent beneath her, but she does not have the strength. She rests her head in the nest of his bear's chest, breathing in its wildness, seeing rainbows burst through the fur's steely glint as if sunlight is bouncing off it, but the sun cannot be seen in the sky's white stillness.

He throws his head back and grunts, the sound of a rutting bull, then collapses back on the bed beneath her. His sexual power is growing by the day, as if he has caught hold of her libido and is slowly screwing it out of her, a tapeworm wound on a pencil.

'When are we going to go?' she asks, and her voice sounds weak and echoing, as if she's far removed from its source. 'We have to find Jonny. I mean Jay, whatever his name is.'

'We'll go when you're better,' he replies, sniffing. The cats have spread their allergens like spores in the heat. 'You have a bit of a fever, y'know. You might see and hear some strange things for a while. It's not a good idea to travel with you in this sort of state. Have another painkiller; maybe it'll bring your temperature down a bit.'

A memory of Hunter telling her this before rushes in, but Sol is unable to locate the sliver of thought in time or space. Thank god one of them knows what's going on. In this crashing surf, she is able to feel fear.

'Maybe it's you that's allergic to the cats,' he says lightly. 'That's a thing: cat-scratch fever.'

But she felt ill before the cats. The sea, the sea is when it started. She thinks of ancient viruses ripping through her veins, dredged up from the seabed, uncovered by the melting ice, hewn from arcane mines and bottled by the Chinese.

'I think we should just get there,' she insists, as she feels she must have protested before. She can hear a self doing it, miles away, down a tunnel.

'And what d'ya expect to find there?' asks Hunter. He sounds amused, and very far away as well. They are having a conversation from distant corners of the galaxy.

197

'My father! Obviously. I mean, that's what all this has been for. I've risked everything.' She is aware that only half of the words she speaks are discernible.

'Have you not seen enough yet?' One half of his face is smiling, the other is ice.

Sol does not know what he means by that. She gives in to the blindness caused by the shock of swirling colours and closes her eyes.

When she opens them again, Hunter's are closed and one of the cats, the tiger, is crying at the door to the garden. Sol gets up, or part of her does, and opens it. The cat looks round at her in thanks, then issues a loud miaow, walks a little way, calls again. Sol gets the message and follows; the cat walks slowly, deliberately through the leafy paths, past an empty reception and the demon pillars, away from that human intrusion into the dense jungle lair of the cats.

It stops, sniffs the air, starts to dig.

Sol sits down a little way from it and watches. The cat regards her steadily with something approaching approval, then continues its burrowing work, front paws excavating, hind legs occasionally kicking the soil behind it. The earth is loose; it's coming away easily. Where are the pools of seawater? They can't have dried up so quickly, but the ground would be much less amenable if drenched.

Finally the striped cat desists. It calls again, its green eyes piercing her own, and Sol comes closer, peers into the hole it has created and springs back in alarm, crying out. Bones! A long white bone, stripped of flesh by what – acid, vultures, the cats? An arm bone, a cheekbone, a section of skull and attached … long rust-coloured human hair. She looks back at the cat and sees the same green eyes flash, but the hefty tiger's face has changed and now it is a man, matted with brindle fur, staring straight at her. He opens his hairy cat face and hisses the love song of the Animal Groom to his newest bride.

Sol screams and wakes herself up; she finds she is still wrapped in Hunter's sleeping arms. He stirs, grips harder; she can't breathe. He growls and relaxes his wrestling hold.

Taking back control of her limbs, she goes to Hunter's bag for another pill, not sure whether she will be able to keep this one down, allow it to enter her bloodstream before her stomach rejects it. Not sure whether it will take her away from all this or throw her in further. The pack is empty so she starts to search the side pockets. More pills there – out they fall along with Hunter's dark blue passport. Checking he's still asleep, she has a look, wondering how old he really is.

It's not him.

It's someone else's passport.

It's Finn Garcia's.

She slams it back in the bag and tosses down two of the new pills; dragons, their tails in a circle, each eating the other.

'Shhh, shhhh. Are you OK, Sol? What's the matter, baby?'

She starts to ask about the passport, senses she should not and shuts up. 'A bad dream, that's all. It's nothing.' Her voice is viscous and slurred.

The tiger cat is back on its habitual perch, its own face restored, watching her closely. When Sol makes eye contact it seems to wink at her. The pools of sea outside have come back, if they ever went away. But the sense of menace is around her and upon her. She is hotter than she ever dreamed possible, burning up, sweating out, then suddenly shivering. All the while Hunter is looking at her and as she looks back, she realises something: she does not know who he is at all. That little he says about who he is adds up. The danger she is in.

She must get away from him, she must get to a public place and she must find a way to contact Kit. But when she manages to wriggle free of Hunter's grasp, flail her way to the end of the bed and stand up, she is overcome with sudden vertigo.

In any case, she has awoken the beast. Hunter reaches out and pulls her down – she is tumbling anyway – upon him.

We have to get away from here, she is trying to say, dizzily slurred, but Hunter is all over her like smallpox, newly returned to a post-antibiotic world. His libido is limitless.

'Have a pill, it'll calm you down,' he mutters mid-thrust. 'We'll go down to the port and see what's going on as soon as you're feeling better.'

Sol's mind and body have split. She is no longer aware of what Hunter is doing to the latter. It is dead to her: she lets him have it as she used to with Chase, when he was like this, and before him, Phoenix. But Phoenix was a pussycat if she gave him what he wanted, which of course she always did.

She is in Hunter's power now and she senses that if she does not get away from him, she too will end up on that pile of bones. She can't run, her physical strength depleted, her mind addled, something toxic – virus or venom – making its way through her muscles. So she must persuade him to take her to other people, to the port as he said, on to the next island, away from this strange place with the robot and the cats and the sea.

As she darts to and fro between the borders of consciousness, her body rejected, compromised by illness and by unauthorised entry, the cats enact a strange dark dance as twilight comes. Sol looks down on them from above, where her spirit is floating up by the roof beams. There is the great tiger cat with green eyes, the scavenger that dug up the bones. She realises: why has she come looking for what she already knows, a man she has sought out and found in a thousand men already? The predator that is already in herself, that wants her dead.

Here is the Dreaming. As she falls awake and asleep, slipping from the time spectrum to a shimmering placeless place, the cats follow her. The walls are thin on the borders between the sea and the land. One world is threaded through the other, but the threads are rarely visible. Only when death is threatening, and the intruder is in your house.

ALL AT SEA

Také is as much fish as man, Kit thinks, sitting opposite him on the bench seat of the *sabani* as he paddles, steering them through the still, shallow waters. The more Kit looks into his eyes as they talk, the more he sees a certain marine quality to the slant of his forehead, his shining irises. Také can swim underwater for a full ten minutes, or so he says. Fifteen on a good day. He used to catch fish with his bare hands for fun when there were plenty of fish to be caught, when neither they nor the waters they lived in were toxic.

'I am *uminchu*, a sea person, but I do not like to swim in it much these days,' Také confesses, smiling broadly in the dazzling after-noon sunlight.

'You believe it's not safe too? The water?' Kit looks over the side of the small boat and feels his tongue translator quiver with foreboding – all the things you can't see in that brilliant turquoise. How radioactive is that patch just there? Is it more or less lethal than that one ploughed up by the deep-sea mining, a wave of lead and mercury and newly unfossilised pathogens? The spray on his face has as many grains of microplastic as it does of salt. Perhaps it's the deadness of it that's so disquieting: a sea no longer breathing, its corals bleached to extinction. The sea is death now, an irresistible force threatening all life. It won't stop until the land is blue.

'Oh, the sea is alright – as long as you do not swallow too much of it.' Také grins and, not for the first time, laughs as if he's made a joke. It makes Kit uncomfortable.

Kit knows this was the only option, that he had to take it for Sol's sake. But he'd imagined that a fisherman, albeit a relic of Okinawa's sea-riding, fish-catching recent past, would have at least a motorboat. Not this guileless dugout now navigating the waveless, windless flats, gliding glassily and deceptively out to the dragon's open sea beyond. He tries to relax the tightness that grips him when he sees saltwater all around him, as solid as the choking sand of the desert, only some dead tree between him and it. He thinks of Risa's red-headed *kijimuna* imps sitting on his chest, imagines throwing one off him into the sea and breathes a little more deeply its salt smell: rotting seaweed and marine life, bitter iodine – or some other acrid chemical. He was lucky to meet Risa.

The boat has NAO painted on the side, his daughter's name – short for Naoko. Také is garrulous about everything but this, as if Kit can't be trusted to know too much yet.

'But how can I help you if I don't—' He needs to know the score … Will it mean he can't go straight to Cat Island? He owes Také but he must find Sol.

'I will tell you. Later. Trust me, I will need you. Just relax! You Americans are all so uptight.'

He leaves it for now, goes back to wondering whether they've now missed the new-year cut-off date. A wild idea occurs to him of crossing the vastness of the Pacific in this bobbing, flat-bottomed thing; all the way home to the American coast with Sol. They might as well row a lilo.

Cynical as he is, there's a certain relief in this surrender to the volatile. Kit has spent his whole life anticipating the worst, and dreading it, bargaining with it. And now here he is, living it, being washed over poisonous waters at the mercy of a floating bathtub. He brings himself to congratulate Také on his craftsmanship. 'Do all fishermen make their own boats?'

'Ha ha, you are funny.' But Také looks a touch more serious, as much as his uptwisted face allows. 'There are no fishermen any more.'

'The racers then. Was it hard?'

'I learned from a master in Iejima – it is a dying art, you know. There are only a couple of people left on these islands who know how to make a *sabani* the right way. And she's a winner – a champion! She capsizes very easily.' He chuckles at this horrifying prospect.

'And that's a good thing – is it?'

'Oh yes, a very good thing. Some races require you to do this, and then right yourself. And it makes her perfect for the open sea – and any swells we may meet on the way to Ishigaki.'

'Uh huh …' Kit grips the wet wood.

'You can ride them out under the hull.'

Kit feels a terrific urge to leave his own body, and fights the urge of the contents of his body to leave him.

'Do not worry! Hiding under the high stern of this boat has saved many a fisherman. Not my poor old father of course.'

'What happened to him?'

'He drowned. I think. He never came home anyway.'

So many disappeared fathers. Drowned or war-murdered, invisible or fled, tricksters or imposters. Whatever Sol is seeking, so is everyone else and they're killing themselves in the process. Humanity is the forgotten child of a pissed paternalistic god.

'Is Nao your only daughter?' he asks. The man may be insane but he is a hero.

Také steers sharply to the right, unsettling Kit still further. His sea legs need crutches. 'There are underwater mountains here.' Také ignores his question. 'Look, you can see how shallow it is in places. We have to slide over the deeper parts, paddle round the ridges.'

Kit, swapping fatherlessness for minute-to-minute survival, praises the way Také handles the dracontine boat, its nimbleness through the crags. He can see their peaks penetrating the still sea surface in places.

'This *sabani*' − Také pats the boat as it snakes round to the left − 'has been blessed by a *yuta*, so we are very, very safe.'

Kit recognises the word from his last days in Yomitan, where he took it to mean some sort of female shaman or priestess. The older women, *yutas* themselves, sat on squat chairs in the neighbour's house, discussing the sinister turning of the *gajimaru* and its *kijimuna* tree spirits. Something had happened to make 'the happiness tree' destroy their house − some weakness in one of them perhaps − and they needed a more powerful *yuta* to set things right. Hana and Umitu spent a good deal of time discussing what that weakness might be, much of the talk centring, uncomfortably for Kit, on an American. Not him, Risa tried to reassure him, so it must be *that* one − the guy who came to stay twenty odd years ago and fathered her. But they don't say that. They keep Risa safe from her terrible father by not talking about him at all.

But Kit knows that silence is a kind of poison. Somewhere, it is breeding ghosts, raising animal spirits.

Také is talking about the souls of the sea-dead, which doesn't help Kit's raised hairs and hackles. 'They hold their own races the day after we do. No one would go fishing that day, so as not to disturb them.' And, of course, no one goes fishing now at all. It's all ghosts out there.

Kit tries to distract him from this unsettling trajectory, but Také wants to talk about the sea, not his daughter Nao.

'I was born in a *sabani*,' Také announces, skirting a worried weather question. 'Everyone said I came into the world with gills. My father could swim like a fish too.' He smiles. 'Sometimes I feel I do not really belong in this world, where the sea has rejected its own children. I am a mythical sea beast, the old fisherman!' His laughter is now disproportionately raucous, his whole face creased up at the thought.

Kit smiles politely. 'None of us are a great fit for this world we've made.'

At length Také stops giggling. 'Let us toast to that,' he says, pulling back a cloth to reveal several heavy *awamori* flasks. 'I have been preparing this boat for some time,' he explains. 'You never know what you'll be dealing with at sea – or on Ishigaki for that matter. It is sensible to have plenty of liquor to hand.' He takes a large swig as a forbidding rock appears on their left and then passes the bottle to Kit. '*Karii*,' he cheers as they sail through the jade shallows.

Kit tries to pretend he's a pirate. The ethanol burn is a welcome contrast to slowly sinking into a grave of chemical seawater. He takes another pull on the bottle, wishes he had some weed. Then he remembers the paranoia, the false starts, the lying dreams when he was smoking a lot. He feels grateful that things don't need to be any more surreal than they already are and draws deeply on the *awamori* again. Také hands him a rice ball wrapped in seaweed. Kit can taste the pickled ginger spiked through it, flashes of some pungent vegetable too. But the ginger or the rice, or maybe the brisk calming effect of the alcohol, settles his stomach a little.

'So it's just open water then, is it? All the way to Ishigaki?'

'The best kind of water, ha ha! You may see the Miyako Islands poking up in places when we get a bit closer to Ishigaki. But they are mainly underwater now, reclaimed by the sea dragon. He flooded them beyond repair when the great crab attacked Tokyo.'

'Crab?' Kit half expects one to surface and tweak him on the nose.

'Well the crab and the eel, they are equally responsible.'

'I'm not the biggest fan of either, to be honest.'

'The massive crab is the naughty one, always grabbing at the eel's tail with his claws. But it's the eel writhing about in agony that causes our earthquakes.'

Kit will lose his lunch if he hears any more about giant crabs. He is silent, trying to remember something from school about a Norse god – was it Loki? – who causes earthquakes. Or was it a Greek god, a sea god, the earthshaker? He can't remember, so he says, 'We never heard anything about those islands on the television, just the Tokyo disaster. Tokyo was the only place shown for months it felt like – the international aid campaign. But no mention of whole islands sunk.'

'Well, isn't that a surprise.' It is the first time Také's laugh has seemed bitter rather than nervous. 'These places were off limits to the media, many of them taken over by the American military for …' He abruptly goes quiet, Kit's Americanness filling the boat.

Kit shrugs. 'We're in the middle of nowhere. What were you going to say?'

'I do not know what they do on them,' Také replies. 'No one does who isn't there. Nao heard the whispers. She is a journalist; she wanted to see for herself, to get word of the truth out beyond Virrea – which only shows things as they used to be, thirty years ago. I told her not to go … I begged her. It's my fault, for telling her of the vanishing land I'd observed from my boat, for fuelling the rumours. I am an old fool, and she is paying the price.'

'The rumours – of flooded islands, you mean?'

'I mean of what is happening on those islands. What was happening on them before the sea took them back.'

'What was? What is?'

'I only know what they say: that the military uses them to torture spies. That there are laboratories of chemical weapons there, that there are toxic rubbish dumps. That there are camps of people who may not leave, though the islands are sinking.'

'And did sink?'

'Some of them, yes.' The smile on one side of his face has developed a tic.

'What? With the people on them? Surely that can't be the case.'

'What is to stop it? Who is to stop them? You said yourself, nobody knows what goes on here. I am a fisherman here, or at least I was, and even I do not know for sure. But you hear things. You see things.'

'And do you think this is happening in Ishigaki too? That's where your daughter went?'

'Ishigaki is just by the disputed Senkakus – and they are the reason America and Japan can justify doing whatever they want on our islands. Retaliation against China, "self-defence". Nao went to investigate the new base there.'

'So that's where you're going first?'

'That's where we're going. They won't listen to me, but you can get us past the Americans; you can make up a story they'll believe. You're looking for someone too, yes? And the base is the place to start – the marines will be the ones moving people about after the typhoon damage.'

Kit thinks he should go to Cat Island first. But wouldn't Hunter have gone to his marine brothers if they were in trouble? Find Hunter, find Sol. He hopes. 'I'm so sorry your daughter's missing. I'm sure there's a reasonable explanation – and we'll find her, and bring her home.'

Také doesn't say anything. Kit realises he is crying.

On the third evening, Také announces that the sunken Miyako Islands are near.

The boat is lit by a vast pollution sunset of red, orange and violet. Kit can see shadows emerge like shipwrecks from the water but nothing of land.

They are sailing by lost worlds. He thinks of the terror he felt on that first ferry to Okinawa. Floating past ghost isles, he knows now.

'Land is running out,' says Také, who seems to have warmed to him. Last night he had let Kit steer the *sabani* while he took a rest. It brought a freedom he had never felt before. 'So keep people where they are, say the rich; if their land is sinking, let them go down with it. Do not allow them to ruin the Good Land, riot for space, food and water. That is what this ban on flying is about, you know.' Také chuckles and coughs – a way of resetting his humour, like a cat licking its nose to shake off a smell. But he hasn't finished. 'So maybe they're right, the politicians. We all stay where we belong and sort out our own problems, and if that means you sink with your island, that is that. Hard luck.'

'But that policy doesn't mean that Japan will allow Okinawa to become independent, does it? Or that the Americans will just go home ...'

'No, you may not go backwards. You are as you fall when the deal comes in, I suppose.'

'All this bullshit about national pride and independence. It's just an excuse. Humans need to pull together as a species, figure out how to be human without causing constant damage.'

'We need to learn how not to be human.'

Kit stares up at the stars speckling a now clear black sky. Its stillness is a small relief.

'You should try to get some sleep now,' says Také.

Kit lies back in the hull as Také navigates, looking up at the mountains of stars, so many stories of men held like crystal in them. We have even militarised space, he thinks. Militarised and robbed but still not colonised. We are doomed to stay put on our own ever bluer planet, just like the island people.

The dark sea looks on.

Kit dreams of a great storm cat wailing over the waves and sending them sky-high. He dreams of Sol; of thrashing eels and turbulent crabs.

He is dreaming and yet he is not, he is not: the boat is cresting, surfing a giant swell. And then Sol turns into Také, urging him to cling to the sides of the boat, yelling, 'Remember what I said, the boat capsizes to keep you safe! You can breathe in its hull; it will be your life raft.'

But the cedar wood sides slip out of his wet grasp, and Kit feels himself thrown from the dragon boat, the great weight of the sea hurling him downwards, churning him round and pressing on his chest like hope, pinning him against still more water underneath the great waves into the darkness.

THE HUNTED

Sol senses that something has shifted when she comes to. The heat fever has ebbed and the morphing terror moved elsewhere. Calm clarity remains, her body purged of whatever sickness was in it. Hunter is not there and nor are any of the cats. The sliding doors leading on to the beach are open and, as Sol stands looking out, she is conscious of a freshness to the sea-spray air. She senses she has been trapped in a nightmare, one that never quite allows the dreamer to surface and see that they are in fact dreaming.

The disturbing oneiric landscape beneath the unweather has been replaced by expansive sunshine, a flush of optimistic rays. Stepping outside, she sees that the sea has receded, the seabed, whorled by storms, clearly visible. When she tries to remember how she came here, to draw a linear thread through the days of waiting trapped in the room, she cannot. This lucidity extends only to the present moment. But it is enough. She remembers the passport – he could have picked Finn's up by mistake at the bar, she reasons. Or did she hallucinate it like the bones, the dancing cats? It's hard to tell what's real. She needs to get herself together, get out of here while she can.

Back in the room, Sol quickly gathers her belongings. She tries not to notice the tinselled fir tree in the corner and what Christmas means for the prospect of flying anywhere. She needs to get back to Kit, wherever he is. Back to Okinawa, initially – maybe she'll find someone prepared to sail that way. She made Kit upset, she knows that, but she also knows him. He wouldn't have just left her in Japan and gone home alone, she's sure of it, now that the madness and confusion of that night in the American Village has passed. At Dreamtime she and Kit had made a pact: if you get lost, stay still and I will come and find you. They never knew which one of them was lost though.

This, her father's hotel, is the place Kit will know to find her, if he comes. When Sol pictures him she thinks first of the speculative way he used to look at her; a kind of wry private amusement, baffled yet admiring. She would give anything – *anything* – to see that expression now. With the exception of her time at Lights, they have never been out of touch for so long. This whole thing is just a crisis of communication. She is adrift without her Virrea – but Kit must still have his. If she can just get back to the port, away from this freakish cat place, she can surely find some way of contacting him. When they are together they can figure out the next move. Trains and boats across the continents, a very big adventure, together, and home.

The door opens and she cringes away from it.

It is the doll-like figure of Anita. 'I need to get out of here,' Sol says. 'Can you help me?'

Anita seems to recoil, even in her robot perfection, from the state of Sol. 'I've come to tell you your evacuation boat will be leaving this morning. You need to pack and get ready.'

'What evacuation? Where? I need to find my friend.'

'Your friend will be back soon. He's gone to make the preparations in Ishigaki.'

'I don't mean Hunter.' Or whatever his name really is. 'My friend Kit and I split ways in Okinawa. Where are we being taken?'

'Mr Finn said Iriomote. That's where you said you wanted to go, isn't it? It's not safe to stay here. There is disease spreading across the island, and the flooding is still out of control.'

'I need to go back to Okinawa. I have to get home.'

It is as if the robot hasn't heard her. 'You can ask anyone when you get to Iriomote if they know Mr Carter. Hard to hide one of you Americans, even in the jungle.' Anita smiles an easy smile; the teeth are perhaps a little too perfect, but aren't everyone's. 'If he's there.'

The tide is in.

Hunter leads Sol back across the long bridge, dodging stagnant pools of seawater where they can. The sea is colonising the land, occupying it inch by inch. Her feet in sandals look filthy.

There's the now-familiar Marine Corps camouflage on every corner. Uniforms are shunting people towards the port or away from it – menacing them with machine guns. As they draw closer, she sees they are wearing white surgical masks.

'What are they doing?' she whispers to Hunter, bending over to catch her breath. The nausea is back; it comes in waves. At one point she didn't think she'd be able to leave the hotel at all, but Hunter said they had no choice. He urged her to conceal her sickness as best she can. They must just get off this island, and then he will look after her, or find people who can. He has promised.

'They're sorting 'em.'

'Why? I don't understand.'

'Look, the whole of this island's gonna be underwater soon.

Everybody knows. So they're trying to get the hell out. Rats leaving a sinking ship.' Hunter grimaces. There's a jitteriness to his movements that Sol has not seen before, and his voice has quietened to a hiss, the old accent back but muted. She may not know what his game is but in this hostile environment he is the devil she knows.

'So the marines are evacuating the island?' Sol coughs.

'Don't do that!'

'I can't help it.'

'OK, well don't let them see you doing it. Not exactly evacuating. They – we've been instructed to stop people heading to the mainland ...'

'What, to land above sea level? What do you mean?'

'It's standard policy for climate change refugees, y'know. People fleeing floods aren't eligible for asylum. It's not the same as leaving somewhere compromised by conflict.'

'But it is the same! That's totally fucked up. And I don't get it – what do you mean "sorting"? Why are they sending people in different directions?'

'They're separating the fit from the unhealthy. They'll send the healthy on to Iriomote.'

'And the others?'

'They're ill. The guys are sending them to the military base – it's just inland and north. They'll get the help they need there.'

'Quarantine while the island sinks, is that it?'

'They're dying, Sol. What good does it do anyone to let them infect the next island?'

'Oh my god, what's wrong with them?'

'Keep your goddamn voice down!'

Sol wheezes, 'Is it the same thing as what's wrong with me?' The steady sense of fear in her bones is ratcheting up, grinding away at her.

'I don't think this particular sickness is what you have.' Hunter places a heavy hand on her diminished form. 'I think, y'know, if you just take a pill now, what you're experiencing might miraculously go away. We're gonna have to chuck the rest.'

She stops to prevent herself from buckling, a cramp coursing through her abdomen. Could she be pregnant? Not for long, she imagines, with all the pills she has taken. And then she remembers: Janet's habit didn't stop Sol's birth.

'Don't you recognise withdrawal by now? Seriously, take this.'

And yet she had felt almost normal by herself this morning. To be cleansed of Hunter is detox enough, perhaps. Or she was still high. Why so hard to commit to reality, to leave the many-coloured confusion?

This is the last pill then. She will conserve what little energy she has in appearing healthy, and not be left behind to drown with the island, incarcerated in some military base that even the military may leave.

Hunter throws the remainder of the packet away – she knows she will grieve for it later. If Hunter is some sort of spy for the marines, as he's stated, he's a good one. You wouldn't know he had anything at all to do with the men in uniform, the way he's behaving.

The sun has reached new levels of inferno. In shallower puddles, the stinking seawater steams at the edges leaving thin crusts of white salt to scar the land.

'You didn't go in the water, did you? Get stung by a cone shell? Bitten by a rabid fruit bat?' Hunter's rasping tone is light-hearted, puzzling her. He is probably trying to distract her from the scenes of devastation around them. A small child is screaming, carried away from the ferry – away from parents? – and back through the streets by a masked marine.

'You know I didn't. I was with you the whole time, hiding out in that crazy-ass hotel.'

But Sol feels afraid that she can't remember half of it. She's hazy on almost everything since she and Kit arrived in Japan; it's been like entering some sort of interzone, a place between two worlds where nothing quite makes sense and nothing is as it seems. It is a liminal place, its very foundations broken along the lines of four tectonic plates that shudder and judder. It is a place of cracks; anything can enter. Phoenix would just love it here.

Down a small avenue of boarded-up bars, they enter the water-logged grid of streets leading to the seaport. There's a group of marines on the corner.

'Keep your head down,' he whispers to Sol, as if they are the enemy. Her head is already wrapped in a white cloth taken from the hotel, as instructed. It conceals most of her face. Hunter has his hood pulled up in spite of the renewed blaze of heat. Hood or not, his size alone is revealing. He has tied a handkerchief around his nose and mouth too, a less effective mask than those worn by the marines but some defence, she supposes, against … whatever this is.

'If they see we're American – tourists or military men – they won't let us get on the boat.'

Why not? Who to trust least … 'I don't want to get on that boat. I want to go back to Okinawa,' she says, as she has said several times. 'I have to find Kit.'

'Sol, there's a fuckin' plague, man. We've gotta get out of here any way we can. Trust me, we both want to get on that boat.'

They creep along, and she resists the urge to ask why Hunter needs to keep out of sight of his fellow marines. As brothers in arms you'd think he'd be able to explain the situation, call in a favour even. Get them to Okinawa. But he's not wearing uniform, he doesn't know these men and for whatever reason he's trying to be someone else. He's trying to be Finn Garcia.

As they move through the port, observe the neon signs saying no tickets are required and join the boarding lane for the Iriomote ferry, they see the marines patting down each and every person, removing Virreas and implants and sending them through to the dock. There's a large pile of technology accumulating behind them.

'What's going on?' she asks quietly.

'I'm not too sure,' he whispers back, hard to hear through the muffling of the handkerchief. 'Let's just get on the boat and I'll fill you in with what I know as we go. Not long till we find your pop!'

Near the front of the queue, two marines take them in hand, each wearing protective visors over their masks. One inspects her passport with gloved hands. 'We need your Virrea and other electronic devices, ma'am.'

'Yeah, sorry, but I lost them in Okinawa.'

'Really, ma'am? No device?' He seems distracted, keeps glancing at Hunter. 'OK, move along – that way.' He points to the far right of the port. 'This boat here is for Iriomote. You need to wait over there please, ma'am.'

'She has family in Iriomote,' Hunter says calmly and forcefully. Whatever his story is, he's still trying to protect her. She can't stay here, she understands that.

The marine laughs. 'That so, eh? Whatever, then. On you go.'

Hunter nods to her and she moves forward warily, trying to keep a safe distance from the crowd of men, women and children boarding. She looks over her shoulder as he shows his suspect ID. Something's up. They're not buying it. Back, onwards, nothing is safe, no one can be relied upon – except Kit …

Then she hears it: 'Captain Garcia – step this way please, sir.'

A yell behind her, *for* her? The cluttered commotion of voices splinters:

It's him, it's him!

Yes, positive, this is the guy!

The name you said ...

... Hunter ...

Hunter Macfarlane.

No, you don't understand!

Look, here's the passport.

Finn, Finn Garcia it says.

Seriously, I gotta get on that boat. You're making a big mistake.

Hey, come over here.

Hunter's trying to push into the throng of passengers, disease or no. Those already on the boat are clustering over the railings above them. Marines surge forward and she stares frozen as Hunter's hairy arm is twisted up behind him and handcuffed to the other.

'Hunter Macfarlane, you're wanted in connection with abduction and rape. We need to take you in for questioning.'

He stops pushing. It is as if all the energy has suddenly drained out of him. What is he looking at? Sol cranes to see and there it is: one of the men surrounding him is Finn.

'Thanks, fucker,' Hunter spits at him as he's marched off.

'Don't forget theft and fraud.' Finn's voice is strangled behind the visor.

Sol is terrified Finn will recognise her through the headscarf. Or Hunter will give her up and she'll be detained too. She ducks down below head height to conceal herself and dodges her way through the rows of people into the boat.

Where now?

Somewhere with a lock. Quick. Stay hidden. At least until the ferry gets going.

Sol heads away from the communal areas, finds the least crowded deck and enters the bathrooms there. She sits on the can, breathing nausea, determined not to come out until they're on their way and she is safe.

SEA, SKY, LAND

Hunter a rapist? But could they have known how he'd been with her on Cat Island? She wouldn't call it rape exactly. He hadn't kidnapped her. It must have been something that happened before. Something so bad he had to fake a passport and get the hell away ... The something that had broken his arm?

Finally – *finally* – the boat shudders forward. She feels briefly better just for being away from Hunter, not so sick at least. But then she remembers: no Hunter, no pills. Pain is on its way.

She stays put for a few more minutes, then rearranges her makeshift headscarf to cover as much as she can and moves slyly through the boat, keeping an eye out for Americans in uniform but seeing none, thank god. Even before she has connected her translation pieces, furtive survivors of the mysterious technology cull, the hum of Hunter's arrest is on the sea breeze. And another name: Yui. She recognises it. So familiar and yet she can't place it ... until ...

The bar in Naha.

The angry girl who came in shouting about her friend who'd been abducted, raped ... Hadn't she said she'd died? That *her* name was Yui?

Yui, Yui, Yui, that's all she can hear now, chanted like an incantation, echoing around the boat.

No wonder Hunter had been interested in her father's story: another marine who'd done what he had and gotten away with it. Jonny started again – a new life, a new woman, paradise on a faraway island. Why couldn't Hunter? Away from the law, away from the consequences. Jungle life. He never wanted to go back to America anyway. Was he hoping her dad would hold out his arms to one of his own, like Phoenix calling in his flock of women? Offer him protection and a job or something?

'Where will the marines take him? Back to Okinawa to stand trial?' Sol asks a man with age-faded hair, forgetting to conceal her identity in her urgent need to know. Too late now.

But the old man stares at her blankly until she remembers to start her tongue translator. He's wearing a mask, as are most of the people here. Between coughs that can only now be released, he manages to hack something out in Japanese. The jaunty electronic voice in Sol's ears translates: 'I don't know. Maybe he'll go back to America on that military ship. Good riddance.'

Oh god, was that where the marines at the port had been trying to direct her? Home? But who and what is safe? It's so hard to know. She will get the next boat back from Iriomote, then beg the marines to take her with them. Or will they just arrest her too? Harbouring a criminal or something …

A younger woman with a birthmark on her forehead speaks in English: 'They'll keep the big marine on Ishigaki, I think, with the sick and dying quarantined on base. They'll need people for that, won't they? Someone to clean up their mess. Friend of yours, is he?'

'He's no friend of mine. I had a lucky escape.'

'Ah dear, we all did. We were not sent to the base.'

'You don't think they'll take him back to his own country?'

'They might let him go back, I suppose. A public trial, so they can keep claiming they're protectors of the peace here. But who's to know about his crime over there? Better to keep it hushed up in Ryukyu. And the base will be punishment enough. Why aren't *you* going back to America?'

'I need to find my friend Kit. He's probably still on Okinawa, I think.'

'Shouldn't you have got on the boat to Okinawa then? I tried to; my family's there waiting for me. I had no choice but to go on this one, to Iriomote.'

'Why?' Sol asks nervously. 'How long are you planning to stay there?'

But the woman moves off to look over the side of the boat. 'At least we're going above sea level! For now. Not like poor old Taketomi – look at that.'

Sol can see nothing at first.

'Look down,' she tells her, and through the clear swell, Sol glimpses flashes of red tiles on the seabed, coral streets and the wrecks of buffalo carts. A Ryukyuan village beneath the sea.

Something is very wrong.

She shouldn't be here.

Oh god, if only she'd stayed with Kit.

Sol tries to focus on the scenes of Iriomote playing out on various screens about the ferry. The island appears idyllic, its inhabitants laughing and dancing in waterfalls and green mangrove swamps. It could be the Amazon. Accompanying woody smells of undergrowth are pumped out too. Sol can see the Virrea logo in the upper-left corner of a screen, displaying its sponsorship.

The video shows the port as well, and nearby a small town, full of life and trade. There is talk among the passengers of people living in the forest, a jungle community who have all they desire there. That Nirai Kanai, the unknown faraway land where the Okinawan gods live, is there – a life preserved from American and Japanese invasion, where the fish are still safe to eat and extinct animals flourish.

'We are going to be free. Look!'

What is going on? Who is in charge of this boat? There are no American marines here, only Japanese navy.

'Does anybody know how often the ferries leave from Iriomote?' Her voice wavers near hysteria through the translator.

Everyone falls quiet.

'Dear, this is it,' a woman says gently through a floral mask.

'There are no boats back,' says someone else as Sol dizzies. That can't be true.

'Oh yes,' others say. 'This is for good.' They seem to view it as liberating in some way. At least they will be away from marines and bases, seems to be the general consensus – what does it matter where on earth they are? A Ryukyuan island beyond the networks and politics, at one with nature, its own people. Sinking, yes, but perhaps not for a lifetime if they are lucky, and, if not, they can build their own boats and sail for China, once a friend to the former kingdom, surely a future ally too.

It is hard to understand this sense of hope. Easier is the cowering distrust of the unhealthy; people turn away from the maskless. The old man who was coughing has been shooed away to a less populated section of the ferry. Sol realises that she is truly alone. Here on the waves, surrounded by strangers, she surrenders. There is a perverse sense of freedom in submission to fate, in being no longer responsible, or failing to be responsible, for herself, her poor decisions. She might as well not be an individual person at all, not a citizen or an escort or an addict. She is a human animal swept along by tides, geographical and political.

An island can be seen in the distance, vibrantly green, rearing up out of the sea. It is mountainous terrain, alive with thick primeval jungle. This must be Iriomote. Sol hears an elderly couple talking about an undersea volcano, the likelihood of it erupting any time soon – impossible to say, of course. These islands, always volatile, now defy expectation all the time, exploding and crushing, dissolving and drowning, the chaos and brutality of nature matching the chaos and brutality of the human activity upon them.

Sol asks what is known about the disease sweeping Ishigaki.

'We think it's from the storm swells, the sewage washed up on to the island,' says a boy with a bandanna hanging over his face, tucked into a baseball cap.

'It did not come from the sea!' cries the woman who spoke English before. She is a journalist, she tells Sol. 'It came from the base!'

'What do you mean? The military base they're sending the sick people to?'

'"Military base!" No way would they allow any of their own fine military men to be based there.'

'How come? Where are all those marines going then?'

'Some will be shipped home, the others, back to Okinawa, I'd think. When they've done their job of delivering the sick to the scientists on the base. We are like animals to them. Guinea pigs. They wanted to test our reactions – and now they can.'

'Reactions to what?' Her heart is rattling her ribs.

'To whatever bioweapon they've modified in that lab now. *That's* what's in the base. Or what was in it before the typhoon. Insanity to build a seaside germ factory in the Pacific Ring of Fire! On a place like these islands, built on fault lines, every day disappearing into the sea. Like the chemicals they stored on the islands that sank—'

'*Bakekujira*! *Bakekujira*!' The sudden cries of other passengers interrupt the journalist. The group that has gathered around her rushes again to the side of the boat.

'That is just the skeleton of a whale, Hiro. It's no demon. The sea is full of them. Poisoned, like the rest of us. It's not moving, see? Just being moved by the choppy waves.'

Sol looks down at the vast whale bones, animated by the sea. In a rush she remembers the cats, the pile of bones beneath the soil.

The dark of the treetops forms a sinister canopy as the ferry pulls up to the port.

But her father. If her father is here then there is still hope and everything's not as dire as it seems. She *is* an American citizen, and on this boat by mistake. She is not a criminal, trying to escape to the end of the world to hide there; not a refugee, being shunted by the government to the end of the world to be hidden. She doesn't belong here, and she has to believe that an ex-marine will know how to get his daughter home.

A THIN PLACE

The crab that greets the passengers is the size of a dog, darkest blue and melanic red, clawed and jointed. It scuttles out from the undergrowth and draws itself up a few metres from the port exit. The crab seems to be a messenger, a spokesman, waiting for an invitation to announce itself. An army of its comrades lurks in flashes of colour some way away as the leader greets the boat people, dumped on the dock before the ferry speeds away.

'Uh, god, a robber crab.' Someone – it is hard to distinguish people, wrapped up in scarves and make-do masks – runs at it shouting and flapping their arms. The vast crab stands its ground for a second, flicks a ninja claw out like a switch blade, hesitates … then clatters off. For reinforcements? Sol has never seen anything like it. She doesn't trust that she *is* seeing it. Sweats, shivers, sickness are here … next come the withdrawal visions. The journalist took one look at her and withdrew too. She's keeping well away from Sol now, and who can blame her?

Nobody seems to be interested in sharing names. Civility would feel too normal. There is a thanatic smell rising from the waves banging against the docks, the scent of something rotten.

The old port looks decrepit, as if it hasn't been in use for years. Not much like the shiny movie; Virrea had shown the ferry's arrival at a pristine white modern building. How long ago did they film that, she wonders. Then, they probably never filmed it at all.

There are no signs of human life. No one at the ticket desk, no tannoy, no information signs … Nothing. How could her father be here on this island? How could anyone with those … things at large. It looks like a land after the extinction of the human race, ruled again by terrifying prehistoric creatures, the rightful heirs of the dinosaurs. At least some life's mushrooming on this doomed Earth.

'They can't survive long in water,' says someone. 'They'll drown when the king tides flood the island.'

Sol can see the blue tinge of crab through the grass on the other side of the road from the port. It seems to spread and spread.

'We need to get to the town. There will be people there who can help us,' says a woman veiled in blue.

'Yes, we saw it on the ferry Virrea.' An older covered face in the clamour. Sol saw it too: Ohara, the lively little port town.

'There's a road just outside that leads there – the only road. It goes all the way around the coast, where the jungle's not so dense. I came here with my father when I was a little girl. He was a fisherman, you see.'

'Times have changed. Let's trust our eyes, no?' This is someone else – a man. She can't identify individuals by speech when they're all filtered through the voice of her earpiece, and when they use their different island languages Sol is entirely deaf.

There is nodding all around, but people are edging away from the blue battle line of crustaceans, back into the port. Some of the weaker passengers have collapsed on dilapidated benches in the port itself, unlikely to move any further.

'They will be food for coconut crabs if they stay here,' Sol hears one say.

'I've never seen any as big as that,' says another.

It does not really matter who is speaking, she realises; they are all limbs of one human organism reduced, in a single boat trip, to a biological need for survival.

Sol smells the dirt encrusted on her skin, as if something black has blown in on the air. It is clinging to her small pale hairs like Tucson desert sand. When was the last time she washed? Her wrappings are taut with sweat, her body purging itself of the pills, brain zaps earthed in aching limbs. She has no conception of how long she was mad with them, what day it is in the calendar. It must be the new year, the flight ban in place, migration frozen. None of them can get back without a boat. So she must move forward into the unknown, perhaps towards her father, before it gets dark. The sun is low in the sky but strong and hot as if it were directly overhead. Maybe she is getting closer to the completely familiar. When she finds her real father, she will know him as herself. She will finally know herself. What does it matter where they are? The only reason it matters is that Kit's not here.

Some of the two-hundred-strong group are advocating shutting up the port terminal as best they're able and taking shelter there for the night. Others say on to the road and left, others right. The remainder: 'Safety in numbers.' Sol is reminded of cattle, bellowing, herded into a barn. But the port's doors don't shut. They had once been automatic and it looks like the electricity has gone from the terminal. A pylon some way down the road has seen better days.

'Look, the town's that way,' Sol hears. 'To the right it's all jungle and those evil-looking crabs.' Further along, she can see terracotta, must be the tops of roofs.

Just as she and a few others take tentative steps towards the buildings, they hear a shout go up from the opposite direction. People – by the looks of their varying sizes men, women and children – are coming towards them.

'Don't go to the town,' shouts one of them. 'It's not safe!'

'We're sorry. We would have come sooner ... We saw the boat arrive and didn't know what to do.'

'The boats usually bring waste, you see.'

'And we have enough of that here!'

'But sometimes they bring people. We have to check – if it is people – they won't know ... We didn't. We thought, we have to warn them—'

'Don't go near Ohara; we don't if we can avoid it ... There's arsenic in the land there and god knows what else has leaked.'

As they come closer, Sol sees that they also have cloths tied around their noses and mouths – over their hair too.

One breaks off from the group to lunge at a crab with a long stick. It clatters off. 'Watch out, those things can crush bones. We've lost two of our number to them so far. Torn apart. They've grown strong on the poison here. They thrive on it.'

A small bent figure turns to another and Sol realises that their size does not indicate children. 'We won't have room for them all in the camp, you know. We should have stayed put.'

'We are not monsters. What do we have left if not humanity?'

'Some will need to stay in the port. Those who are already sick can take their chances in the town if they like. There are some perfectly comfortable places to rest up ... if you know you're already dying.'

'Those of you who are well enough can come with us. It's about an hour's walk. You can make it before dark if you follow us now, and you'll find a fairly safe place to lay your heads. The camp's in a sacred spot on hot springs – it used to be a hotel for ecotourism. We're also close to the sea and the crabs don't seem to like the double threat of water. The snakes do not mind it, of course, but we have a *yuta* there and she has blessed it. And, well, it is the best you will do here. It's the furthest point from the dump.'

'The dump?' asks someone.

'Nuclear,' someone replies.

'You should have hijacked the boat, killed the captain. Did you not even try?'

Night falls quickly and absolutely as they walk. The jungle awakens: squeals and hisses, rattles and howls, vibrations as if the island itself is pulsing. Life slithers over her foot; small spotted wildcats flash through leaves lit by neon fireflies and an approving moon. A burst of blue beaded skin from a mangrove, of red and black stripes and scales. If it is true that this island houses something terrible, then it is also a haven for some. Sol passes no other humans. It feels like they've been walking much longer than an hour, the pace slow and deliberate, often steeply upwards. Some fall away at the back. They just sit down where they are, with the snakes of the rainforest, promising to join in the morning. A lie that everyone can be happy with.

'We're nearly there,' Sol hears, as their feet crunch over something alarming.

'Don't worry, that's just salt,' says someone else with a tremulous note in their voice. 'To keep the bad spirits away.'

It's hard to see anything now, though there is a sulphurous smell, and something slightly redolent of sewage behind it. Sol has embraced the anonymity of the new group, has been careful to fall in line and not to give herself away as a foreigner by speaking. Safer, till she knows who they are. Her improvised headscarf has kept her from attention, and now the darkness of a night lit only by stars does the same: no fireflies and the moon has clouded over. The passengers she met on the boat have not spoken to her here. She wonders if they've realised she's trying to remain incognito. Probably they are just thinking of their own survival, and not about her. It's a lonely thought. The group is debating whether to light a fire.

'We don't have any electricity so night is night, I'm afraid. Sometimes we have a fire, but it's risky, there being so much flammable material leaked all over the place.'

'Fire stirs up the topsoil – bad news for everyone.'

There hasn't been a month without a wildfire story in Tucson. Not a day in the States.

'This area was used as a military jungle training camp for a time, so it bears the scars. Or at least that's how they referred to it, but it's clear now that it was a base for what they call extraordinary rendition, meaning torture of the Chinese.'

'It's clear because we see their ghosts, recreating the scenes.'

'Yes, this is a thin place.'

Nobody asks what a thin place is, but the people who live here need to talk. We are on the borders here, they say: land and sea; earth and sky; an extreme meeting point where the veils lift. They sound like Phoenix, the old devil. She has crossed the whole world only to end up back in Dreamtime.

They do light a fire, and in its flare Sol can see steam rising up from pools of hot spring water. That must be where the rotten-egg stench comes from. A waterfall is crashing somewhere, she can hear it. Perhaps it is the sea, insisting it is near, it is coming. She wishes Kit was here, or that she was not. She wishes she had some tobacco.

Some weed, some pills, some heroin. Anything. It has been all she could do to survive the trek here, not to give herself away as sick, as American. She craves the release of sleep.

What must once have been the hotel, or the barracks for the jungle training camp – or perhaps, Sol thinks brightly, a place to stay for those constructing this dump they keep talking about – is more like a system of shacks, as if the original was razed and a replacement reconstructed haphazardly, only to be blown to bits again, recreated piecemeal. They sit outside it, close to the fire.

There's a sequence of caves here, they say, though Sol cannot see them. By the hot springs. The caves keep us safe.

The fire's heat in this intense humidity is crushing. She listens to the old hands of the camp attempt to educate the new arrivals. Oh yes, you see strange things here, they are saying. We don't know if they're real or not.

'You see mirages of people you love, talking fish, the extinct lynx cat.'

The spotted cats, Sol is sure, are as real as the crabs and the fireflies; she saw them.

'Some say the waste frees our minds; some that it takes us closer to the end, and from the end, it is easier to see ahead to where we're going.'

'I saw a dugong the other day.'

In this twilight world Sol wonders if she is dead already. Aching for comfort and beyond hungry she decides to risk breaking her silence. She whispers into her translation piece to one of the men from the camp, who has taken off his mask, 'I'm sorry to bother you, but I'm starving. Do you have anything I can buy to eat?'

'American, are you?' But he doesn't say it loudly. 'We live off what nature provides here.' His teeth have largely fallen out, his hair patchy and scabrous. 'It'll kill you, but what choice do we have?' He draws Sol away from the fire and the others, hands her half a coconut. 'The crabs crack them for us. Pretty useful, provided they don't kill us.'

'What do you mean? Is the fruit not safe here?' Her hand goes involuntarily to her own dark hair, flattened by sweat beneath the cloth from Cat Island. It has grown past the point where it sticks up of its own accord, some indication of the passing of time.

'Safe, ha! Nobody knows anything, do they? We did not until we came here.' The man chews and sucks on the coconut with his swollen, gummy jaws. Sol turns away, feeling she is watching something embarrassingly intimate. Looking around though, she sees broken smiles and toothlessness all about, like an inversion of the American grin. The dazzling white teeth of the blue-eyed dental advert, of the heroic marine planting a flag.

'They've been wanting to use these islands as a nuclear dump for years. Can't get rid of your rubbish? Hide it at the end of the world. As if what you bury will not come back to bite you.'

Though people keep their mouths and noses covered, Sol can see youthful eyes of children in the firelight and hear higher-pitched voices. A girl recrosses her legs and, as she settles herself, strands of her long, uncovered hair catch the orange glow revealing shiny patches of scalp.

'What do you mean?'

'It's not buried any more. They bulldozed the deep earth for the waste, were digging down as far as they could while they stored the containers up on top. But the digging itself was what caused the landslide when the earth shook. It was probably what caused the earthquake too. A great tsunami rose up and over the land, flooding the loose earth. It damaged the storage system, and the poison leaked all over this island and into the sea around it.'

A sense of horror folds in on Sol, nerve endings flayed with stark, unmoderated reality. It simply can't be true. Can it? 'But how can you live here?'

'What choice do we have? They dropped concrete on the waste to try to contain what was left, and as a result, this island is just about habitable. There are animals that survive. The crabs never used to be so big, or so bold with the humans. They sense our weakness and they've grown somehow stronger, fiercer with the radiation. It kills them too – their corpses litter the jungle – but before that, it gives them fight.'

'America did this?' Is this the islanders trying to control the story, to get rid of the Americans?

'Sure, they did and they do. It's military property. Means they can bring rubbish over and dump it anywhere now. Japan calls this place a "climate refugee camp"; they send anyone they don't want around any longer our way.'

The man returns to the fire and Sol follows. They can't be prisoners here, there can't be no boats taking people east. She doesn't believe it. She won't. She will stay here just until the morning and then she will … what? Maybe there are computers in the town and she can get word out. If the world knew! More desperately, if people and rubbish continue to be shipped here, the opportunity to steal their transport is still an option. Or to build their own boats, to get away from this terrifying place … At first light she will go to Ohara and search for clues, and her father. She is an American, after all, and so is he. She must trust that her own people will look after her. Did Hunter know about the disaster here? He can't have done. Or, he must have had a plan to go beyond – get to Taiwan, defect to China or … something.

'This is a death camp!' she hears someone cry, evidently having the same conversation she's just had. She realises it's the journalist from the boat. 'It's a concentration camp with no guards!'

'Yes,' someone else replies flatly. 'There isn't room for our people left on earth now our islands are sinking. We are an inconvenience. Where can we go?'

'You can try to get away!' says the journalist. 'This apathy is what will kill everyone.' She's right. The inertia weighs upon the camp like the chemical clouds dripping over them. It is a cult of inactivity. 'Why are you not making boats, trying to sail to China …'

'Oh yes, throw ourselves on Chinese mercy, or Taiwan, half-sunk, occupied by American troops.'

A different voice: 'You can't get away from sky, land and sea. These, our most ancient ancestors, have been greatly injured; our only hope is to worship them, to win back their favour through ceremonial veneration.'

'We escape inwardly – that is the only resistance left to us now. We tell stories and sing songs, we cry, we sleep, we use the chemicals they left us to reach a different plane – roots from the jungle too. These take us closer to paradise, to the other side of the thin place.'

'To death!' says the journalist.

'We hold on to our good gods; we propitiate them.'

Something resembling a pipe is lit from the fire and a herbal pungency diffuses through the stagnant, swampy air as it's passed around. Something in Sol lights up in expectation.

'You're all insane,' says the journalist. 'And don't share that pipe, you don't know who's contagious.'

'True insanity is modern life, how far we have strayed from our gods and from nature. This place won't be safe for twenty thousand years, yet animals may live here, for a time. If we become animals, we may live here too. We can adapt and mutate, as they have done. Perhaps we can heal too, if we appease the spirits of this contaminated island.'

As the pipe comes round, Sol hesitates. Nothing is safe here. She passes it on, and once the churning craving for relief begins to settle, she knows with pride that this is the first time she has ever willingly done so.

Instead she lies down on her side and imagines Kit is holding her, wrapped around her from behind. She could cope with being anywhere if he were with her. Even here. They'd live off-grid, two people at the ends of the earth. What do they need beyond each other?

THE SECOND TALE OF JONNY

As night continues its passage, the heat relents slightly and a strong wind whips around the island, flustering the trees and rattling the shacks.

Some move inside when the fire goes out, and some say they are going to the caves. Sol, remembering the bandit crabs, follows the former, though no invitation is issued to the people from the boat. Still no one wants to sleep, it seems. They lie around on futons that smell of damp and decay.

The occupants of this shack want to know what has happened to bring the newcomers here. A protest against Tokyo? Another submerged island? Sol stays quiet while others talk of the typhoon and trouble on Ishigaki. The Iriomote people say they hid in the caves here when the storm hit, but supplies had been lost. She senses seeping regret that they had sought out these immigrants, thinking they might have brought … what? Clean food, medicine, a chance of escape, something other than more rotting bodies to feed, water and die alongside.

Another voice, a new tone, and the language is English: 'You,' it says, throaty and female. 'You're American, aren't you?'

The man she'd spoken to must have given her away.

'How did you manage to be swept up with us to this cursed place? We thought it was just us Ryukyuans who are condemned to die on our islands as they sink, suffering the indignities of your people.'

Sol can feel the hostility hovering like a heat wall around her. She takes a deep breath but someone – she can't see who in the encompassing dark – cuts in with, 'No need to hold her responsible for our troubles. She couldn't help being born American.' Others have noticed, then.

She tentatively breaks her silence again. 'I came to Japan and to these islands looking for my father. An American, I'm afraid …' She stops short of saying 'a marine'. 'He was in Okinawa, then he had a hotel in Ishigaki and … people said he'd gone to this island, Iriomote, to search for his wife. That she had family here.'

'Well, that narrows it down,' says someone, apparently with amusement. 'There weren't many people on this island when I arrived. What's her name?'

'I … I can't remember her first name but her married name is Carter.'

'Of course, it's only the American name that counts.'

'Have you heard of a woman or a man with that surname? Jay Carter?'

A hum goes round the shack, extends through the camp like Chinese whispers.

'Do you know him?' Sol asks. 'Is he here?'

'Oh, I'll take you to see him!' The hoarse woman sounds like she is clambering over mattresses.

'Sit down. We don't punish children for the sins of their fathers here. She deserves to hear what happened.'

'Besides, it's not safe. The crabs are most aggressive at night. They don't like the intense heat of the day; the night is their time.'

'The dragons prefer the day,' says a little girl, or perhaps a boy. Hard to tell in the dark. 'The big lizards, I mean.'

'Very well. Let me tell you a story. A story of a man with many names: a shapeshifter, a trickster. It is an ancient story, and yet it is also a tale for our times: a Western fairy tale brought to the East. I think you'll like it.'

That sounds extremely unlikely, Sol thinks, unease creeping through her. Something's not right. 'Is he here?' she asks again. 'My dad?'

Once upon a time, there was and was not a big white man called J. Everything about him was charming, from his pearly-toothed grin and his rosy complexion to the way he treated women. He was very tall and extremely handsome, and his uniform glinted in the sun, telling the girls he was coming.

One day, he caught the eye of a maiden of Okinawa. She was a dancer: beautiful as a fox, her hair red as flames. Lieutenant J. looked so dashing that the beautiful maiden, whose name was Yuna, instantly fell in love with him and he with her.

The lieutenant said, 'Let's get married and start a family.'

'OK,' said Yuna. Her mother had run off with a marine a decade earlier.

'There's only one thing,' said J. 'I have to leave Okinawa and go to another island, to Ishigaki, to make my fortune. Will you come with me?'

Yuna hesitated, for everything she knew and loved was on the beautiful and blessed isle of Okinawa: her whole life so far, her friends, all her family, save a long-lost aunt who lived not so far away on Iriomote. But Yuna loved J. so she agreed to follow him, to the ends of the earth if he so desired.

'We have to leave immediately,' he said. 'I can't tell you why.'

There was no time to say goodbye to her father and six brothers as they had to begin the sailing trip in secret, overnight, for they would be in danger, he said, if anyone saw them. In any case, she did not want to tell her family what she was doing, as she suspected they would not approve. So, as night fell, the pair eloped in a boat.

It was an adventure. And Yuna was crazy about him.

She was much younger than him, still a child. He could lift her up and carry her in one arm, like a cat. She didn't understand much of what J. said, but she gathered a little English along the way.

They sailed to Ishigaki, and there they were married. Yuna took J.'s name but kept her own too. J. thought she should be able to change it as easily as he did his, but Yuna means the moon in Ryukyuan, and that is a good thing to hang on to.

They bought a patch of land on a man-made island that had fallen into disrepair. It had become a haven for cats. They decided to build a hotel. It was very luxurious and people from abroad loved to stay there and paid a lot of money to do so.

But while Yuna was happy on Ishigaki with J., the island had a dark side. Young women kept going missing. It made Yuna feel unsafe, even though J. promised he would protect her. It was unsettling.

One day, Yuna was walking in the sugar-cane fields when she thought she saw her husband far off in the distance. He'd said he would be in the town all day on business, so she was puzzled to see him. She decided to follow him, surprise him … and perhaps seduce him there in the fields, away from prying eyes.

But as she drew nearer, she saw that he was not alone. A girl from the island was with him. Distraught, fearing her husband's infidelity, she followed the pair into a forest, tracking them like a vixen, until she saw them stop suddenly, as if they had found the spot they'd been looking for. Although fearful of snakes, she quietly and nimbly climbed up a *gajimaru* tree, as she had in Okinawa as a child, the better to see what was going on. From here she could see that the girl was wearing a gag. Her eyes were bulging with terror, like a calf's.

Her husband started scrabbling at a pile of fallen leaves, moving them aside to reveal a makeshift door in the ground. As he bent over, she could see thick, curly red hair poking out of the back of his trousers, dense as a feral pelt and fiery as her own dyed flame hair. How, she wondered, had she never noticed that before? J. opened the door to reveal a pit in the earth. He steered the girl there and showed it to her in silence; her screams were stifled by the gag. Yuna could see bones poking up from the wounded earth. She saw her husband hold up part of a skull – the skull of a long-haired woman whose head had been bashed in.

She watched J. turn the girl towards another tree. He lifted up her skirt and began to push himself inside her, still in silence. The girl calf didn't protest aloud when her face rubbed up and down against the bark. She just leant against the tree. Yuna could see she was trembling; a silver bracelet was jangling. She wanted to scream herself; she wanted to come to the aid of the girl, but she knew the strength of her husband. He was a trained killer; he could snap her like a twig. She was afraid.

Yuna watched in horror, trying not to rustle the leaves of the *gajimaru* as her husband quietly put his hands around the girl's neck and, still moving in and out of her, slowly strangled her to death. The girl went limp and, eventually, the man did too. He removed the silver bracelet from her wrist and put it in his pocket. Then he lowered the girl's still-warm body into the pit. Yuna saw it all, and she vowed that she would not be silent.

She waited until her husband had left, and had been gone a long while, before she came down from the tree and made secret plans. When the good lieutenant came home that night, he gave Yuna the silver bracelet she had seen him lift from the dead girl. Yuna put it on, and then she felt she must be next, that her animal husband was marking her for the slaughter.

She told him, 'I have an aunt who lives nearby on Iriomote, and she is unwell. I'm going to stay with her for a week.'

Her husband grumbled but did not stop her from going. When she failed to return, J. came here to look for her and bring her back. But Yuna had told her father and brothers about him; they were waiting at the aunt's house, and when J. arrived they hacked him all to pieces.

Sol feels very cold, even as the heat is pouring from her. She is aware of rock-like paralysis, the air, her body, the flickering muscle of a finger, the fluttering of an eardrum. But dead … 'Dead?' Her voice is thick with disbelief. Then something else occurs to her … They are glad he is dead because he is American. Is there some additional danger for her here, then, something beyond the horrors of a poisoned island?

'Yes, the man is dead. You can see his bones. They're here, stripped clean by crabs. The man is dead.'

'Your father is a legend in these parts. You should be proud!'

'You can understand why we love this story here. Finally, some sort of justice served. We kept the tale of Yuna Carter secret, as they had kept secret so many American crimes against us, and it gave us hope.'

'Yuna was here in this very camp, you know, but she disappeared. There are many stories about her too. Some say she died of the poison. Some say she was no mortal but a *kitsune*, a shapeshifting fox demon who used her magic to avenge Jay's victims. To these people, there was no aunt in Iriomote; it was Yuna who lured him here by taking the form of a different young woman, promising him everything and then tearing him apart as her wild animal self.'

'We'll show you your father's pile of bones in the morning, if you like.'

'We'll never see the washed bones of our own ancestors again.'

She wonders if they are going to kill her.

One says, 'You were coming here to kill him yourself, weren't you? We saved you the work.'

She wonders, closing her eyes, if this is true.

LAND OF THE RISING SUN

The dawn seems to have been breaking for an eternity, yellow and purple lights shining in his eyes like some obscene medical experiment. There are so many different types of pain coursing through him that it's difficult to separate them, identify one from another. He is drifting in and out of a fantasy, a world of seawater and dragons and dugongs, but every so often he comes to, opens his aching eyes to a sore blur and the feeling of solid soil or sand beneath him. He is still bobbing up and down, a message in a sea-tossed bottle, but for the first time he can sense something static resist the perpetual undulation of his body.

He tastes of salt; he is saturated with the stuff, choking it up like sand. It has pickled him, drawn out all the moisture of life and sucked him dry, a husk. He trembles against the scratching ground, remembers being smashed against a rock or the seabed and held there as the waves crashed above him, the whirling sand and salt filling his ears and eyes and mouth until he blacked out.

He cringes as the glare of sunrise penetrates his swollen eyelids. His naked skin, blistered and burnt, recoils from it as his thoughts crystallise into one iterative word, the sand-bound cry of his youth:

water, water, water. His brain is bashing against the confines of his skull demanding it. Beneath this, the old howl: Sol. Where is she? He thought he had seen her in the sea, that she had saved him. It was Sol and yet it was not; the flaming hair, the fish-scaled tail. He was drowning, dying, unable to reach the surface when she had swum to him, taken his hand and drawn him upwards and upwards for an eternity till they struck against the moiling cedar planks of the upturned boat. He clung on and she swam away with a powerful flick of her mermaid's tail while he called and cried for her.

The *sabani* had been constantly moving as one with the sea; whatever he is lying on is still and soggy. He prises his agonised eyes apart and there it is: his enemy, the sea, lying quietly before him; he clatters back away from it, face and body up, propelled by arms and legs, crabwise. Is this hell? Is he dead? Some sort of curse to eternally face the thing which destroyed you, suffer destruction over and over again.

He forces himself to look around. He is on a bristling beach, thorns spiking up through the sand; one has flayed a piece of sun-burned skin from his back. Plastic debris is strewn in all directions. But the boat! The boat is there, just a little way away. Even with his sea-beaten eyes he can tell it's taken a pounding. He tries to crawl towards it, to pull it from the water's grasp, but he falls back exhausted. If he could just have something to drink … He feels himself tumbling from consciousness again.

He's uncertain whether he's been out for a second or a day. The sun is still rising, vast and threatening, blood red on the yellow-streaked horizon. He had dreamed of Také, that he too had been nudged back to the boat, had hung on, that he had been washed up here. But he is nowhere nearby. And Kit had not seen him since the moment the storm swell first overturned them. A tear adds more stinging salt to the wounds on his face.

This time he is able to crawl gingerly to the boat, to drag what is left of it up on to the beach, away from the hungrily lapping sea, home of monsters and darkness and terrible all-devouring power. He dives under it in horror as a diabolical noise comes from overhead. But when he dares to look up through the holes in the hull, he sees an American Osprey overhead, circling in the sky with that familiar waspish menace. He picks himself up and, fighting the faintness that wants to force him back down, he waves both hands in as wide an arc as possible. The aircraft dips and Kit thinks he has been spotted, but then he remembers the lopsided, clumsy way they fly. Before he knows it, the Osprey has careered away and Kit collapses again, too exhausted even to drag his body out of the cinder-making beams of the risen sun and into the jungle behind him. Why would the jungle be safer though? All of nature is hostile to humans now: the sea, the sun, the beach, the trees. And what new order of creatures are they sharing them with?

Také was a creature of the sea, and the sea has most likely reclaimed him. Or maybe he has been swept up on a different beach somewhere. Death is something people are more familiar with these days. A thousand climate migrants have died trying to make the crossing, or a thousand perished in the landslides, or ten thousand or a million died of drought, dehydration, famine, pestilence. The constant throwing out of numbers has inured most people to the reality, and as all distant reality has been replaced by the virtual, it is easy to stay inured, even to deny completely.

Kit can't deny this.

Out on the boat he had found himself wishing Také was his own father. He had shown him what a father should be like. But Kit had not been a good son. He had not stopped Také from putting himself in mortal danger, though he knew the women who loved him had tried to. He should himself be dead.

'All in good time,' he thinks he hears, but the voice echoes as if it's within his head, or within the broken boat. He thinks he must be dreaming, or hallucinating. Dehydration can do that. But he has woken enough to crawl back under the seafaring wood, scant barrier against the vaulted inferno. The guilt he feels merges into his guilt at letting Sol go, for not persuading her to stay in America, protecting her from herself, vulnerable in the first stages of recovery. He saw a chance with her here; a chance for himself. That's why he didn't stop her. He tries to cry again, but finds himself a pillar of salt, no moisture left even in his tear ducts.

He looks at the boat above his head, the gaping holes in it. He wonders why it did not sink, how it was washed up here like drift-wood. Does he owe it his life or were they both spat out separately here, wherever here is? He does not remember much, only the sensation of lungs filling with saltwater, thoughts starting to melt.

Maybe the boat can be mended. Také spent some time describing what he had learned from the Iejima craftsman: the *sabani*'s construction, the design of it, so that it can survive great swells – as indeed it did. He must push on, see where he is – is he on a desert island or are there people here? Is he on a spit of land or on the coast of a great mainland, perhaps in China or carried by the tide and wind back to the Japanese mainland? Wherever he is, there are American airplanes … so there must be something here of interest.

He hears something like metal drumming on the *sabani* that is now, again, sheltering him. He feels the little boat is alive in some way, ancient forests and ancient human traditions protecting him from a more savage new strain of nature. Peering out of a hole, he sees a red stalked eye peer back in, a deep-blue jointed claw poke its great armour through and wave it around, exploring what trespasses on its territory. Kit shrinks back in fear, tries to bat the claw away; the beast withdraws and Kit hears it clack behind him, battering the thorns, heading for the jungle.

He could not say how long he lies there after that, by turns fearful and then lost to reality, diving down deep to the dragon halls of the sea or soaring up, a celestial crane flying over vanishing islands to the faraway land of the gods, or back in the Tokyo hotel room, Sol beneath him, above him, chaining him to ecstasy.

Trees of the rainforest rustle and sigh as a wind starts up from the sea. The tide begins to seep in beneath the boat, withdraws and then floods back in greater volume. Sand inside the *sabani* is thrown up into his exposed irises. Kit knows that he, a hermit crab, must leave his adoptive shell and crawl out naked into this new land. He must save the boat; he must save himself. But the danger of the jungle, the danger of the sea … He does not know which way to go, or how far he can walk, only that he must find fresh water or die.

He reminds himself that he has survived. Something wants him to live. He sucks strength into his battered lungs, Sol into his spirit, and drags the boat back as far as he can from the hungering waves. The pain has left him weak and numb. He is shocked every time he sees the yellow flesh of his body, raw where the skin has departed. He has been stripped to his soul: first clothes, then skin. On the boat, the sensation of being trapped in his own skin departed; now his shell has opened and is allowing what is him to bleed out, a diffuse spirit of sea and sky and land.

He crawls, naked crab unhoused, blown by gusts along the beach. There's some higher rocky ground jutting into the sea here and he can't see beyond it. If he can climb up there, he will be safe from the tide and have a better idea of where, if anywhere, he can go before the sun reaches its zenith. But he falls back again, exhausted. He thinks of his parents. The cosiness, the smallness, the respectability and safety of their pharmacy. It is a different planet. Or the thinnest of veneers on the same planet. Civilisation is nothing to nature.

This way, he thinks he hears. Sol? He raises his head and sees a flash of red hair disappearing into the forest. Chrissie? Is he dead too? Come on.

There is a path.

Up it leads from the beach, through the jungle, yes, but at least the way is not untrodden. The sun has been moving in that direction and Kit limps after it, trying to focus on placing each foot safely on to ground free of habu snake and other monsters, trying to ignore the sharp cries of the jungle around him, which seems to live and breathe. To seethe. Eyes peep from every leaf.

He rounds another corner, then … a mirage – or it really is a road shimmering before him? An actual tarmac road, and a rusted yellow sign with a leaping spotted lynx upon it. There are Japanese characters underneath it but, of course, his eyepiece is long gone, snatched by the great sea dragon, like his clothes. His hand goes to his ear; the earpiece too has gone.

The presence of a sign, of a recognisable language, even one he cannot read, fills him with hope. He may have nearly died – but he has not even left the country. If the land has not sunk, it will be inhabited. He feels a surge, surely his last, of an energy he thought he'd fully drained and limps along the road towards the sign.

Around the next bend he sees people approaching. He tries to shout, his voice nothing more than a squeak. He feels himself collapse as someone runs forward and holds a plastic water bottle to his mouth and he drifts out of consciousness again.

Kit is wrapped in a cloth of some sort, a roof shielding him from the terrible sky but there are no walls, just poles holding up the roof. The wind blows through the shack, breaking the heat wall, and the crackle of fire provides some light. There's the smell of something cooking, baked beans and Spam heating up.

'Where am I?' he tries to ask.

Immediately a flurry of what sound more like orders than answers. He can't begin to understand what is being said. He can just make out the word 'America', but clearly that's not where they are.

His eyes, scrubbed with abrasive sand, are struggling to work out how many there are here. Eventually, one of the many comes into closer view, evidently the most confident speaker of English.

'You,' he says, 'sick.'

'Yes,' croaks Kit, 'but not dead. Thanks to you. Where are we?'

'Iriomote. Island, island.'

He does not know where that is. His hope that he might have washed up on Ishigaki is dashed.

The foggy man-shape continues, painfully pulling out words learned at school then never needed. 'We bring here … See Miss America, in camp here.'

'There's another American? I must talk to them – please.'

'Yes, woman – you talk her. Now, you rest.'

Kit has little choice. He closes eyelids on sandpaper and sinks back down into the painful familiar, the infinite desert. He wanders from dream to dream across the plains, far from the sea, searching for Sol.

He finds her everywhere.

Once he thinks she's there in the hut with him – he can feel her holding him – and then she spreads dragons' wings and he realises he's still dreaming.

Once she is a fox, a coyote, a crow. Once she is the moon.

And then, the sun. In she walks. It is Sol. She is real. She is really here. He is certain of it, but he begs her to tell him – to bite him so he feels it, so he knows it in his bones.

'You're mine,' she says. 'Don't you know we belong to each other?'

'There is a boat,' he begins.

ACKNOWLEDGEMENTS

I'll be forever grateful to Jen Hamilton-Emery for rescuing this novel after its original publisher, Quartet, failed to survive the pandemic. Salt has been just amazing – a glorious, generous port in the storm – and I'm so honoured to join its briny family. Thanks, too, to James Pulford, Neil Griffiths, Sam Mills and Hector Macdonald, who gave great advice when things were looking dicey.

My thanks always to the late Naim Attallah of Quartet for taking that first chance on my writing and changing my life. I'm enormously thankful to Peter Jacobs who edited *Dreamtime* with real flare, Mandi Gomez who guided me on an early draft, Tony Lyons for his extraordinary artwork, Alex Billington for crab-strewn typesetting and Grace Pilkington for some exciting publicity.

Many wonderful people helped me on my travels in Okinawa, Ishigaki and Iriomote, both local and American. I'm indebted to Rob Kajiwara, an Okinawan activist who offered valuable feedback that I have tried to incorporate. Needless to say, any mistakes are my own.

I would like to thank Lucy Binnersley and Jack Solloway at *The London Magazine*, who published an extract from *Dreamtime* at the beginning of a tumultuous 2020.

Some of the novel was written at a writers' retreat I was lucky enough to attend. Hector and Rosemary Macdonald, Sophie Campbell, Sarah Murray, Perrie Hennessy and Bonnie Dunbar were excellent company. Many thanks to all my bright, wise and energising writer friends for a great deal of fun.

Greatest thanks and love always to my brilliant husband Charlie (whose birthday I missed in Okinawa, trapped in the eye of Typhoon Trami) for his vision, wit and unfailing belief in this book and in me; to my son Hal for being awesome; to my mother Suzanna for inspiring me to write with her own stories and for her fantastic support throughout; and to my father Charles and my sisters Zinnia and Isadora for their vastly appreciated encouragement.

This book has been typeset by
TETRAGON
using Apollo, a font designed by Adrian Frutiger
for the Monotype Corporation in the U.S. It is manufactured using
Holmen Book Cream 70gsm, a Forest Stewardship Council™ certified
paper from the Hallsta Paper Mill in Sweden. It was printed and bound
by Clays Limited in Bungay, Suffolk, Great Britain.

CROMER
GREAT BRITAIN
MMXXI